# I Am Kiko

A Novel By

K. U. Helsley

I Am Kiko
By
K. U. Helsley

This book is a work of fiction. References to real people, events, establishments, organizations, or locales are intended only to provide a sense of authenticity and are used fictitiously. All other characters, and all incidents and dialogue, are drawn from the author's imagination and are not to be construed as real.

I Am Kiko. Copyright © 2026 by K. U. Helsley. All rights reserved. Printed in the United States of America. No part of this book may be used or reproduced in any manner whatsoever without written permission except in the case of brief quotations embodied in critical articles and reviews. For information, contact Ken.Helsley@yahoo.com

*Cover art was AI-generated using DALL-E.*

ISBN: 9798243819909

# Chapter 1

I first met Leonard Boyce, or "Lenny," as we called him, when I was 24. I was young and brash and believed I was destined to become a great singer and musician. I was living in Austin, Texas, the indie music capital of the world, or so it billed itself, attempting to build a career among the hundreds of other Indie musicians doing the same. I was good, well, to be honest, in my mind I was great, but after six years of working the nightclubs of Sixth Street and the occasional music festival or opening spot of a slightly better-recognized performer than me, I was dead broke, and if not for the goodness of a dear friend, nearly homeless. But I suppose if I'm going to tell this story properly, I need to begin with a little background about myself.

My name is Kiko Davis, a Japanese woman who was born in Japan and adopted by two American parents when I was just ten days old. I grew up in Colorado Springs, Colorado, and in my later teen years, in Denver. I knew absolutely nothing about my biological parents until I was 26, and when I finally learned the truth of the circumstances that had produced me, I was amazed that I had even been born at all. But that's a story for later on, for now, I'll begin with my first memories of growing up in Colorado.

My adoptive parents, William (Bill) and Katherine (Kate) Davis, were a US Air Force couple stationed in Yokota Japan, when they adopted me. Kate was in an automobile accident when she was 18, which did a great deal of damage to her internal organs, resulting in the need for a hysterectomy, so she always knew that adoption was her only option for ever having a child.

Bill was a young Air Force mechanic stationed in Colorado Springs when he and Kate met at a social event. After dating for only six months, Bill received orders to the Air Base at Yokota, Japan. Kate was afraid it would tear them apart, so they decided to get married after getting to know each other for just a few months.

They were both in their early twenties, in love, and excited about this new adventure that was offered to them to transfer to a base in a foreign country.

Kate was a devout Catholic, raised by an Irish Catholic mother and father. Bill was ambivalent about religion but was willing to do what was needed to keep Kate happy. Although they did break with tradition and got married in Las Vegas, as there wasn't time for Bill to go through the requirements to qualify to marry in the Catholic Church, they promised Kate's parents they would do so as soon as the opportunity arose to get Bill baptized and confirmed, which they were assured he could do at the airbase in Japan, so Kate's parents gave their consent, and they drove to Las Vegas and got married so that Bill could take Kate with him to Japan as his wife. That was in early 1984.

Life in Japan was wonderful for a young American couple experiencing a foreign country for the first time. The meager military salary of an Air Force Sargent went a long way in Japan with an exchange rate of over ¥100 to $1 in those days. With base housing that was somewhat of a higher quality and built to meet American housing standards, more than what was available out in the local economies, they were living quite well. They quickly made friends with other couples, and Kate busied herself by volunteering with the Ladies Auxiliary at the base chapel.

The base had several Chaplains assigned to it: a Catholic Priest, a Protestant (Lutheran) Pastor, and a Jewish Rabbi. Father James was the Catholic Priest, and Kate collaborated mostly with him, through the auxiliary, to help coordinate services and other activities for the Catholic service members who practiced their faith at the base chapel.

One day, Kate was helping to coordinate a christening for a newborn infant and was surprised to discover that the infant was a Japanese-born orphan who had been adopted by an Air Force Officer and his wife from a Catholic-run adoption agency that operated in the city of Yokota. She was curious and asked Father James about the orphanage. He confirmed to her that the Orphanage was opened nearly 100 years before, when the Catholic church was working hard to establish a presence in Japan, and even though they never made great inroads into the religious life of the Japanese people, they had managed to establish several orphanages that gave young mothers a better alternative, if they happened to find themselves with an unwanted child they could not care for. These institutions survived even WWII, due to a very loyal group of Japanese Nuns, many of whom had been orphans themselves and raised by the Spanish, English, and Italian Nuns who had established the orphanages. The adoption agency in Yokota was established by English-speaking Nuns, the Sisters of the Immaculate Heart, so it was quite popular with Americans seeking to adopt a foreign-born child.

Although the practice of abortion became legal in Japan in 1948, under certain circumstances, foreign adoption was still believed to be a more humane option by many young mothers who found themselves unable to raise a child. In the early 1990s, the Japanese government began to tighten the restrictions on foreign adoption in favor of keeping its children in Japan. However, in 1984, Bill and Kate Davis found themselves sitting in the reception parlor of the Our Lady of the Sacred Heart Catholic adoption agency of Yokota, Japan.

They completed the required paperwork and were told that as soon as the church had approved their request, they were prime candidates for receiving a child. Less than two months later, they got the call. A new baby girl had just been born, and they were next on the list. They arrived at the agency, which was also a home for unwed teenage mothers, and were told that a new baby girl, just ten days old, was ready for adoption. They were taken to the nursery window and allowed to see the beautiful little girl, all cozy and bundled up in my swaddling cloth. A young Japanese girl was standing next to the window, looking at the little girl, as she was the only baby in the nursery that day. As Bill and Kate approached, she turned to Kate and said, in broken English, "She is Kiko," and before Kate could even respond, the girl turned and walked down the hall and disappeared into a room.

Kate turned to Bill and asked, "Do you think that was the mother?" Bill just shrugged and replied, "Who knows? Look at her, she's so beautiful. Look at that gorgeous smile," referring to me, all bundled up in my crib. At least that's how he always relays the experience. After a few moments, they returned to the office and said to the Sister who was managing their adoption, "She is wonderful. When can we take her home?" as if I were a new car or bright shiny new appliance of some sort.

I apologize. That was unfair of me; they truly believed they were doing "God's work" by adopting me, or at least my mother did. Bill just fell in love with this beautiful little life lying so peacefully in my crib.

"Everything is approved, so you can take her today if you like," the sister told them.

"So soon, I never imagined it would happen so fast," Kate replied.

"We've found that the earlier the child begins to experience the new parents, the faster they bond and begin to develop familial tendencies," the Nun said.

"My gosh, Bill, we haven't even bought a crib yet."

"The base exchange has everything we'll need, Kate. I can get whatever is needed as soon as we get back to the base."

The Sister asked, "Have you chosen a name yet? I need to write something down on the birth certificate."

Kate whispered to Bill, "The girl at the window called her Kiko. That's a beautiful name. Why don't we call her Kiko?"

"Kiko! I like it." And he turned to the Sister and said, "Kiko, her name will be Kiko Davis."

The Nun just smiled and said, "Okay, Kiko Davis it is."

That's the story that my adopted mother always told me. I later discovered that it was somewhat of a different story, but I'm sure she was just seeing things through her own rose-colored glasses.

Before meeting Kate Griffin, Bill Davis had given little thought to becoming a father. He just assumed it would happen when it happened, and that it would be a child of his own. He could never have imagined how fast and how hard he would fall in love with this little bundle of joy. Kate was also ecstatic about now having a child of her own, but she always looked at me as her adopted daughter and always introduced me as such, even into my adult life, as if she was afraid someone might get the mistaken notion that she had married and given birth to the child of an Asian man.

I'm sorry, that's not fair either. I really don't know what was going on in her mind. I sometimes let my own mental projections creep in when telling this story. I'll try to do better.

But for Bill, I was just his daughter, completely and in every way, and as I grew, the paternal bond between him and me became quite evident.

I never knew what it meant to be adopted, although I had heard the word hundreds of times as a child, I just thought it meant special or something like that. My parents and I returned to the US when I was two; my father's enlistment contract being completed. Kate always wanted him to reenlist and make a career out of the Air Force. The Air Force was all she ever knew. She grew up in Colorado Springs, and both of her parents were civil servants working on the Air Force base. Kate could not imagine a life that didn't include access to the Airbase and a life that revolved completely around the military complex. But Bill had other desires. He grew up working with his hands. His father was a carpenter and Bill learned that trade growing up, but he joined the Air Force to earn the G.I. Bill, so he could go to school to learn a new trade. He worked on crew life support systems on the large tanker aircraft, so he chose to enroll in Air Conditioning and Heating school and then went to work for an HVAC company after completing his school, but he actually wanted to own his own business more than anything.

Bill knew he needed experience and was willing to spend the time working for someone else to gain that experience, but his goal was always to have the independence that came with not having to work for anyone but himself. Kate never ceased trying to get him to take a job on base, "Maybe in the maintenance department," she would constantly chide him. She had taken a job at the Base Officer's Club, first as a server, then working up to an assistant manager position, but Bill always resisted the temptation to go into the Civil Service, even when Kate's father offered to hire him into the Department that he ran.

When I was six, I was in school one day, and my mother had dropped me off at the curb and driven away, as was her usual routine, when two little boys came up to me, and one said, "You're not a real kid, you're adopted. That's why you don't look like your Mom." I was shocked, and I didn't understand what he meant. I was so disturbed that I began to cry. My teacher came to me and asked, "Kiko, what's wrong?"

"Timmy said I'm not a real kid, because I'm adopted. It's not true, I am a real kid!"

My teacher, Mrs. Knutson, was so kind, and she said, "Oh, sweetheart, being adopted doesn't mean you're not a real kid, it just means that your parents adopted you from some other parents. Timmy was confused about what it means to be adopted."

I know she was just trying to be kind and explain to me what adoption meant, but that confused me even more. "That's not true," I insisted, "My parents did not take me from my real parents." By this time, I was so upset that Mrs. Knutson had to take me to the office, and the Nurse called my mom, and she had to come back to school to pick me up. My mom was so mad at the lady in the office and started to yell, "You had no right to tell her I'm not her real mother. That's not your job, and it's none of your business," completely ignoring the fact that she had been telling people that, since I was born.

The poor lady at the office tried to explain to her what Timmy had said, and Mrs. Knutson had told her what she did, but when Kate Griffin-Davis invoked her righteous indignation, she was not someone who was going to back down. She took me and stormed out of the school, drove home, and called my dad and insisted that he come home right away. My poor dad must have thought that I was in an accident or something because he was home in less than ten minutes.

That was the first time my parents, or I should say my dad, sat me down and explained what it meant to be adopted, but that just confused me more. Kate tried to placate me with that adage about me being chosen while other parents have to just accept who they get, and I will confess I used that card on more than one occasion to other kids when they tried to make me feel bad for being adopted. But the older I got, the more I knew that was just BS. It didn't change the fact that I was still unwanted by my parents. I eventually came to realize that other parents don't have to just accept who they get because I was living proof of that, as I was not accepted by my birth parents.

So, as you can imagine, my childhood only created questions and uncertainty as to who I really was and why my birth parents didn't want me, but Bill and Kate were loving and very good to me, and I managed to push those questions to the back of my mind for most of my early childhood.

Then, almost in an instant, everything changed. When I was nine, I came home from school one day and saw my dad loading suitcases into his car. Being a rather curious child, I of course asked, "Daddy, where are we going?"

He looked down at me and cupped my face in his hands and said, "Sweetheart, Daddy has to move out of the house. I won't be far away, and I promise I will come and see you every day that I can. Come inside, me and Mommy will explain everything to you." He took me by the hand, and we walked inside. My Mother was sitting at the kitchen table. We sat down together, and they explained to me that they were getting divorced.

I knew what divorce meant, or at least I thought I did. My friend Jenny's parents were divorced, and that meant she only got to see her dad on weekends and holidays. I was, of course, too young to understand the intricacies of marriage, but I was beginning to dislike the very concept of marriage if it meant families had to become separated. In retrospect, I suppose it was only inevitable, as my parents fought constantly about everything. But I just thought that's how all parents were. In my mind, everything was perfect, so I didn't understand why this was happening. But since my dad was the one leaving, I of course blamed him for the break-up. I now know how wrong that was, but I was nine, what did I know?

My dad moved into an apartment not too far away, and he came to pick me up every Saturday and we would return home every Sunday evening, at least for a while. I believed that it was just a temporary situation and that soon all would go back to the way it was, but it never did.

After about a year of this routine, my Dad announced to me that he was moving to Denver. He had completed all his certifications as an HVAC technician and was now classified as a Master Technician, and it was time to follow his dream and start his own business. When he went to work for the company that trained him, he had signed an agreement that stated that if he left the company, he would not open a competing business within 50 miles of Colorado Springs, which meant he would need to move to another city to start his own business. Denver was the closest city large enough to absorb another HVAC company without impacting existing companies, so he told me that he was going to have to move to Denver.

I remember how hard I cried when he told me that, but he made me a promise that no matter what, he would always come to pick me up and take me to spend my weekends with him every two weeks, and he never once failed to keep that promise to me, even when the snow was so bad it was unsafe to make the drive, he would put his snow chains on and make it anyway. I can't tell you how much that meant to me.

Two years after my dad moved, he remarried to a woman whom he had hired to manage books for his business. Her name is Janice, and 18 months after they married, they had a child of their own, a little girl whom they named Zoe. I was twelve when she was born, and as much as I loved her as a little sister, our age difference was enough to ensure that we were never very close, not like I always envisioned sisters should be, at least not until we were both adults.

My teen years were filled with bitterness and teenage anxiety. The older I got, the more I understood that it was my Mom who had been the instigator of my parents' divorce and my increased awareness of that made my resentment towards her grow all the more.

I was given my first guitar for Christmas in 1997. I was 13. I had asked my dad for a guitar after my friend Julie had received one for her birthday that same year, and we thought it would be cool to play together and maybe form a band. Julie grew tired of playing by the time she was 15 and stopped, but music stuck with me. I found it to be a good outlet for everything my young brain was going through. I began experiencing a real crisis of identity during my early teenage years. I was unsure of who I was. I developed a rich fantasy world of alter egos and got into gaming with Dungeons and Dragons and other role-playing games.

For a while, this world, and the friends I had in it, seemed to give me a sense of belonging, but that was short-lived. The only thing I knew was true about me, was that my dad loved me, just for who I was, and I think that kept me from falling into the world of goth or witchcraft or any of the other extreme directions that so many of my D&D friends seemed to fall into as they progressed through their own teenage crisis. I was always too afraid of disappointing my dad, so as more and more of my friends went down these extreme paths, I tended to just withdraw more into my own fantasy world of becoming a great musician and a singer, only now, I know, I didn't really have the self-discipline to become very successful in that world either.

When I was 15, and my mom was now the full manager of the Officers' Club at the Air Base, she was drinking more than before and there was a parade of boyfriends coming in and out of her life. Most were younger Junior Officers whom she met at the club, and as a result, we fought constantly. But I also was not very understanding of the self-esteem crisis that she was going through as well.

She was nearly 40 and single and struggling with me and she didn't know how to deal with all of that, not to mention that she was also struggling with how easily my dad had found it to move on with his life and now had a child of his own. That led her to take every opportunity to criticize him in front of me, and when I defended him, she would get even angrier at me. I was not very sympathetic. I had too much of my own mental crisis going on and I was not going to allow her to tear down the only good thing I had in my life.

This all came to a head one morning when I woke up to a man sitting at our kitchen table and my mom, wearing nothing but a robe, standing at the stove fixing him breakfast. She never even tried to introduce us; she just acted as if this was the most normal thing ever, and asked "Can I make you some eggs, Kiko?"

The man just smiled and said, "You must be Kiko. Your Mother has told me about you." As was my typical teenage way, I didn't even acknowledge him; I just grunted and turned, and walked out. But what broke me, was about twenty minutes later when I was coming out of the shower, I opened the bathroom door, wearing nothing but a towel, and he was standing right there. My Mom had gone to her room to get ready for work and left him alone, and there he was, staring at me like I was a young Gazelle abandoned by its mother and he was a hungry lion. I screamed and ran into my mother's room and yelled at her to, "GET YOUR PERVERTED BOYFRIEND OUT OF THIS HOUSE!" My mother, of course, had no idea what had just happened. She only knew that she had come out of her room in time to find her new friend quickly leaving through the front door as he decided he did not need this much drama in his life. My mother then came back into my room and yelled at me, and we had the biggest, and I dare say, last fight we ever had. I packed my backpack that I used to take to my dad's and left for school. That day I called him from the school office and asked him to come and pick me up after school.

When he picked me up, I wanted to go straight to his house in Denver, but he took me back home as I explained what had happened. He told me to go pack all of my things, and we waited for my mom to get home from work that night. It was a Friday, so she usually didn't get home until after 8:00 pm. But he called the club and told her that he was waiting to talk to her, so she came home early. I didn't hear everything they said, as they were outside, but it was a rather loud discussion, when they were finally done, my dad simply said, "Put your stuff in the truck, you're coming home with me." That was the last time I lived in my mother's house. We did visit from time to time, but I always made her drive to Denver to see me.

The next few years of my life were fairly stable. I lived with my dad, Janice, and Zoe. Janice, for the most part, was okay with that, as she now had a live-in babysitter, which gave her and my dad a bit more freedom to have the occasional date night or not have to be overly concerned if they had to work late at the office. Dad's business was doing well. A friend of his was retiring from a plumbing business with 7 employees, and my dad saw that as an opportunity to expand his own business, so he bought him out. Between the HVAC and plumbing sides of the business, he now had nearly 20 employees.

As a teenager, I learned to work the phones for him in the evenings, setting up appointments for the techs, and Janice showed me how to do bookkeeping, which comes in handy much later in my story, as you will see. I continued to play guitar and write my songs, and I met a boy who was in my music class at school. His name was Derik. We were really good together. He was not so much a musician, but he loved the art of mixing and producing others. Derik's dream was to be a music producer. We talked about him becoming my producer as soon as we graduated from high school.

So from age 15 to 18, I had a fairly settled life and was mostly happy. I loved Zoe, she was a very sweet little girl, and she thought I was the best person in the world.

Then my world came crashing in once again. It was just weeks from high school graduation, I was in my room, and I guess my dad and Janice did not know I was home when I overheard Janice and my dad arguing about me. Janice asked, "How long are we going to let her stay here after she graduates?"

My dad replied, "What do you mean, she'll stay as long as she wants to. If she goes to a local college, she can stay here to help save money."

"We need our house back Bill. Don't get me wrong, she's been a great help with Zoe, but I think Zoe's becoming too close to her. Every time I ask Zoe if she wants me to help her with something, she says, 'No, I want Kiko to do it.' I'm starting to think it was a mistake to let her stay here for so long."

"She's my daughter, Janice."

"Yes, but she's not your real daughter, Bill. Not like Zoe."

"She is my daughter, and nothing can make me think of her in any other way."

"She's eighteen Bill, she is old enough to be on her own. I'm not saying we can't help her, but I want my daughter back. Zoe is your flesh and blood; she should always be your first priority."

My dad just went silent. Clearly, he did not know how to respond to her and didn't want this issue to come between them. He quietly replied, "I'll talk to her."

My heart was broken. The one person in the world I thought I could count on had just failed to come to my defense. I didn't say anything to him about it at that time. But at dinner that night, I announced, "I have something to tell you. Derik and I are going to move to Austin as soon as we graduate. We've been planning this for a long time. The music scene there is really on fire, so we think that will be a good place to launch our music careers."

Dad looked at me and said, "Kiko, are you sure that's a good idea? I thought you'd go to college here. I mean you have been accepted to the University of Colorado already. Why do you have to move so far away?"

"The Indie music scene is taking hold in Austin, Dad. Derik and I both want music careers, so why would we wait? I think this is the best thing for me."

Janice smiled and said, "If you think that's the best thing for you, Kiko, who are we to stand in your way. We'll support you in any way we can. I'm sure you're going to be a great singer with just a little bit of experience and development."

I just smiled in return but did not say anything. This is what Derik, and I had talked about, but only after college, so now I needed to convince Derik that he could just as easily study sound engineering in Austin as he could here in Denver. It took some discussions, but by graduation day, we were both on board and ready to make a move.

That's how I came to be in Austin, on that August night, several years later, when I met Lenny Boyce.

# Chapter 2

As graduation day approached, a sense of panic began to come over me. I had painted myself into this corner and even convinced Derik to move to Austin with me, but I wasn't sure of anything. How were we going to live? How were we going to find music venues that would hire me to play and sing? Was I even good enough to get hired, after all, the only people who had heard me sing to this point were friends and family, and they weren't exactly what you could call an objective group of critics. Suddenly, my mind was filled with images of a young singer standing before a celebrity panel to try to get a spot in their TV competition, and being awful and laughed at.

Was I just fooling myself about my talent? It was a very stressful time for me, but Derik was wonderful during it all. He was my rock, and he just kept us moving forward. He believed in me, and that, I thought, was all I needed.

The day before we left, my dad took me out to dinner, just the two of us. While we were at dinner, he handed me an envelope with $5,000 in it and said, "Your mom and I have been saving for your college for a long time. We discussed this and decided to turn this over to you. This is not all, but I'll send you checks periodically for as long as there is still money in the account. There are some tax implications if we just take it all at once, so I can only take quarterly withdrawals without having to pay penalties. This is what I can remove for now." I was so surprised! At least I knew we weren't going to starve.

Derik's parents had given him a very expensive mixing board as a graduation gift, and, not knowing that my folks were giving me money, they also gave him several thousand dollars. Together, we thought we were millionaires. We were young and carefree and never thought about anything but having fun, but we soon learned that having fun was expensive.

We arrived in Austin on June 30, 2002. We found Austin a wonderful place for two young music junkies like us. The downtown nightclubs were bustling every weekend, with tons of college kids who loved anything Indie related, and the clubs were always looking for new talent and good soundboard operators, so within a few weeks, Derik and I were both beginning to earn some money. If I didn't have a gig to play, I could always pick up a shift as a waitress or a barback in one of the clubs that got to know us pretty well, and at least share in the tips for that night. It wasn't too long before Derik met some studio owners who let him come and spend time watching and learning from more experienced sound engineers. They were happy to have him come in and help set up amps and mics and the like, especially since he was willing to do it for free, just to be around the studio and learn and watch the producers and engineers do their thing. He was not interested in the bands or singers who would come in to record, but in the recording process itself.

Sometimes we would be sitting in our apartment listening to music, and he would stop it and say, "Did you hear that? That was awesome."

I'd say, "What?"

He would say, "That, that triangle in the background, that's genius, you can hardly hear it, but it rounds out that sound." It was all about the arrangements and subtlety of the different sounds to him. It wasn't too long before he was hired full-time by Rondo Records, a small label in Austin, working as an engineer. Rondo was small, but it was a wonderful learning ground for Derik. Derik wanted more, though – he wanted to be a producer.

In our first couple of years in Austin, we thought we owned the world. Everything was going well. I was gigging regularly, Derik was working full-time, and my dad would send me a bit more money every few months. It was a great life, and we thought it would never end.

The same year that we moved to Austin, the City decided to hold a new Music Festival called Austin City Limits. For the first three years of the festival, I was given spots to perform. They were not prominent spots, usually early afternoon and on a smaller stage, but Derik would come and run the mixing board for me, so I always sounded so good at the festival.

When the fourth year of the festival came around, I didn't receive an invitation, so I called the lady who did the line-ups and asked if I was going to get a spot. She told me. "I'm sorry, Kiko, but we need to make room for newer and better-recognized artists this year. The festival is growing so fast. We're adding stages this year, and we have so many applications. We even have record companies offering to pay to get their artists showcased, so we need to make room for them. But we do need lots of volunteers to help with the crowds and in the vendor booths. I'd be happy to sign you up if you like. That will get you free admission."

I was devastated, but after talking to Derik, we both signed up as volunteers, believing that just being around the bigger artists who would be performing might lead to some opportunities. This paid off for Derik, but not so much for me.

At the end of the fourth Festival, Derik was offered a contract with a band that had some recognition and was beginning a six-month tour of 25 cities to run the soundboard for them for their live shows. This meant he would be gone for six months. I was very happy for him, but not so much for what this meant for me. My hopes for a music career were not completely dashed at that point, but they were rapidly dwindling.

Indie fans and college kids were looking for artists who wrote and performed their own music. I was still primarily a cover artist. I tried to write and perform my own stuff, but it was not great. I never got booed off the stage or anything, but it just was not at the level that some of the most talented artists were performing at, and I knew that. But not all was lost. Bobby Barnes, the owner of the Top Hat club on Sixth Street, liked me, and his crowd was not so rowdy as some of the other clubs, so they kind of liked the covers more than some avant-garde Indie music. He let me come and play regularly for tips, and the tips were not bad.

As soon as I turned twenty-one, I got my bartender's license. Bartending in Austin, at that time, pretty much meant dispensing beer, wine, shots of tequila or whisky, margaritas, and the occasional mixed drink. I was really good at the first three and had a menu for the mixed drinks, but the people who frequented Sixth Street didn't know if what I served them was correct or not; they were mostly just trying to impress a date by ordering something more sophisticated, so I managed to do okay even with those.

One night after I had done a late-night spot at the mic, the bar was closed, and Bobby had closed the cash boxes, I walked into the office to say goodnight. He was sitting at his desk making entries into a ledger, and I asked, "Do you still do that by hand?"

"Yeah," he replied.

"You know they have software for that, right?"

"I'm not so good with that stuff. I've always done it this way; it works for me."

"I know how to use that kind of software." I can set it up for you. I learned how to keep books when working for my Dad when I was still in High School."

"Really?"

"Yeah, I mean, how do you even know if you are making money or losing it every week if you just enter receipts every night and then just pay bills as they come in? Don't you have an accountant? How does he calculate your taxes?"

"No. I've always just done it myself. I just guessed how much I made based on my personal expenses and what my business expenses were. Nobody has ever questioned it."

"Wow, I hope you don't ever get audited." I laughed, "My dad was audited two years in a row. It was serious; they wanted receipts and invoices, and everything needed to match perfectly. Luckily, Janice keeps good books; she was strict about that."

"Janice?"

"His wife, my stepmom. She's the one who taught me how to keep books."

"So you know how to do this, then?"

"Yeah."

"Okay, how much do you want to try and make sense of all this?"

"I don't know. $300 a week."

"What about your singing and bartending?"

"That will be separate from the bookkeeping, like an independent contractor."

He thought for a few moments and said, "Okay, that's good, but only I get to handle the cash. I will close the registers every night, make the bank deposits, and bring you the receipts."

"That's fine, I can deal with that."

And so for the next year and a half, that's the way it was. He handled the cash, and I did the books.

In the meantime, Derik was beginning to get the recognition he had worked so long for. He sent me money for the rent every couple of weeks and would call every night, at first, but slowly the nightly calls became once or twice a week, and then just occasionally. When the tour ended, he came home and was there for about two weeks when he got a call from another, even better-known artist to come and run their sound system during a six-week tour. This included a few performances in Las Vegas, which he was very excited about. I even flew out there for the opening show to see him work, and it was so much fun. The artist he was working for was very well known, the crowds were large, and it was all very exciting.

But then, when that tour was over, he came back home, but I could tell that something had changed. He seemed lost in thought and distant most of the time. I would ask what was wrong, but he would just say, "Nothing, I'm fine." But I could see he was not. When he finally mustered the nerve to tell me, I was shocked.

"Kiko, I have an offer from the entertainment director at Caesar's Palace to come and work for them full-time, as the sound engineer for a new show they're producing, and I've decided to take the job."

"Wow... that's great, Derik. I'm willing to move if it means you'll be able to continue to grow your career. At least your career is actually growing – mine seems to be going nowhere."

But then he hit me with the news that shocked me to my core. "I'm going alone, Kiko."

"Alone, what do you mean alone, Derik? We're a pair, we're partners, you always told me so."

"I know, Kiko, but you'll be fine, you're doing okay, and earning some steady money now with your bookkeeping. Maybe you should go back to school and study accounting, you're good at it."

I just began crying. I was devastated. I never imagined that he would just leave me like that. "Have you met someone else?" I asked.

"No, it's not like that. I just need to be alone for a while. We've known each other since our freshman year in high school. I just think that for us to each grow, we need to experience life in different ways. We both know that our lives have gotten a bit stale. How can either one of us become who we want to be unless we get to know ourselves better? I'm sorry, Kiko, you know I love you and always will, but I need to go out on my own for now."

His words seemed to make sense, or at least I convinced myself they did, until one day I realized it was just a long-winded version of the old, it's not you, it's me, speech. I was still very naive in those days. Imagine how I felt when word came back to me that he had gotten married just eight months later, to a Vegas showgirl, nonetheless.

If it's any consolation, it only lasted a couple of years. The last I heard, he has been married and divorced twice now.

Somehow, I managed to carry on. He was right, I did have my bookkeeping gig along with bartending and the occasional turn at the mike. I did take one piece of advice, though: I enrolled in a couple of accounting classes at the local community college. I wasn't looking to get a degree or anything; I just wanted to make sure I was doing everything right, since this was now my primary source of income. But then even that rug was pulled out from under me.

One night, I was working as a Bartender at the Top Hat, and it was a really good night—the 4th of July weekend, and the club was packed. The till was almost overflowing. I told Bobby that he needed to cash out what was in the till and get it put in the safe, so that we would reduce the risk of being robbed. He did that, and the night continued. I stood at the register and watched him count the cash and restart the till, and then walk into the office. The next day was Sunday, and then on Monday morning, he took the cash to the bank to deposit it. When he brought me the receipt, I knew it was light, meaning I knew we had made much more money than that, several thousand dollars more, actually. My accounting classes had taught me the importance of accuracy in these matters, and so it weighed heavily on me. Then I began to wonder if this was a regular practice with Bobby.

I talked to one of my accounting professors, generically, of course, about the culpability for something like this, and as a former IRS Agent, he told me that, if it were proven that the bookkeeper was aware of the practice of undercounting or reporting, they could be held just as liable as the owner. And now I was aware. I was not all that close to Janice, but I did trust her to advise me on this issue, so I called her. She told me I either needed to confront him and let him know he was putting me at risk as well, or I just needed to walk away. So I got up my nerves and went in to talk to Bobby about what he was doing.

He just laughed at me and told me that it was a common practice among the club owners to barely show enough money on the books to look like they were breaking even.

"But that's illegal!" I said.

"What are you, some kind of goody-two-shoes now? Get with it, Kiko!"

"I...I can't be part of that, Bobby."

"So what, you're going to shake me down now. How much more do you want? Will another hundred a week help ease your conscience a bit?"

I confess, another hundred a week was tempting. I had been struggling since Derik left. I even had to move into a smaller studio apartment in a not-so-nice part of town to make ends meet. But I couldn't get the image out of my head of IRS agents crawling all over the bar and asking me to see all the register tapes.

"No, Derik, I can't keep doing your books if they're not 100 percent legit."

"I'm sorry to hear that, Kiko. It's been nice having you around here, but if you can't do the books, I really don't need you as a Bartender or singer either." And just like that, I was out of every gig and vestige of hope I had left.

After licking my wounds for a day or two, I began hitting the other clubs looking for work as a Bartender, Gig Artist, Bookkeeper, or anything I was capable of doing, but I soon learned how fast news travels in that world. All the bar owners know each other, obviously, as many of them own several clubs. They talk regularly, and Bobby had put the word out that I was a potential troublemaker and not to hire me. Even chain restaurants like Chili's and such, that had bars, seemed to have received the memo not to hire me. Of course, it was not an actual memo, just word of mouth, but it might as well have been. I knew just about every Bartender, Barback, and Gig Artist in the Austin music scene, but they would barely speak to me now. One, who turned out to be the only real friend in the bar community

I had, told me that I had been "Blacklisted." I couldn't believe it. What was I going to do now? Where was I going to go?

After about six weeks. I had to give up my apartment. Thank goodness for Gina, the only friend I seemed to have left, who let me come and couch surf until I could figure things out. I was just about to give up on my dreams and go home to work for my dad, as he always left that option open to me, when, just by happenstance, I met Lenny Boyce.

I was sitting in the apartment one afternoon, about 3:00 or so, and looking very down, when Gina said, "I'm going out to Liberty Gardens to listen to Lenny tonight. He's really gifted and insightful. You should come with me; you might get something out of it.

"Lenny, what is it, some kind of lecture or something?" I asked.

"Kind of, but his lectures are like something I've never experienced before, and they'll be food – at least there's usually food."

"You've been there before?"

"Yeah, a few times. Come with me, Kiko, I think you'll like it. I mean, what's the alternative, sit around here alone all night?"

She was right, I certainly did not want to sit around the apartment all night alone, so I took a shower, put on the cleanest clothes I could find, and drove with Gina out to this place in the hill country, just off of Highway 290, to hear a Lecture which I was sure I was going to hate.

We pulled the car off the road and drove under a wooden sign with the name "Liberty Gardens" carved into it. We drove about another 50 yards up the gravel drive and then pulled into a parking area off to the right. Several cars were already parked there. We parked and got out of the car, and followed a few other people up the gravel path for about a hundred yards or so, past an old house that looked like it was a hundred years old. The entire property was covered in natural flowers and shrubs, but no trees, yet the property itself was surrounded by a thick forest of wild oak and cedar, and nearly every variety of natural Texas tree. It was like this place had been carved directly out of the forest.

We approached a large, covered pavilion, which had another wooden sign hanging over the gabled opening. Which read, "Where the spirit of the Lord is, there is Liberty." I immediately got a sinking feeling in my stomach that I had somehow been roped into attending a church meeting of some sort. I looked at Gina and asked, "Is this a church?"

"I call it church without walls. But it's not really church, it's just Lenny."

"What does that mean?" I asked.

"You'll see," was all she said.

As we entered the pavilion, I could see off to the right side were steps leading down into a small amphitheater, with concrete seating in a semi-circular fashion, with a concrete pad at the bottom. It was only big enough for a hundred people or so, and at the bottom was a chair with a microphone sitting in front of it. We sat there for about 10 minutes while a few people who recognized Gina came to say hello. Gina introduced me, and everyone seemed very kind and friendly, and always said, "We'll talk later, Lenny's about to begin." Suddenly, all eyes turned to watch a tall, thin figure of a man descending the steps.

## Chapter 3

As I turned to look at the man everyone else was looking at, I was somewhat surprised. I had assumed, or at least my past experiences with such outdoor churches, that the pastor would be some thirty-something, good-looking guy who everyone thought was "Hip" or "Cool," but what I saw was not that at all. This tall, very slim man was old, maybe mid-sixties or early seventies even, with a full white beard and long silvery white hair. His hair was not tied back in a ponytail, as I had grown to expect from old men with long hair, but hung loose about his shoulders. He navigated the steps with much more agility than I would have expected for someone of his age, greeting people sitting on the aisles as he descended, and then went to take his seat in the chair on the stage.

He sat in this big rattan chair with a fanned back and just looked out at all of us for a few moments. This man looked like he was in his natural element – comfortable and relaxed, as if this was exactly where he was supposed to be. He was wearing jeans and a long-sleeved white button-down shirt with an open collar and leather sandals on his feet. *Oh God, a Hippy*! was the thought that ran through my head for some reason, but that was just my own prejudice, I suppose.

Nearly 40 or so people were sitting in the seats. He smiled and said, "It's nice to see so many familiar faces here tonight," and he seemed to look directly at me when he then said, "And some new ones as well." His voice was deep and clear, but had a rhythmic quality to it. On certain phrases, it would go up about an octave or two, and then come right back down to his normal, steady, lower pitch. And then he began to speak, without an introduction or forewarning—he just went right into it.

"We have this rather peculiar idea in our culture that helping others is always the right thing to do. We've been taught from childhood that to be a good person, a spiritual person, a loving person, you must always say yes. You must always give, you must always be available, and if you hesitate, if you pause, if you dare to set a boundary, well then, something must be wrong with you. You must be selfish. You must be unkind.

"But what if I told you that this entire notion is backwards? What if the compulsive need to help everyone, to fix everyone, to rescue everyone, is not actually love at all, but a form of interference, a way of disrupting the very lessons that life is trying to teach? There's a distinct difference between serving others and helping everyone. You see, to be of service means always to be looking out for the other person's best interest, but to help, at least in this modern world, usually implies just giving something to anyone who asks. Think about it. When you continually rescue someone from the consequences of their own actions, what are you really doing? You're not serving them. You're keeping them trapped. You're preventing them from learning. You're standing between them and the wisdom that only comes through experience. Before offering help to anyone, you must ask yourself, if I do this, will I be empowering them, or limiting them?

"Now, I'm not suggesting that we become cold or indifferent. That would be another extreme, wouldn't it? The question is not whether you should care. The question is how you care. And more importantly, who you choose to pour your energy into. You see, certain types of people will drain you dry. They will take and take and take, and no matter how much you give, it will never be enough. And the tragedy is not that they are taking. The tragedy is that you are preventing them from growing. And in addition, the people who only know how to take seldom learn how to give themselves.

"Today, I want to share what I have learned about the types of perpetual takers that you must learn to recognize. Not so that you can judge or condemn them, but so that you can protect your own energy and allow them to face the very experiences that they need to learn the lessons that life is presenting to them. Now, keep in mind, we are not talking about starving children who cannot fend for themselves; I am only talking about fully grown adults who refuse to make good choices for their own lives.

"First, there's the chronically lazy. There is a difference, you see, between someone who is struggling and someone who has simply given up. The person who is struggling will take your help and use it as a stepping stone. But the chronically lazy person will use your help as a hammock. They have made a decision, whether consciously or not, that life is too difficult and someone else should carry their burden for them. And the moment you step in to help them, you become their 'someone else' – you become their co-conspirator in laziness. And this is not because they are not capable of doing for themselves, but because they have discovered that someone will always do it for them.

"Now watch what happens in nature. A bird does not bring food to a chick that refuses to open its mouth. A tree does not continue to nourish a branch that bears no fruit. Nature is very clear about this. If something is not producing, if something is not contributing, it is eventually cut off. Not out of cruelty but out of wisdom.

"The chronically lazy person will always have an excuse. They will tell you about their difficult childhood, their bad luck, their unfair circumstances, and some of this may even be true. But here is the question you must ask. What are they doing about it right now? Are they taking any steps, however small, to change their situation? Or are they simply waiting for someone to come along and fix it for them?"

I suddenly felt very convicted, like I was taking advantage of Gina in this same way, and I looked over at Gina, but she was just looking straight ahead and didn't seem to feel the same or gain the same sense of being taken advantage of as I did about taking advantage of her, so for a moment, anyway, my guilt was lessened. But then the question went through my head, "Is this why she brought me here tonight, to send me a subtle message that it was time to leave?" Lenny then went on.

"When you help someone who refuses to help themselves, you rob them of something precious. You rob them of the satisfaction of their own accomplishment. You rob them of the strength that comes from overcoming difficulty. You rob them of the very thing they need most, which is the discovery that they are capable. Some of you have been carrying people for years. You pay their bills, you solve their problems, you clean up their messes, and every time you do it, you tell yourself you are just being kind. But what if your kindness is actually keeping them weak?"

Again, another arrow went straight to my heart, but Gina never looked at me as if she felt that way at all.

Lenny continued, "What if your help is the very thing preventing them from standing on their own feet? The lazy person needs to feel hunger. They need to feel discomfort. They need to experience the natural consequences of their choices, because it is only when they feel the pain of staying the same becomes greater than the pain of change, that they will finally move.

"Next, there is the perpetually ungrateful. Have you ever noticed that some people can receive an extraordinary gift and treat it as if it were nothing? You could give them your time, your money, your energy, your very heart, and they will take it without so much as a second thought. No thank you, no acknowledgement, no appreciation whatsoever."

Oh my God, was he trying to destroy me? This man doesn't even know me, and yet every word he says seems to cut right through me like a knife. By this time, I was feeling very uncomfortable and wanted to leave, but I knew I couldn't – I had come with Gina, and she was driving, so I just had to sit there and listen.

"This is not an accident. This is a character issue. Gratitude is not just good manners. Gratitude is the sign of a person who recognizes they are part of something larger than themselves. A grateful person understands that every blessing, every gift, every kindness is not owed to them but given freely. And when you understand this, you treat gifts with reverence. But the ungrateful person believes the world owes them. They believe your help is their right. And the more you give to them, the more entitled they become. It's a strange paradox, isn't it? The more you pour into them, the less they appreciate it.

"I once knew a man who helped his brother pay his rent for three months straight. Month after month, he sacrificed his own needs to make sure his brother had a roof over his head. And throughout the entirety of the three months, the younger brother complained. He complained that he couldn't go out drinking with his buddies. He complained that he couldn't go out to restaurants like he used to. He complained that he was missing out on all his friends' activities. Not once did he say thank you. Not once did he acknowledge the sacrifice. And when the three months ended and his brother could no longer help, do you know what happened? The needy brother became angry. He felt betrayed, as if the help he received was not a gift but a debt that was now being unfairly called in. This is the nature of the ungrateful.

"They don't see kindness; they see weakness. They don't see generosity; they see opportunity. And they will take and take and take until there is nothing left of you. When you help an ungrateful person, you are not sowing seeds. You are throwing them into a bottomless pit. And no matter how much you throw in, the pit will never be filled."

Okay... I felt a bit better now, that certainly was not me. I am always very grateful for all of Gina's help. *Do I really express it, though?* I wondered.

"Then there are the arrogant and self-righteous. Some people don't want your help – they want your validation. They don't want your wisdom – they want you to confirm what they already believe. And if you dare to offer anything that challenges their worldview, they will reject you entirely. The arrogant person is not suffering from a lack of knowledge. They are suffering from an excess of pride. They believe they already know. They believe their way is the only correct way, and anyone who suggests otherwise is simply wrong. Now, pride is a curious thing. It masquerades as confidence, but it is actually fear. The arrogant person is terrified of being wrong because their entire identity is built on being right. If they admit they don't know something, if they acknowledge they need help, their whole sense of self begins to crumble.

"And so they double down, they defend, they argue, they reject. You can't help a person like this. Not because they're beyond help, but because they don't believe they need it. And until they come to that realization themselves, anything you offer will be wasted.

"Jesus walked away from people like this. He didn't chase them. He didn't beg them to listen. He simply said what needed to be said and moved on, because he understood something very important – you cannot force wisdom on someone who is committed to their own self-delusions. The arrogant person must fall. They must experience the consequences of their pride. They must hit the ground hard enough that they finally look up and realize they do not have all the answers. And only then, when they are humbled, when they are broken, will they be ready to receive help. Sadly, so few arrogant individuals ever get humbled in this way."

Amen to that, I thought, but then I remembered all the times Derik and I argued, and I refused to give in because I was always so sure I was right and he was wrong. But Lenny wasn't finished yet.

"This brings us to the habitually iniquitous. Now, I want to be very careful here because we don't like to use a word like iniquitous these days, and I most certainly do not use it lightly. We prefer softer language. We say someone is troubled or misunderstood. But there are people in this world who are not confused. They know exactly what they are doing is wrong, and they do it anyway. The iniquitous person is not someone who makes a mistake. We all make mistakes. The iniquitous person is someone who has made iniquity their way of life. They lie, they cheat, they manipulate, they harm others without remorse. And when confronted, they do not repent – they justify. When you help an iniquitous person, you become an accomplice, you enable their behavior, you give them the resources to continue harming. And let me tell you something, they will use what you give them, not to change, but to go deeper into their iniquity and drag you right down that rabbit hole with them.

"There is a reason why traditions across cultures warn against supporting those such as the iniquitous ones, and even the Bible refers to Satan as being iniquitous. It is not because we lack compassion. It's because we recognize that some people have chosen a path that leads to destruction. The iniquitous person does not want to be saved. They want to be empowered. They want someone to fund their schemes, to cover for their lies, to clean up their messes. And if you step into that role, you are not helping them – you are partnering with darkness."

I've definitely known a few of those, I thought. Bobby, for some reason, popped into my mind, but maybe that was unfair to him – I don't know. I really don't know what was in his mind or heart. But there were still more types that Lenny talked about.

"Now we come to the incurably foolish. A fool is not someone who lacks intelligence. A fool is someone who refuses to learn. They make the same mistakes over and over again. This is akin to insanity. A wise man once defined insanity as the act of 'taking the same steps over and over again and expecting different results each time.'

"The fool ignores advice. They reject wisdom. They touch the hot stove repeatedly and then wonder why their hand is burned. The difference between a wise person and a fool is very simple. A wise person learns from experience. A fool does not. Now, here is what makes this particularly difficult. The fool will often come to you in distress. They will be in crisis, they will be desperate, and your heart will go out to them. You will want to help. You will want to rescue them. But if you look closely at their history, you will see the pattern."

"This is not their first crisis. This is not the first time they have needed rescue. In fact, they have been in this exact situation multiple times before. And each time someone helped them, they went right back to the same behavior that got them into trouble in the first place. The fool is like a person drowning in the ocean who refuses to grab the life preserver you throw them. Instead, they keep thrashing and splashing and going under. And if you jump in to save them, they will pull you under, too.

"You cannot save a fool. Only life can teach them. Only the consequences of their own actions can break through their stubbornness. And if you keep intervening, you prevent those consequences from doing their work.

"This brings us to the master manipulator. The manipulator is perhaps the most dangerous person on this list, because they are the hardest to recognize. They do not come to you with demands. They come with stories. They do not take from you directly. They make you want to give. The manipulator understands human nature. They know that good people want to help. They know that kind people feel guilty when they say no. And they use this knowledge like a weapon. They will tell you exactly what you need to hear. They will play on your emotions. They will make you feel special, needed, important, and before you know it, you are doing things for them that you would never do for anyone else."

Wait, was this me? Am I the manipulator? I didn't feel like a manipulator, but is that how Gina sees me, especially after hearing this lecture? I was now so confused and so depressed. *Coming here tonight was not a good idea*, I told myself.

"The manipulator is a shape shifter. With one person, they are the victim. With another, they are the hero. They change their story depending on who they are talking to. And if you compare notes with others who have dealt with them, you will find that the stories do not match. When you help a manipulator, you are not helping a person in need. You are feeding a system. You are providing resources for them to continue their games. And the moment you stop giving, the moment you see through the act, they will turn on you. They will paint you as the villain, they will tell others how you wronged them, and they will move on to their next target.

"So what do we do with all of this? Do we become cold and indifferent? Do we stop helping people altogether? No, of course not. We learn discernment. We learn to recognize the difference between someone who is struggling and someone who is stuck. We learn to distinguish between someone who needs a hand up and someone who wants a hand out. We learn to see clearly without judgment but also without illusion. True compassion is not enabling. True compassion sometimes means stepping back and allowing people to face the consequences of their choices. Because it is often through difficulty, through hardship, through hitting bottom that people finally wake up."

*Is that me*, I wondered? *Have I hit bottom? Maybe I had, but what do I do now?*

"When you help the right people, you see fruit. When you plant in good soil, you see growth. But when you give to those who are not ready, who do not want to change, who will only use you and drain you, all you will see is waste.

"Your energy is precious, your time is finite, your resources are limited, and you must be wise about where you invest them. Not everyone deserves your help. And that is not cruelty. That is wisdom. So ask yourself today, who am I helping that I should let go? Who am I rescuing that needs to fall? Who am I enabling that needs to face their own consequences? And when you find the answer, dare to step back. Not with anger, not with resentment, but with the understanding that sometimes the most loving thing you can do is allow someone to experience the full weight of their own choices. Because in the end, you cannot save anyone. You can only point the way. And whether they walk that path or not is entirely up to them.

"Now, are there any questions from anyone tonight?" Lenny asked.

Everyone looked around, and no one seemed to be brave enough to raise their hands.

"Wonderful," Lenny said, "It looks like we are going to have an early supper tonight. I believe Irma has cooked her incredible chili con carne, so please, I invite you all to join us in a meal and time of community."

Lenny stood and began to ascend the steps back up to the top, and was the first person in line to fill his bowl. I looked at Gina, feeling like I just wanted to leave, and she looked back and said, "I love Irma's chili, come on, you'll love it too."

Gina and I went and got in line. Behind the counter were two women, one with coal black hair, maybe in her late 30s or early 40s, and the other much younger—late teens, I guessed.

We got our bowls of chili and went and sat down, and two other women came and sat at our table as well. They knew Gina, and Gina introduced us, but to be honest, my mind was still focused on what the teacher had said, so their names kind of went in one ear and out the other. But they were nice and they asked me questions about what I did and what I thought about Lenny's oratory.

"Oratory?" I asked. "Yeah, that's what Lenny calls them. In fact, he calls this entire theater an "Oratorium," like the old Greek philosophers would use.

I just replied, "It was nice, and that the speaker was a very good speaker, and he gave me a lot to think about."

"Yeah," said one of the other girls, "a couple of times I felt like he was talking just to me. He always makes me feel that way." Gina and the third girl agreed that, sometimes, they get the same sense when he speaks. I was just happy to hear that I was not alone in that feeling.

Meanwhile, Lenny was moving from table to table, speaking with every person, one at a time, until he finally made his way to our table. He greeted each of my three tablemates by name and asked each a question, indicating that he actually listened to them in their past conversation with him, and he remembered what they said, as if each of them really mattered to him. I had never seen anyone like him before. Then he came to me and said, "And so, who is our new friend?" as he held his hand out to shake my hand.

"This is Kiko, and she came with me tonight, Gina said, like she was very proud of herself for having brought someone new into the community.

Lenny replied, "Well, Gina, thank you so much for bringing us someone new to share in our joy and fellowship." He did not ask what I thought about his talk, and I thought that a bit unusual. My experience in these kinds of situations is that the speaker wants to know what everyone thought, so they can make the evening all about them, but Lenny did not seem to care at all about what I or anyone else thought about his lecture.

Then the lady behind the serving counter called out to Lenny with a heavy foreign accent, Hispanic, I thought, "Lenny, don't forget about our announcement before people begin to leave."

"Oh yes, of course. Can I have everyone's attention, please? I have a wonderful announcement. He held out his arm, and the young girl who was working behind the serving counter came to stand by Lenny's side. "This is somewhat of a difficult announcement for me, as our friend, Suzanna, here, is leaving us on Monday to head off to college. I am so proud of her, I can't believe how quickly she has grown up. I have known this wonderful young lady since she was just a few weeks old, and as you all know, she and her mother, Irma, have been here with me for nearly two decades. But at long last, the time has come for this one to go off and leave her mother's nest and head off to University. She's not going too far, just up the road to the University of Texas at San Marcos, but far enough that she will be living in the dorm, at least during the weekdays. So, I know you all want to join with me in wishing her a wonderful career at College as she begins her studies to become a Registered Nurse. In honor of this occasion, all tips placed in the tip jar tonight will be given to Suzanna to help her get her dorm room furnished and take care of any unexpected expenses she may have as she makes this transition, so please give generously. And, if anyone is looking for a job, please let Irma know. She will need a new assistant here in the gardens."

People began to rush up to the tip jar that was placed on the serving counter, and I also felt compelled, so I went up and put a five-dollar bill in. I saw lots of twenties and even a few hundred-dollar bills, so this was obviously a very well-to-do group of attendees. After Gina had her chance to say her congratulations, it was time for us to leave, as others were beginning to leave as well.

As Gina and I were driving home, we sat in silence for about 10 minutes, both processing what Lenny had said, then I broke the silence and turned to her and said, "I want to thank you, Gina, for all that you've done for me. I know these last few weeks have been a burden on you."

"A burden, Kiko, you couldn't be a burden even if you tried. Just the fact that you think you might be is proof that you are not capable of being a burden."

"Thank you for saying that, Gina, but I know it's not easy carrying the load for two people, and I don't want you to think that I am taking you for granted."

"Kiko, didn't you hear what Lenny said? 'We need to plant our seeds where we know they will grow, and you are the very best kind of soil.'"

"Do you really mean that, Gina?"

"Kiko, over the last few years that I've known you, I have seen you work as a Barback, a Bartender, a Singer, and a Bookkeeper, sometimes all in the same week. I've never known anyone who works as hard as you. What's happened to you is a shame. It happened because you made a good ethical decision, and someday, that decision is going to repay you in ways you never imagined.

We drove the rest of the way home without saying a word, but just listened to the radio and sang along like we were teenagers again.

# Chapter 4

We arrived back at the apartment at around nine o'clock, and Gina went directly to bed, as she had an early shift in the morning. I was making up the couch, getting ready to call it a night myself, when my phone rang. It was my Dad, just wanting to know how I was doing. I walked out onto the small patio we had that was furnished with a little round metal tea table with a marble top, and I said, "Hi, Daddy."

"Hey Kiko, I just wanted to check in to see what's going on. Any luck finding a job yet?"

"Not yet, but I have a few leads that I'll look into this coming week." That was a complete lie. I really hadn't been looking much at all. I was still too self-absorbed to even consider looking very seriously. But I now knew I couldn't keep taking advantage of Gina like I was.

"Good, glad to hear it, but you know, sweetheart, you always have a job here if you would like one. Janice has been hinting that she would like to spend more time with Zoe, now that she's twelve, so I could always use the help with the books and scheduling."

At that moment, I wanted so badly to say "Yes," and just pack everything up and move home tomorrow. I missed my dad so much, and Zoe too. The last time my dad came to visit me, Zoe and Janice came with him, and I couldn't believe how big Zoe is getting. She was so excited to see me, and I had missed so much of her life. Even Janice has been quite lovely to me since I moved to Austin.

My Mom was also finally settling into some kind of reasonable life and dating a man who seemed to be very good for her – a retired Air Force officer, and she was in a twelve-step program, so really trying to make some changes in her life for the better. With everything that I had been through these last few months, I missed them all so much more than I ever expected I would.

But those words spoken by Lenny just kept running through my head, and all I could think of was not wanting to become some kind of "taker" who never gave back. I knew that if I went home, my Dad would allow me to become Lazy, or Manipulative, or any of the other kinds of people Lenny had talked about.

Then, suddenly, Lenny's words finally registered in my brain. "There is a job opening working here at the gardens if anyone is interested." I don't know why I didn't pay attention when he was talking before, too much in my own head, I guess. I was now asking myself why I didn't at least go and ask Irma about the job. Maybe it was something I could do. Maybe it was only part-time or doesn't pay enough to be worth the effort, I don't know. That place looked like it was in desperate need of a makeover, so who knows what they can afford to pay, but I should have at least asked about it.

"You know what, Daddy, I think I may have a lead on a job here in Austin that I want to look into before deciding on coming home. I'll call you later in the week and let you know how it works out. If it doesn't work out, then we can talk about me coming home and taking that job."

"Does that mean coming home is still in play?" he asked hopefully.

"We'll see, Daddy."

"Okay, sweetheart. Well, that sounds promising anyway. We'll talk later in the week, and you can fill me in. Just remember, if you need me to fly out to help you move or do anything, just let me know. I love you, Kiko, but it's getting late there, so I'll let you go for the night."

"Thank you, Daddy, and I love you too. I'll talk to you in a day or so. Good night."

"Good night, sweetheart."

Before I went to bed, I walked over and opened my laptop and printed out a copy of my resume, and thought that I would go and enquire about that job.

The following morning, Gina was up and out by 5:00. She was working as a shift manager at a local restaurant, and it was Sunday morning, so the breakfast crowds started coming in early. I stayed in bed until about 7:30, and then got up, showered and dressed, made some breakfast, just toast and strawberry jam, and some juice. Gina was always willing to give me shifts at the restaurant when I felt up to it, or when she was short-handed, she would ask me to fill in, so I wasn't desperate for pocket money, but she knew it was not what I wanted to do.

I sat down, picked up my guitar, and began to play. That always cheered me up. I wondered if I should go out to "The Gardens," that's what Gina called the place we had gone last night, on a Sunday. Something inside me kept saying to go. Then I thought, what about that woman, Irma, would she even be there on a Sunday? Does she live there? What was her relationship with Lenny? He said he had known her daughter since she was just a few weeks old. Were they married? Was he the stepfather? I had so many questions, but something just kept saying, "Go today. If you wait, someone else may get there first." My Grandpa Kellen always used to say, "If you snooze, you lose. Never put off until tomorrow what you can do today." So at about 10:00 AM, I decided to drive out to The Gardens to at least hand in my resume.

I retraced the route that Gina and I had taken the day before, and just hoped I would be able to find this place again. It was kind of out there in the Hill Country, as that part of Texas is called. It was actually closer to a city called Dripping Springs than it was to Austin, but still, there was very little else around it. But I have always had a pretty good sense of direction, so I pointed my 12-year-old beat-up Toyota Camry in that direction and drove out.

To my surprise, I found it with very little difficulty. The parking lot was empty, so I pulled up in front of the house. The house was built of all timber that had never been painted, so it had a very rustic gray look to it, but as I approached the front door, I could tell it was built as a solid timber-frame construction. I had been in enough homes with my dad up in the mountains of Colorado to know different types of construction – stick frame, timber-frame, log-frame, and steel-framed buildings, so I could see, now that I was up close, that what I had assessed yesterday as a rickety-looking home was anything but that. It was a solid timber-frame, and timber-framed homes were built to last, sometimes hundreds of years.

I knocked on the door and stood there for what seemed like 5 minutes, but I'm sure in reality, it was less than a minute. Then the door swung open, and there stood Lenny, a big smile on his face, and hair and beard looking a bit disheveled. I don't know what I was expecting, but I was shocked to see him standing there, kind of like seeing a celebrity out in public doing normal things, like at Home Depot or something. He was tall, about 6 feet 4 inches, and looked even older than I recalled from last night. His face was weathered and brown, like he had worked out in the sun most of his life, and his teeth were a bit uneven, but they looked all natural. His tall, thin frame filled the doorway as he took one look at me and said, "Kiko, what a pleasant surprise!"

I was even more flustered that he remembered my name and acted as if he was quite familiar with who I was. I took a step back, took another moment to collect myself, and then stammered, "I'm so sorry to disturb you on Sunday, but I wanted to give Irma my resumé for the job opening." My lack of confidence was glaring as I stuck out my hand with the resumé dangling from my fingers.

"How wonderful." He replied. "And an actual printed resumé, impressive young lady." Even before he had looked at it. "I've heard about these, but I've never actually seen one before, most impressive indeed."

I had no idea how to respond to that. Was he making fun of me, or was he serious? I really couldn't tell. Then he said, "Today is Irma's day off, but she usually comes in the early afternoon on Sundays to tend her garden and harvest what's ready to harvest. Why don't you come in and have some tea, and we can have a wonderful chat while we wait for her?

I wasn't sure what to do now. I didn't know him, and he wanted me to come into his house alone. I could hear my dad's voice screaming in my head, "Don't go, Kiko, don't go in." But there was something about him that was very disarming, a kind of childish innocence, or a playfulness, so I turned off the alarm bells and went into the house. The inside was not at all what I would have expected given the outside appearance. It was warm and kind of cozy. As we entered the entryway, I saw what appeared to be an office or library to the right, with open French doors. I could see a big desk and floor-to-ceiling oak bookcases filled with books, and some beautiful wood paneling on the walls, more like something you would see in a Victorian home.

We walked into the living room, and it was a completely different vibe, much more farmhouse shabby-chic, I would say, with ship-lapped walls, an overstuffed chair, and a big sofa with a solid wooden coffee table in front of it. "So, how may I serve you, Kiko? I can brew some hot tea, or I have some iced tea, and I believe I have some lemonade in the Frigidaire as well."

I can't remember the last time I heard someone refer to their refrigerator as a "Frigidaire." Perhaps I had only even heard that term in an old movie or something, I really couldn't recall.

Why don't we go out onto the patio? It's such a lovely day. So we went through a set of double French doors, and he motioned me to have a seat at a glass-topped steel-framed patio table with beautiful metal ornamentation on it. I sat at the table, and I responded to his question, "Iced tea will be fine."

"Sweetener or none?"

"Yes, just a bit."

"Wonderful, I'll be right back. He then entered another door off the patio, which I assumed led into the kitchen, and a few moments later, he returned with two tall glasses of iced tea and a bowl of sugar on a platter and set it down on the table, and then took a chair opposite where I was sitting. After he got comfortable, he said, "So, you are interested in the position we have open, are you?" as if he was conducting a serious job interview, and then he laughed. I couldn't help but laugh because he was laughing.

"Why, yes, I am," I replied.

"Well, as you can see," he said as he gestured to my single resumé sitting on the table, "we have several applicants to sort through."

Finally, I got what we were laughing about. At least up to that point, I was the only person who showed interest in the job. I wasn't sure what that meant about the job. Was it too little pay, too few hours, too much work? "Oh, I see, well then just let me know if you see something that makes you think I might be a fit." I didn't know what else to say.

Lenny picked up my resumé and began to read, and he just nodded as he went down the list, "Singer, very interesting, Barback, that could come in handy, Bookkeeper, oh well, that could be very handy to have around here, for sure." He laid it down and he said, "So, Kiko, what makes someone as qualified as you want to come and work for us? You seem very well suited to do the work you've been doing, so why change jobs now? And before you answer, look around at where you are, on a Sunday afternoon. Does this seem like the kind of place or job that you have ever worked before? So tell me, why here?

I didn't know what to say. I still didn't even know what the job was, or how much it paid, or anything about it. But I could tell, by the way he asked the question, that this was definitely not a typical job interview, and that he was not looking for any kind of typical job interview answer. Now my dad's voice began to say to me, "Just be honest, honesty is always the best tactic in the long run."

Anytime my dad had to bid on a job, especially for new construction, he would never try to underbid to win a contract, because even if he lost to the cheapest bid, he knew his reputation was such that he was often the first call they would make when they had to fire the winning contractor for going over budget or otherwise not being able to fulfill the contract. So I decided I was just going to tell this man exactly what had happened to me, including the ending of my long-term relationship, and just see what happened.

"I don't have many other options at this point. I either get this job, or I move home to Denver and spend the rest of my life working for my dad." That probably sounded much more dramatic than I intended it to, but Lenny just sat there, with that reassuring smile on his face, and nodded as if to say, "Go on, tell me more."

So I laid it all out for him. Everything that I had done, including how I had been black listed by the nightclubs as a "Troublemaker." After I was finished, he just smiled and said, "So do you still think that refusing to keep false books was the best decision you could have made?"

Oh, Geez, now what do I say? What answer does he want to hear? No, this is about being honest with him, so I said, "Yes. I can sleep at night, and even though these last few weeks have been difficult, at least I have that."

"I agree, Kiko." And he held out his hand and said, "Welcome to Liberty Gardens."

"Oh, okay, umm, do you mind me asking how much it pays and how many hours a week you will need me?"

"The job starts at $17.50 an hour, and is 40 hours a week."

"Oh, full-time, alright, I thought maybe it was only a couple of days a week or something."

"Can you work full-time, Kiko?"

"Yes, of course."

Just when I was about to ask more, a car pulled up over near a fenced area. Lenny said, "And right on queue, here's Irma. She'll be happy to tell you everything you need to know about the job. Lenny stood up and called out, "Irma," and motioned for her to come over to the patio where we were sitting. Irma walked over and, as she approached the patio, Lenny said, jokingly, "I got you a gift, Irma."

In a thick Hispanic accent, Irma replied, "Oh, really. I hope it's what I asked for." As if I were a Christmas or birthday gift of some sort.

"I think she's just what you wanted," Lenny said. "This is Kiko, and I just hired her to help out around here."

"Wow, thank you, Lenny, I've been wanting one of these."

There was obviously some inside joke going on between the two of them, and I was somehow now part of it, but I wasn't sure what my role in the joke was or how to respond to all of this banter between them. Irma held out her hand to shake mine, and so I extended my hand and said, "Hi, I'm Kiko."

"Hello, I'm Irma."

I picked up my resumé from the table and handed it to her, and she asked, "What's this?"

"It's my resumé, Ma'am."

"Oh, fancy!" she exclaimed. "And Irma will be fine; we don't have much formality around here." Even with the heavy accent, I could tell she was very well-spoken, which is usually a sign of education, so I was immediately intimidated, as I did not go beyond High School myself. She didn't even look at my resumé, which disappointed me, so I said, "I'm very excited to work for you!"

She smiled and said, "We'll see how excited you are when you get started. There is a lot of work to get done every day."

"I'm a hard worker, I can handle anything, I promise."

"Okay, if Lenny is convinced, then you're okay with me. Lenny, did you tell her about the…" and she pointed to the right side of the house.

"Oh yes, I nearly forgot. The job comes with an apartment, if you're interested. You don't have to stay there, but it is available if you would like."

"An apartment!" I think I squealed when I said that."

"Yes, it's not large, but it is clean and dry and safe. I repainted and put in all new appliances about 5 years ago, but it's only been used a few times by visiting guests over those years, so it's almost like brand new."

"And how much does it cost?"

"Well, I spoke with my accountant when deciding how much I should pay for this position, and he told me that if I don't charge for the apartment, the IRS may decide for themselves what it's value is and consider that as part of your compensation package and tax you accordingly, so we decided $200.00 would be sufficient to keep them off your back."

*$200, that can't be right. He must mean per week*, I thought to myself.

"Per week?" I asked.

"Oh dear no, per month."

"200 a month, really!"

"Yes, why, is that too much?"

I could tell by the look on his face that he knew that was not too much, but I was beginning to understand his sense of humor, I think. "No, 200 will be acceptable."

"Wonderful, I have some work to attend to, next week's lesson won't write itself. I'll leave Irma to show you around and explain everything. She'll show you the apartment, and the two of you can work out the details of getting started and all of that. I'll see you both later then. Lenny turned and walked into the house, and then Irma said, "Let's begin with a tour, and I'll show you the apartment and explain your duties as we go along."

Irma and I began by entering the door Lenny had gone into to fetch the tea, and as I suspected, it was the kitchen. The door was that old kind of door that was split in the middle, so you could open the top half and keep the bottom still closed. The kitchen was large with a big six-burner gas stove with a stainless steel vent hood above and a large island with a farmhouse sink in the middle with a butcherblock countertop on all the lower cabinet counters. The cabinetry was nice, but nothing fancy or ornate, just plain. I guess you would call them Shaker-style cabinets. The floors were hardwood, *oak*, I thought. There was a dining table with six chairs. There was a split across the middle of the table, so it could be extended with a leaf if needed. "This is nice," I told Irma.

"Yes, I'm very lucky to have such a nice place to work. You know, Lenny built all of this with his own hands. At least everything that is made of wood. He's a wonderful woodworker. Even to this day, he loves to go out to his workshop and make things."

"Really, I think even my dad would be impressed with this place."

"He built this house, too," Irma added.

"All by himself?" I asked.

"No, he had a partner that he worked with back then. But he died before I came here. Okay, so this is where I do most of the cooking, but there is another stove out at the pavilion that we use to keep the food warm before serving."

"Okay, and will you want me to cook as well?"

"Can you cook, Kiko?"

"Yeah, I can hold my own in a kitchen. Nothing fancy, but I can make a meal."

"Good. Yes, you will get some cooking time as well. Now that Suzanna is in college, I may need to take the occasional Saturday off, so it will be nice to know that you can do that if I'm gone. Okay, let's go see the apartment next."

We left the kitchen and went back out to the patio and down a few terraced steps to a door. Irma opened the door, and we walked into a space that was pleasant and homey. It wasn't fancy, but it had a kitchen with apartment-sized appliances and decent cabinetry, and a small dining area with a simple table and two chairs. The living room was off to our left, with a couch and a coffee table, and a side armchair that looked in good condition. The floors were hardwood, and the walls were painted a bright white, which made the place feel larger than it was, with a beamed ceiling at about 9 feet. We went into the bedroom, which had a queen-size mattress with a big four-poster bed frame. There was no closet, but instead a large Wardrobe sitting against the wall with four drawers on the lower half. Irma said, "There's no closet, so I hope the Wardrobe will be okay?"

"Yes, it's lovely. Did Lenny make this, too?"

"Of course. He made all the furniture and cabinets in the house and the apartment. I even have some in my own home that he made for Suzanna and me. We lived here, in this apartment, when Suzanna was very little, but as she grew, we needed more space."

"Through that door is the bathroom." We went in and looked, and it was very nice, but it was tiled in a kind of peach colored tile with black tiled accents. It reminded me of a bathroom my Grandma Davis had in her old house, where my dad had grown up. The sink was connected to the wall and had two steel legs on the front to hold it up, and one of those old dual faucets with ceramic knobs. "It's not much, but it's quite functional. There is a medicine cabinet behind the mirror and a cupboard there for towels and tissues, and such."

"I see, that's fine. So do you live on this property, Irma?" She could tell by the tone of my question that I was kind of fishing for some clues as to her relationship with Lenny, to see if it was more than employer and employee."

She smiled slightly and replied, "No, we have our own place, a few miles away. Okay, let's go and look at the pavilion. We walked out behind the house to the pavilion and the oratorium, as she called the speaking theater. As we walked to the Pavilion, she turned to where her car was parked. "That's my vegetable garden. I try to grow as much as I can to use in our recipes. Lots of peppers, tomatoes, carrots, green beans, peas, like that."

"And chickens – you have chickens too?"

"Yes, for eggs, and to help eat the bugs that are trying to get into the gardens. You can see the chickens have a separate run around the garden, which is fenced off from them, but if caterpillars or other bugs try to get to the garden, the chickens will eat them before they can make it." If a chicken stops laying eggs, then we have fried chicken for dinner."

"Really, do you kill the chicken?"

"No, Lenny will do that."

"Where did you learn about the chickens and bugs?" I asked.

"I learned when I was in college, back in El Salvador. I wanted to be an agriculturalist, but sadly, that did not work out, so I try to do what I can here to put what I learned to use."

I didn't ask her any more about her past, at that time. She showed me the Pavilion, which I had seen the night before, and just said, "We use this every Saturday, unless the weather is too bad. All we need to do is keep it clean."

Then she pointed to another building that was about 30 yards behind the Pavilion, one I had not even noticed the night before, and said, "There's the storage and clean up room. Come, I'll show you."

The building looked as old and weathered as the house, and it was built with the same timber frame construction. It had a concrete floor, and as we entered, it was lined with storage for plates and bowls, and silverware of all kinds. "This is where we keep all the dinnerware and silverware, and do all the cleanup. There is a deep sink for washing pots, pans, and dishes, and two dishwashers."

It had not dawned on me the night before that we were eating the Chili out of ceramic bowls, but now that I see them, I couldn't help but wonder why they didn't use paper bowls and plates and plastic utensils. I asked Irma, and she replied, "Lenny is kind of old school that way. And so am I, I suppose, but he would never dream of serving food to guests on a paper plate or bowl. Next Saturday, I'll show you what needs to be done, and you will see it's not that much work. So, that's pretty much the tour. You can start on Tuesday if you want. We take Sunday and Monday off, and work Tuesday through Saturday. But on Saturdays, you don't need to be here until 1:00 PM. Because we work until the dishes are all finished."

"Okay, that will be fine. I'm happy to be working with you, Irma."

"Me too, Kiko. I hope you'll like it here."

As we walked back to the house, I asked her, "Did your daughter get paid to help you as well?"

"No, but when she entered High School, Lenny made her a deal. He told her that if she came and worked with me anytime I needed her to be here, he would pay for her college. So she never failed to be here when I needed her to be here."

"Wow, that's very generous of Lenny, and a lot of trust to put in a promise."

Irma turned and looked at me and said, without a hint of a smile, "If Lenny makes you a promise, he will keep it. That's one thing you need to understand about Lenny, Kiko. You will never meet a more trustworthy person in your life. Besides, Lenny is the only father Suzanna has ever known, and she is as close to a daughter to him as he has ever had."

I felt as if I had just been scolded, but then she smiled that warm smile she has, and I knew we were okay. I said my good-byes to the two of them and drove back to Gina's place. I couldn't wait to tell her and call my dad and tell him that I had secured a job. I knew they would both be so relieved.

# Chapter 5

When I arrived back at Gina's apartment, she was sitting out on the patio, drinking a soda and reading a magazine. I stepped out, and she said, "There you are, where've you been, Kiko?" but before I could answer, she added, "Oh, I have some really good news to share."

"News, what news?" I asked.

"Mr. Rennolds, the restaurant owner, came in this morning, and he asked me if I wanted to become the full-time manager for the entire restaurant. Reggie is leaving to move to California, and Mr. Rennolds said that he's very impressed with my work, so he thinks I'm ready to step up to be the full-time manager."

"Wow, Gina, that's incredible. I'm so happy for you and proud of you. You've worked so hard for that place."

"Yeah, and that's not all, I get a salary now, not just hourly with tips, and I can get health insurance through the company."

"That's big, Gina."

"And, Mr. Rennolds owns 15 other franchises and seven other restaurants, and he said he has his eyes on me for even more opportunities down the road."

"That's wonderful. No one deserves it more than you. You've been with that restaurant for seven years now. It's about time they recognized your worth."

"Thank you, Kiko. So what have you been up to?"

"Well, I have some news of my own. I got a job."

"Really!" Gina squealed. "That's fantastic, Kiko, I'm so happy for you. Where is it?"

"Remember last night, that teacher, Lenny, he mentioned that there was a job available at the Gardens. So, I drove out this morning, just thinking I would give them my Resumé, and he ended up hiring me on the spot."

"You're kidding! Well, look at you, taking action like that. I'm so proud of you. So what exactly will you be doing? I mean, I've only really ever been there on Saturday evenings, so I have no idea what goes on during the week."

"Well, mostly just helping Irma clean and cook and keep the place up, I suppose. It's a big property, and she said there's a lot of work that needs to be done daily, so I'll just be doing whatever needs to be done."

"Oh, and what about your music?" Gina asked.

"Lenny said it might come in handy, although he wasn't very specific as to how, but you know, it's a job, and for now, it's at least something."

"So how much does it pay?"

"$17.50 an hour, and it's full-time, so that's not too bad, right?"

"Most of the people I know who are earning an hourly wage are making $12 to $15, so I guess that's better than most. The economy is starting to get pretty bad, and a lot of factories and other businesses are laying off, so I guess you're pretty lucky to get that."

"And there's one more thing, it comes with an apartment."

"With an apartment? What... where?"

"It's a basement apartment, but it has its own entry, and it's pretty nice. I mean, it's not fancy. But it has a bedroom and bathroom, a kitchen, and a living space. You know, everything you would expect in an apartment."

"In Lenny's basement?"

"Yeah."

"I never would have guessed. So how much will it cost you?"

I didn't want to tell her how cheap it was, because I was kind of embarrassed about how little he was charging me for it, so I told her, "It's part of the compensation for the job, so it just gets calculated as part of my income. The IRS sets a price based on the square footage, and Lenny said his accountant will do all the paperwork."

"Oh, well, okay then. Lucky you. When will you be moving in?" I could hear the disappointment in her voice. We have really enjoyed living together. She's a great roommate, and I guess she feels the same, so I said, "I'm not sure. I start work on Tuesday, so I'll work out the details with Irma then."

Gina just smiled and said, "Well, look at us, Kiko – it looks like things are working out for us both. Didn't I tell you it would?"

"I won't be going far, Gina, and we'll see each other every Saturday when you come out to hear Lenny speak."

"Yeah, yeah, you're right, Kiko."

But I could hear a kind of sadness in her voice, like I had taken something special, something that was hers, and I felt bad for her. But what else could I do? I mean, just yesterday, she introduced me to Lenny and the gardens, and now, I'm going to work there and live in his basement apartment. Up until now, I didn't even know she knew about this place. When she took me there last night, she was sharing something really important to her, and now, standing here telling her my news, I felt like I was stealing that from her. But I had to make a change, and I couldn't keep taking advantage of her by staying in her place and not paying rent. "Well, I need to call my dad, and let him know also. He'll be so excited."

"Yeah, of course, Kiko."

I walked into the dining area of the apartment and sat at the table, and called my dad. He answered, "Kiko, what a surprise, I wasn't expecting to hear from you until later in the week."

"I know, Daddy, but I have some news. I got the job I was looking into."

"Really, so fast, and on a Sunday, what kind of job is it?" I could hear the skepticism in his voice."

I wasn't even sure how to explain what Liberty Gardens was and what Lenny did, so I just did the best I could. "It's working for a man who gives lectures, but he has a place that's like a big garden or estate. That sounds too formal – it's not like a formal estate or anything, it's more like a natural garden. But I'll be working as an assistant to his assistant, if that makes sense."

"Um, okay, I'm not sure what that means. I'm trying to wrap my head around this. So how are you going to get paid?"

"Oh, it's hourly, $17.50 an hour, and he has a basement apartment that I can rent for just $200 a month."

"Wait, you're going to be living in his basement?"

"It's not like that, Daddy. Well, it is, but there's a separate entrance to the apartment."

"And who is this man, whose home you will be living under?" He insisted.

"His name is Lenny Boyce, and he gives lectures on his property every Saturday evening, and he teaches people, you know, about life and philosophy and stuff. I mean, I've only heard one of his lectures, but it really made me think about a lot of stuff."

"Huh, so you just met this man, he offered you a job, and now you want to move into his house."

"Not into his house, Daddy, into a basement apartment."

"Kiko, have you thought this through? It sounds like you might be grasping at straws here. Who else lives on this property? Are you sure this isn't a cult of some sort? Who got you involved in all this?"

Now, thinking back on that conversation, I can only imagine how bizarre it must have sounded to him. "It's not like that, Daddy. I don't know how to explain it so that it makes sense. The only other person living on the property is Lenny. It's not a cult, I promise you that." Then it dawned on me, it's not a cult, is it? I have only been to one meeting. It didn't feel anything like a cult, oh God, maybe I was a bit hasty getting involved in all of this. But no! I spoke with Lenny and with Irma, and there was nothing cultish about either of them. Irma said I can trust Lenny, and she trusts her own daughter with him, so I have to trust her.

"I don't know if I'm comfortable with you living on the property with him alone, sweetheart. How well do you know him?"

I wasn't brave enough to tell him that I just met him, but I said, "It's okay, Daddy. Irma also works there, and she is there every day."

"Who's Irma? I've never heard you mention that name before."

"She's Lenny's assistant, and I'll be working for her mainly."

"I just don't like the idea of you living on that property alone with that man. Especially someone I have never met. Promise me you won't move in there until I have had a chance to meet him. I'm booking a flight today. I'll be there on Wednesday or Thursday. I want to speak with this man before you actually move into the apartment."

I was hesitant. How was I going to tell Lenny that I couldn't take the apartment until my Dad came to speak with him? How embarrassing was that? But the other side of my brain was yelling, Yes, he's right. "Okay, Daddy. I start work on Tuesday morning, so I'll talk to him then."

"Okay, Kiko, I'll see you later in the week, sweetheart. I'll send you my flight information."

"Okay, Daddy, see you in a couple of days." I suddenly felt like I was sixteen again, but I know he loves me, and he is just worried about me.

Monday, I spent most of the day alone, as Gina was working all day. But I wanted to do something really nice for her, as she had done so much for me, so I went shopping and prepared a really nice dinner. Steaks and a salad, and I made a Tiramisu for dessert, and a bottle of good red wine for dinner, and white for dessert. When she got home, she was so surprised, and we talked and had a really nice time. She did confide that she was caught off guard by my sudden announcement and that the reason she hadn't told me about the Gardens before was that she was a bit embarrassed that she went there to listen to Lenny. It was like a guilty pleasure that she allowed herself. His teaching was very esoteric, and she knows a lot of people from religious backgrounds don't like what he teaches. She knew I was raised as a strict Catholic, and wasn't sure what I would think about it.

She said she had seen lots of people, over the two years that she had been going to the Gardens, come and try to challenge Lenny or prove his teaching was incorrect, "But Lenny, he just smiles at them, lets them vent, and never argues with them. His silence is usually so disarming that they just leave frustrated. It's kind of funny to watch, actually."

"Really." I said, "I gave up being super religious when I moved to Denver to live with my dad, so I'm pretty skeptical about any kind of religious teaching."

"That's the thing about Lenny, his teaching is not really religious, it's just enlightening."

"Well then, maybe I'll get some good out of it. Anyway, you'll continue to come, and we'll still spend time together, I promise."

"I know we will, Kiko."

I felt so much better by the time I went to bed, and even though Irma had not given me a start time, I wanted to make a good impression and get there right at 8:00, so I was in bed by 10:00 PM, and anticipating the next day.

The next morning, at 8:00 AM sharp, I knocked on Lenny's front door. He opened it and said, "Good morning, Kiko, I'm so happy to have you here. Irma is not yet here, but she should be shortly. But in the meantime, I have paperwork spread out on the kitchen table for you that my accountant has sent over. You know, the Government loves its paperwork." I noticed as we walked into the kitchen that the top half of the kitchen door was open.

"I understand, Lenny, it's not a problem. But I do have something to discuss with you, if you don't mind." I had been dreading this conversation all morning, but I figured the sooner I got it out of the way, the better.

"I'm all ears, young Lady."

"Um, when I called my dad to tell him about this job and the apartment, he said that he was a little concerned that I would be living on the property. He said he wants to meet you before I move in. Do you mind if he comes to meet you?" I asked very tentatively.

Lenny laughed. "Of course, Kiko. Your father is welcome to come here anytime, in fact, I have a spare room in the house he can use if he would like to. It might save him a few dollars on a hotel. If my daughter were to move into an apartment in the basement of a man I had never met, I would be alarmed as well. I would be more surprised if he were not concerned."

I was expecting a lecture on being an adult and why I can't make decisions for myself, but I didn't get any of that from Lenny. "Okay then. His flight gets in at 8:00 PM on Wednesday. I'll bring him with me on Thursday. I'll tell him about the room, but he usually likes staying at a hotel."

Just from behind where I was sitting, I heard Irma's voice standing at the open kitchen door. "Whose flight, from where?"

"Oh, my dad's. He wants to meet Lenny before I move into the apartment."

"Oh, Oh, Lenny, you better hide your drugs and needles." And then she laughed.

"As long as you cut down those funny-looking weeds you have growing out in your garden." He responded, and they both laughed. I assumed they were both joking, but then I really wasn't sure about any of this. I mean, I just met these people, and who knows what they might be into.

I smiled and just said, "Good morning, Irma."

"Good morning, Kiko. I hope you're ready to get your hands dirty today."

"I'm ready for whatever you need me to do." I was never afraid of hard work and was willing to learn new things and try just about anything, so I was up for whatever the day had to offer.

The rest of the day was spent doing tasks around the grounds. I discovered that the word Gardens, was meant in the truest sense. What looked like a bunch of wild, overgrown plants was actually some very cultivated and curated native species of flowering plants that were perfectly suited for the hot Texas Hill Country. Irma turned out to be a wonderful teacher and explained to me about each type of plant and when they flowered. "You must see this place in the Spring, Kiko, it just explodes with color. It's the most beautiful place in all of Texas in the Spring." So for the next two days, we just did that, cleaned a bit, weeded a bit, and ate a midday meal together that Lenny had cooked for us. It was actually very pleasant work, and I found I liked it a lot.

Wednesday night, I picked up my dad at the airport, and as he got in the car, he asked, "So, did you tell this Lenny character that I was coming?"

"Yes, and he's very eager to meet you. In fact, he offered to host you in a spare room he has in the house, if you're interested."

"I have a room booked at the Double Tree for three nights, but maybe if I stay at the property, it will be a good way for me to get to know this guy a bit, so, yeah, tell him I'd love to take him up on that offer."

"Okay, you can come with me in the morning. I'll take you to the hotel for tonight, and pick you up at 7:00 AM. Be out front with your bag."

"Okay, I'll be there."

So, I dropped my dad off at the hotel, and after he checked in, we went down to the bar to have a drink together and I told him all about what I had been doing for the last two days.

"Well, look at you, Kiko, the farmer. I would have never imagined." And he laughed.

"Yeah, me too, but I've enjoyed it so far, and Irma and Lenny have been very nice, and I'm really enjoying the job, so far anyway." After a glass of wine, I said goodnight and drove back to Gina's.

The next morning, I picked my dad up at 7:00 AM and we drove to the Gardens. It was just before 8:00 when we arrived, and I could see Lenny already out and working in one of the garden areas, pulling some weeds. "There's Lenny, over there, Daddy. Come on, I'll introduce you. We walked over to Lenny and said, "Good morning, Lenny. Lenny, this is my Dad, Bill Davis."

"Mr. Davis, what a pleasure. I must tell you what a lovely daughter you have." I had not told Lenny or Irma that I was adopted, but the obvious difference in appearance between my dad and me didn't even cause Lenny to bat an eye.

"Thank you, Lenny, I'm very proud of her."

"And you should be, she is quite accomplished, this young lady, and I can tell you with confidence, that in just two days, she has already begun to make a difference here in the Gardens. If you would like to go into the house, I believe Irma is cooking breakfast, and we can all sit and have a wonderful chat. I'll be right along as soon as I sort the debris and get the compostables into the compost pile."

"You compost, do you?" Daddy asked.

"Yes, of course. Irma insists on it."

"Okay, Lenny, we'll see you in the house then," I said.

"I won't be long, and you can put Bill's luggage in the spare room."

We walked a few dozen yards to the house and entered through the Kitchen door. As we walked, Daddy said, "Why didn't you tell me that Lenny was an old man. I pictured you living here with some guy in his twenties or thirties, not some septuagenarian."

"Sorry, I didn't think about it. Does it matter?"

"Well, it certainly puts my mind at ease a bit, that's all."

We entered the house through the Kitchen door, and the top half was open, so I could smell bacon frying as we approached. I introduced my Dad to Irma, and I went to retrieve his suitcase from the car and put it in the spare room.

When I returned, Daddy was sitting at the table, and Irma was standing at the stove, scrambling some eggs. They were both being quiet, so I said to Daddy, "The eggs are fresh, Daddy, from the chickens here in the Gardens. I'll show you later."

"Yes, I gathered them just this morning," Irma added."

"Wow, I'm impressed," Daddy said.

Just then, Lenny showed up, and Irma said to him, "Don't bring those dirty boots into this house."

"Yes, Ma'am." He replied.

Over the last few days, watching the two of them together was like watching an old married couple, yet there was never any kind of what you could call, public display of affection, but it was obvious that they cared a great deal for each other, and it was difficult for me to understand why they were not married, or at least living in the same house together. But I suppose it was really none of my business.

Lenny went to the sink, washed his hands, and came and sat at the table. Irma put the food on the Island counter Buffet style and said, "Okay, it's ready, come and get it."

This was truly a wonderful breakfast, something like you would see in a farm household with bacon, sausage, scrambled eggs with diced onion, green and red peppers, and some kind of seasoning that Irma had added, orange juice, coffee, biscuits, and gravy. It was fabulous!

After we had all filled our plates and were seated at the table, Daddy asked Lenny, "This is quite a place you have here, Lenny. How did you come by it?"

I was so embarrassed, "Daddy!" I said, "That's not polite."

But with no sense of irritation at the question, Lenny replied, "Oh, that's a wonderful story. This is not my place; I'm just the trustee of it. My friend and mentor, Sam Eustes, established it. Sam bought this land and hired me to help him clear it, and then we built this house, the pavilion, and the workshop. Sam was the original lecturer, but when he passed, he placed the entire place into a trust and made me the trustee, and I've been here ever since."

"So you don't really own this place then."

"Can anyone ever really own a piece of land, Bill? At best, we are all just caretakers of whatever goods or wealth have been entrusted to us for as long as we tarry in this life, and when this life is completed, so will be our responsibility towards any earthly goods that were placed into our hands for safekeeping."

Daddy nodded and replied, "I suppose that's true."

Then Lenny added, "The reason so many people in this world have such a self-righteous attitude over their possessions and land ownership and such is that they are so short-sighted and look at this life as the only life that matters. I tend to take a longer view of the whole thing, and view this life as just the beginning of a long, beautiful life full of adventure and experience throughout the entirety of the cosmos."

"So you're a religious man, then, Lenny?" Daddy asked.

"The word religion has such a limiting connotation to it. I prefer to think of myself as a Deist – a child of the infinite creator, who has designed an infinite journey for me that will ultimately lead me back from where we have all come."

"Irma, then interrupted, "Lenny, this isn't the time for a discourse on your universal perspective."

"Yes, you're quite right, Irma, so Bill, Kiko tells me you own your own business."

The next 30 minutes or so were just filled with polite small talk and Lenny explaining to Daddy about the Gardens. Then finally, Irma stood and said, "Well, Kiko and I have work to attend to, so Lenny, we will leave Bill to your capable hands to show around the Gardens and get settled in."

Irma and I began to clear the plates and get the dishes done before going out to the storage room to make sure we had everything needed for next Saturday's meal. "I'm fixing Hungarian Goulash on

Saturday. It's one of Lenny's favorites. Have you ever cooked Goulash?" she asked me.

"No, I don't think I've ever even had goulash," I replied.

"Yeah, me too, until I came here, and Lenny taught me how to make it. In fact, Lenny taught me how to make almost everything I make for the meetings. He's actually a really good cook."

"Really, so how did you meet Lenny, Irma?"

"Oh, that's a long story. Are you sure you want to hear it?"

"Yes, of course, I mean, you've been here for 18 years, Irma. Lenny must be very special to you."

"Lenny saved my life," Irma said, "I don't mean in a literal sense, like he pulled me out of a burning building or anything, but he found me at a time when I had nothing but a small suitcase and a month old infant, and no idea how I was going to even survive more than a week at a time."

"Really, that's terrible. How did that happen?"

"I grew up in El Salvador, and my family was very wealthy. My father was the largest exporter of agricultural goods in the country, and he was very successful. That's where I got my love for agriculture. But when I was a teenager, the troubles started. The socialist people took over the government, and they took his company from him and took almost everything we had. They arrested my father, and I never saw him again. But he was smart, and somehow, I guess he saw what was coming, he made sure that my mother had money to raise my brother and me, and so when I was 18, I was able to go to college.

"So I was in college, and my brother went to join the rebels. There was so much fighting, a Guerra, what do you call it... a civil war. But none of that mattered to me – I was just carefree and in school, and then I met Franco. Oh my God, he was so handsome, and he could dance! Nobody could salsa, like he could salsa, and he liked me, so we began to date, and we got married."

"You were married, Irma?"

"Yes, for nearly three years. Franco was also a college student and a socialist, and so he studied politics. He wanted to become a politician. I think he really wanted to become president someday. We were so idealistic and thought we were going to solve all the problems of the world. We would have long talks about everything. Every time I went home, and I would talk all these socialist ideas to my mother, she would get so mad at me and tell me, 'You better not let Raul,' my brother, 'hear you talk like that.'"

"Wow, you were married to a politician, that was good, right?"

"No, at least not in those days. Remember, there was a war going on. Franco was three years older than I, so he graduated and got a job working for the mayor of San Salvador, the capital city.
I was still in college, but I was not bothered because the government wanted more students to study agriculture because they were socialist, and they thought that agriculture would be the salvation of the nation. So Franco began to build his career, and I finished school, and we were very happy. Then one day, a group of men showed up at our home, and they put a gun to my head, and they dragged Franco out of the house and shot him dead. They wanted to send a message to the mayor, I guess. I think the only reason that I was not killed that day was that I was Raul's sister, and he must have told them not to harm me."

"So, you lost your father and your husband to the civil war?"

"Yes, and ironically, they were on different sides of the ideologies."

"That's terrible."

"The Mayor vowed retribution, and I was with him – I just wanted those men to pay for what they had done. But then, I found out I was pregnant, and suddenly, nothing else mattered. Someone told me that if I could make it to the US, I could ask for asylum, and all I wanted was to be out of the war and away from all the violence and talk of killing and revenge. I was just two months pregnant, so I went to my mother, and I told her I was leaving and I wanted her to come with me. But she refused. She had no more money. She had spent it all on my college, and my brother was all she had left, so she was going to stay with him and his wife."

"But your brother was with the people who killed your husband?"

"Yes, I was married to a man who was blamed for killing our Father. Such is the craziness of war. I understand better now than I did back then. But anyway, I got on a bus and headed north, and made it country by country, little by little, stopping every few days to work for a few days to pay for the next part of my trip. By the time I made it to the Border at Laredo, I was nearly eight months pregnant. I approached the border, asked for asylum, and since El Salvador was in a recognized Civil War, they had to accept my application."

"So it was that easy to claim asylum?"

"No, there was much more than that. Lots of paperwork and background checks, and they had to check out my story. I had a case worker assigned to me, and I was sent to a motel to stay while my case was reviewed. I was still living in the motel when Suzanna was born. But once she was born, and she was a U.S. Citizen, my caseworker was able to get my hearing expedited, and I finally got my asylum approved."

"How did you get here to Lenny's?" I asked

"That's where the miracle happened. I had met a lot of asylum seekers at the motel, and had made some friends, and they all said, 'Come to Dallas. I have family in Dallas, and they are going to help me find a job, and I will help you.' So when I got my papers, Suzanna was just 4 weeks old, and I was given $150.00 in cash and a bus ticket to anywhere I wanted to go. I asked for a ticket to Dallas. They gave me the ticket and a list of resources in Dallas that I could contact for refugee assistance.

"So every day, a van would come and take people to the bus station. I was walking out to the van, with my suitcase in one hand

and Suzanna in the other, between the motel and the bus, there was a man, standing there, just leaning up against his car, holding a sign in English and Spanish that read, Housekeeper needed. Apartment provided. Lucky for me, I was the only woman going to the bus station that day, and all the men were looking for construction work, so they were not interested. But the real irony is that I had hardly even noticed Lenny; it was his car that I noticed. It's this old 1957 Continental, and it was the same car that my Grandfather had when I was growing up in San Salvador. I couldn't help but walk towards that car, and then Lenny said, 'Are you interested in the job?'

"Job," I said, now I noticed the sign he was holding. "Oh, yes, I can do housekeeping." And that's how I met Lenny. Suzanna and I came here, and we have been here ever since."

"Wow, that's an incredible story. What are the odds that he would have the same car as your Grandfather?"

"You tell me, but I can only assume there must have been some divine hand behind what happened."

"So, what happened to the car?" I asked jokingly.

"It's still in the garage. I love that car. Lenny doesn't drive anymore, but anytime I have to drive him somewhere, we take that car. You'll get your chance to drive it, I'm sure."

We finished our work at about 4:00, and Irma said, "I think that's enough for today. Tomorrow we need to do grocery shopping for Saturday, and I have some steaks to grill for tonight's supper. What do you say we head up to the house?"

We arrived at the house and found Lenny and my dad sitting on the Patio, in deep conversation, and I asked, "So what have you two been up to today?"

Lenny replied, "We have had a splendid time, and Bill even took a look at my Air Conditioner and Heater to make sure they were in tip-top shape for the coming fall and winter."

"Daddy, really!" I asked with obvious scorn in my tone.

"What, I figured as long as I'm here, I might as well be useful. Tomorrow we're going to fix a fascia board that's coming loose on the south side of the house."

I just shook my head in disbelief and laughed.

# Chapter 6

That evening, sitting there with my dad and Lenny and Irma, was one of the most enjoyable times I could remember in my adult life. We had the most engrossing and enlightening conversation I had ever had. We talked until about 9:30, and even Irma remarked that she could not remember the last time she was free to just sit and converse with other people and not feel like she needed to rush home to be there with Suzanna.

As we sat on that patio talking, I decided I was going to ask Lenny any question that came to my mind. If ever there was going to be an opportunity to ask him these questions, now would be it. As he kept answering, I, my dad, and even Irma, just kept asking, and Lenny never hesitated to answer. I had heard him say earlier in the week, "Never volunteer your opinion, unless you have been asked, but once asked, endeavor to be as honest and sincere in your answer as is humanly possible." Well, this was my chance to ask, so I was going to take full advantage of it.

I began by saying, "Lenny, you seem to talk about God a lot in your lectures, but do you think there is any such thing as one true religion?"

"I do believe in revealed religion," he began, "but I don't believe that any revealed religion can spread to the world when it makes the serious mistake of becoming permeated with some national culture associated with an established racial, social, or economic practice. Our current predicament, where certain individuals are attempting to turn their religion into an ethnic or nationalistic affiliation, will only limit that religion's appeal to the broader world."

My dad then asked, "So how do you think we can become a better and more humane civilization?"

"The secret to a better civilization is bound up in teachings based on the fatherhood of God and the Brotherhood of Man. But adoption of these teachings can only be propagated one heart and one mind at a time. Only when individuals accept this principle, and begin to live individually as sons and daughters of the Father, and seek to live according to His will, will we achieve a lasting and humane global civilization.

"So... Lenny, why do you think this world is in such chaos?" Irma asked, as if she were truly trying to understand the reason or existence of Evil.

Gently, and knowing her background, he answered her, "You have to remember, my dear, that we all look at the world, and only see the black patches of evil, as they are displayed against the white background of good. There is so much more white than black, more good than evil, we simply choose not to see it. I know what terrible evil you have endured in your life, but look at what goodness has come out of it today. You have turned this place into a garden that thousands, every year, can come and enjoy. And Suzanna – just imagine how many thousands will benefit from her beautiful and healing hands in the years and decades to come. That is not to say that the evil that befell you in El Salvador was done to put you here. Life is never about the evil that happens to us, but only about what we choose to do with that pain when it does, and you have done so much to see the white, despite the blackest of patches. You could so easily have chosen to hate and seek revenge, but you didn't – you chose to move towards the good.

Lenny, I asked, "I was always taught when I was growing up in the Catholic church, that Jesus' teachings were all prevailing in this world, but all I can see is a world filled with materialism. Even among my really religious friends, they all just want to get rich and have lots of things. How can we stay focused on Jesus' teaching, when all around we see so many who proclaim his gospel and then refuse to live his message?"

"No matter what the apparent conflict between materialism and the teachings of Jesus may be, you can rest assured that, in the ages to come, the teachings of the Master will fully triumph. In reality, true religion cannot become involved in any controversy with science, philosophy, or materialism. Truth is in no way concerned with material things or the false stories we tell ourselves as humans, struggling to understand that which we cannot ever fathom as reality. True religion is simply indifferent to, but sympathetic with, the material world, while it is supremely interested in the materialist. All true religion is personal, and only concerned with the individual's growth and purpose."

So, are you saying we should not be even conducting science, or involved in scientific exploration?" my dad asked.

"No, not at all, Bill. But the pursuit of mere knowledge, without the attendant interpretation through wisdom and spiritual insight of God-knowing experiences, eventually leads to pessimism and human despair. A little knowledge is truly disconcerting if not tempered with some grounding in spiritual understanding." Lenny replied.

"I'm not sure what you're saying exactly, Lenny," Irma said.

"I'm saying, and maybe I'm not the best at explaining all of this, my old partner Sam was so much better at it than I am, but what I am trying to say is that unabashed materialism reduces man to a soulless automaton and constitutes him merely an arithmetical symbol finding a helpless place in the mathematical formula of an unromantic and mechanistic universe. But where does all this vast universe of mathematics come from, if not from a master Mathematician? Science may try to explain the conservation of matter, but religion validates the conservation of men's souls – and serves to validate each individual's experiences with spiritual and eternal values. Without these, mankind would have ceased to exist thousands of years ago. Without the understanding of some greater power in the universe, urging us on to an ever-higher moral understanding, we would have destroyed every human on the earth through endless wars and self-interest ages ago. The fact that wars and selfishness still exist shows that we still have a long way to go before we truly understand the Master's teachings, but our individual moral compasses have kept us from total destruction, and stand as proof that there is still hope that we will get there in the end."

"So why do so many priests and holy men use so much warlike jargon in their calls to us to take up the armor of a spiritual battle, and then equate our material wars as being battles for our spiritual souls?" Daddy asked.

Lenny replied, "Religious leaders, from every faith system, are making a great mistake when they try to call modern men to contemporary spiritual battle with the trumpet blasts of the Middle Ages. Religion must provide itself with new and up-to-date slogans if it is to carry men forward into a new and better way. Neither democracy nor any other political panacea will take the place of true individual spiritual progress. False religions may represent an evasion of reality, but Jesus, in his Gospel, introduced mortal man to the very entrance door upon which an eternal reality of spiritual progress can take place."

"So, how can we know when we have found God, Lenny?" I asked

"My dear girl, the very fact that you have set your heart towards finding God is proof that God has already found you. You simply must let him guide you to where He wills you to be.

I then said. "My friend Brandon always tells me that the universe is just one vast machine, and we are just cogs in the machine."

"I have heard that many times, Kiko, but tell me this – if the universe were one vast machine, would a mere cog even know that they were part of the machine. I would argue, no. Only those who stand outside and apart from the machine can recognize that it is a machine. So if the universe is a machine, how could we possibly know that if we were just cogs in that machine? Does a single cell in your body understand that it is only a single cell in a vast body made up of trillions of other cells in a world of billions of individual bodies? Of course not." Only those outside can dive deep enough to see the individual cells.

"And let's take that to a more relatable level. If the universe is one vast machine, then by extension, we are merely machines as well. If we are mere machines, by what technique does a man claim to know that he is only a machine? The experience of self-conscious evaluation of oneself is never an attribute of a mere machine. A self-conscious and avowed mechanist is the best possible answer to mechanization. If materialism were a fact, there could be no self-conscious mechanist. It is also true that one must first be a moral person before one can perform an immoral act."

"Can you explain secularism to me? I'm not sure I really understand what it means, yet I read that term all the time." Daddy asked.

"It is the religionist, not religion, that proves the existence of spirit realities in this world. Secularism attempts to free men from the bonds of totalitarian religions to suppress and limit men's understanding of the spirit world to a limited understanding, which the religion carefully tries to control.

"Secularism attempts to free men from ecclesiastical slavery, only to betray him into the tyranny of political and economic slavery. Materialism denies God. Secularism simply ignores God. At least that was the earlier attitude. More recently, secularism has assumed a more militant attitude, assuming to take the place of the religion whose totalitarian bondage it onetime resisted. Twentieth-century secularism tends to affirm that man does not need God. But this is a double-edged sword, and this godless philosophy of human society will eventually lead to unrest, animosity, unhappiness, war, and worldwide conflict.

"Secularism can never bring peace to this world. Nothing can take the place of God in human society – God's knowing is the greatest civilizing force in the world. But I warn you, do not be quick to surrender the beneficent gains of the secular revolt from ecclesiastical totalitarianism either. Western civilization today enjoys many liberties as a result of the secular revolt. The greater mistake of secularism was in revolting against the almost total control of life by religious authority, and after attaining the liberation from such ecclesiastical tyranny, the secularist went on to institute a full-on revolt against God himself, sometimes tacitly, and sometimes openly. I believe we are entering a great correction phase where we will, sometime in the not too distant future, restore the balance between liberty and God-knowingness."

By this time, our brains had just about filled to the brim with all this information, and we all needed time to digest for a while. I said my goodnight to them all, and I left for Gina's. As I was saying goodnight to everyone, my dad said, "So if you need me to help get you moved into the apartment, Kiko, I can do that before I leave." That was, of course, his way of saying that he approved of me moving to Lenny's property and now felt comfortable enough with Lenny to know I would be safe.

As I was driving home that night, I couldn't help but think about almost every conversation I had had since moving out of my dad's home, and I wondered why they all seemed to be so shallow and meaningless. Derik and I talked a lot, but our conversations were always so trivial – a comment on a TV show we were watching, or a short discussion about a song lyric, or some musician, or some bill we needed to get paid. But never about anything meaningful or philosophical, or spiritual.

Even my conversations with Gina, who was obviously a much deeper person than I knew just a week ago, but our conversations were more about guys, work, fashion, or reality TV. But driving home after that time at Lenny's table, in a really deep conversation about real, universal, and spiritual things, I felt like I was actually having an adult conversation for the first time in my life. My dad even seemed to sense the weight of talking about things that truly made him think and understand, and even question things he had never questioned before. That night left me so hungry to understand more about who I am and why I am here than I ever had been.

I arrived in the morning with three of my six plastic tubs full of my stuff, and both of my guitars and my small Yamaha electric guitar amp, to begin moving into the apartment. This was what my life had been reduced to at that point, just six large plastic tubs filled with pots, pans, dishes, and a few pictures or wall decorations I had felt compelled to keep when I had to give up my apartment, two suitcases full of clothing, two guitars, one acoustic and one electric that was my pride and joy, and somehow, I ended up with that really nice mixing board that Derik had left behind when he moved out. He said the theater where he would be working had all modern, state-of-the-art equipment and that he wouldn't need it, and that maybe it would come in handy for me someday. For some reason, I hadn't been able to bring myself to sell it. So it just sits in my storage closet on Gina's patio.

My dad unloaded the tubs and put them in the apartment, and asked where I wanted stuff placed, and said he would take care of getting everything unpacked because he knew I had work to get done. "So I guess you're comfortable with me living on the property now, then?" I joked before heading out to meet up with Irma.

"Yeah, Lenny is a solid guy. I think living and working here may actually turn out to be a good thing for you."

"How so?" I asked.

"I don't know, you just look very comfortable here, and I dare say, happier than I can remember seeing you for quite some time. Besides, you're close enough to Austin that you can always go and gig there if an opportunity comes up, so maybe, if you don't feel so much pressure to pay your rent, your music will come more easily."

"I'm not sure what you mean, Daddy."

"Well, sweetheart, the last few times I saw you playing in a club, you just sounded stressed, like your life depended on being liked and playing what the audience wanted to hear. The pressure of playing to make a living is intense, and I can see how it's taken some of the joy out of your music. It concerned me a bit. When you were young and just sitting on the couch or in your room, playing and singing, you seemed so carefree, but now that innocence of just playing for yourself or the people you loved has left. Maybe now you can get some of that back."

"Oh… yeah… maybe." I had no idea he could hear in my music what I was feeling these last couple of years. So what did this mean for my music career? Was it over? I was very conflicted at that moment about my life choice to become a musician, and now I wasn't sure about anything at all.

But work was calling, and Irma was waiting. It was Friday, and Fridays are shopping days for Saturday's meal. I had cooked a fair bit over the last few years and was not too bad at it. I began cooking when I was just 13, when my mom was working late, and I taught myself how to cook for the two of us. Janice was also a good cook, and she taught me some things as well. Derek always seemed to like my cooking, as did Gina. But I soon found out that cooking for a few people was not the same as cooking for 60. Irma informed me that we always cooked for 60, as that was most likely the largest number we would have on a typical Saturday evening. "Sometimes, if we have a special event, we may have more, but usually between 30 and 60."

"So, what if we cook too much? I mean, we could have a smaller crowd, right?" I asked.

"Yes, of course, but there are always people and families we know that can use it, so we'll take the leftovers to people who we know can use some good food. But Lenny would never allow us to run out of food for our guests, so we cook for sixty, and it usually works out about right. Okay, are you ready to go?"

"Yeah, sure, do you want me to drive?"

"No, we'll take Lenny's car. It has a very large trunk."

We went into the garage, and there it was. The car that Irma loved so much – the '57 Continental. Not Lincoln Continental, mind you." She made sure I knew the difference. "No, this car was built before the two brands merged, so this is a very special car." She explained. She seemed to know everything about this car and its history, and didn't hesitate to tell me.

It was a beautiful car. Dark gray color, red leather interior. It had a strange automatic shifter lever that sat under the center of the dashboard. I had never seen anything like it before, but Irma told me about the one her grandfather drove in San Salvador, and how she always loved that car. "Driving this car makes me feel like a kid again, when everything was right with the world." She said.

So, off we went, like two high school girls driving daddy's car on a Friday night. We drove to the south side of Austin to a COSTCO warehouse store and stocked up on everything Irma had on her list. After the food shopping, we took a small excursion and did a bit of girls' shopping for ourselves, then had some lunch before we headed back to the gardens. When we arrived home, my dad saw us drive up, as he was standing on a ladder leaning up against the house, fixing that fascia board that had come loose, and he came to help unload the groceries. He said that Lenny was in his study preparing his remarks for tomorrow's talk. "Irma, is this your car?" he asked.

"No, Bill, it's Lenny's, but he doesn't drive anymore, so he lets me use it when I'm running errands for the gardens."

"Wow, it's a beauty."

Irma just smiled, and we went on about our business. We spent the rest of the day preparing for the next day and then doing some minor gardening work around the place. As we were working in the vegetable garden, I asked Irma, "Where did you get your love of plants?"

"My family has been farmers for generations, and my grandfather began the export business way back in the 1940s. He built the export business, and it became very successful. But I was always in love with the farming part. I studied Agriculture in school, because I wanted to teach the farmers new and better ways to grow their crops, so they could get more yield from every hectare of land. But when that all fell apart, and I had to come to America, I came here. Lenny pretty much just lets me do whatever I want with the land here. Someday, I want to expand the gardens to the entire 110 acres owned by the trust."

"The trust owns 110 acres?" I asked.

"Yes, but right now, we have only cleared and cultivated about 10 acres, which is what you see here. But all this land surrounding the gardens, the trust also owns. Early in my stay here, I met a man from the Texas Gardener's Association, and he showed me how to grow Texas native plants that are good for the environment and are perfectly suited to grow in the hot Texas sun. He taught me how to do all-natural gardening, and over the years, I earned my Master Gardener's certificate, and that's how I became a Natural Gardener. Now, I grow these gardens, and sometimes people call me from the local area, and I go and help them plant or learn about natural gardening as well."

"I had no idea you were so prolific and well known in the Texas gardening community."

Irma smiled and replied with a real sense of pride, " I'm a little bit known."

I came to discover, over my years with Irma, that she was much better known than she was willing to admit. I left early that day, around 4:00, as I had told Gina that I would come and spend one more night with her before I completely moved into my new apartment. My dad seemed to be enjoying his time with Lenny, and when I left, they were out in Lenny's workshop, doing something, I wasn't sure what, but they were both covered in sawdust and seemed to be having the time of their lives, so I just said a quick goodbye and drove back to Gina's place.

When I arrived, Gina was already home, had brought home some food from the restaurant for us, and had planned for us to have a movie night, watching a couple of our favorite movies together.

It was a fun time, and we laughed and ate popcorn and drank some wine, and had a real girls' night. When Gina finally went to bed at around 1:00 AM, I sat on the couch and looked around, and realized that this was probably the last time I would ever sleep on this couch or watch a movie with Gina and laugh at silly characters in a movie together. We promised each other that we would do this on a regular basis, but change can only move our lives forward, never backwards. Both of our lives have changed so much since that night, but it is still such a lovely memory to hold, and I cherish it deeply.

Gina had been there for me at a time when I so badly needed someone to be there, and I could never repay her for that. Lenny had said to me, just the night before, "The people that are there to save us from the deepest moment of despair in our lives are never there by accident, but by divine providence."

I thought about those words as I sat on that couch, and I wonder how divine providence works. How does God know when we are at our deepest point of despair?" How does God know who to send to pull us out of that pit of self-pity? It's not like Gina wasn't already there. She had moved to Austin from Oklahoma, just as I had from Colorado, but just for different reasons. She came to attend UT, and she did. She got her degree in business and then decided she was going to build her career in restaurant management and spent the last seven years doing just that, beginning as a late-night shift manager. That was always her goal, and now it was working out just as she had planned, so how could her being there when I needed her have been anything but a coincidence?

I met Gina because she used to run the late shift at the restaurant, and I would go there after I had finished a late night myself at a club, either playing or bartending. Often it was just me, maybe one of two others in the place, and so we began talking to each other, and I invited her to come and hear me play one night. She did, and we just became fast friends after that. But none of this screamed divine intervention, and yet there she was, when I had been abandoned by Derik, lost every job and income-producing gig I had, she took me in, she lifted me, she gave me time to heal, and she was my best friend. If this was how divine intervention worked, as Lenny had suggested, I knew, sitting there on that couch, that I needed to know more, and something inside of me was telling me that Lenny Boyce was my best hope for understanding it.

# Chapter 7

I woke up Saturday morning very early. Gina and I had said our goodbyes last night, and she had to be in at 5:00 for the breakfast rush, so I wasted no time getting the remaining tubs and other things I had left in the apartment loaded into my car, and headed out to the gardens to try and get unpacked before I need to begin work at around 1:00 to start cooking and setting up with Irma.

My dad was already up and about when I drove up, so he helped me unload the car, and I began to get things unpacked. I was still having a difficult time believing this place was mine. It was unlike any place I had ever lived, and it was right where I worked, so there was no commute, not to mention the cost was something most people would kill for.

Lenny did not own a TV, but he did use a satellite dish for internet service, so my dad went to the local big box store and bought some cable and connections, and then stopped at another place and bought me a small, but good enough, flat screen TV as a housewarming gift. He got everything connected and set up, so I had something to watch at night. That was very thoughtful of him, but as it turned out, I found I didn't use it all that much, and discovered I didn't really miss watching it. This place was actually beginning to feel like a home, and I had just gotten started.

After I had been there for about an hour, Lenny stopped in to see how I was settling in, and when he saw my acoustic guitar setting on the couch he asked me, as casually as was possible, "Kiko, I know you're going to be very busy today, but do you think you could open the festivities tonight with a song? It doesn't need to be anything special, just something you already know and play. I'm sure our guests would love to hear something from you."

"Umm... yeah...okay, Lenny. I'm sure I can do something."

He just smiled and said, "Thank you, Kiko, I can't wait to hear you perform." And then he left, as casually as if he had just asked me to do the dishes.

I looked at my dad, and he looked at me and said, "And you thought your playing days were over, I think you need to reconsider that."

Soon enough, it was time to go and help Irma, and my dad went to find something to do with Lenny. Irma and I began preparing the evening's meal. Earlier in the day, I looked up goulash online because I wasn't sure of what it was exactly. It turns out, there are two kinds: the original Hungarian style, which is a stew-type dish, or an American version, which is more of a pasta dish made with elbow macaroni. Based on the ingredients we had bought yesterday, and the green peppers we had harvested, I assumed we were making the American version, and I was right.

The rest of the afternoon was busy with cooking and setting out bowls and hooking up Lenny's microphone next to his chair, which really was not needed, but Irma said she liked it because it made sure she could hear his talk, while still working in the pavilion. I took a few minutes to make sure my guitar was in tune, and then decided to perform a song that I have loved since I was in High School, called, Somewhere in My Broken Heart, written by Billy Dean and Richard Leigh. It's beautiful and melodic, and one that I think I do particularly well. I had performed this song a hundred or more times in my career, so the lyrics were emblazoned in my brain, and I could play it with little or no rehearsal.

Finally, it was 4:00 PM, "Lenny is always a stickler about starting on time," Irma told me. The talk was well attended this night, it looked like 35 or 40 people, and as Lenny appeared at the top of the Pavilion, he said to me, "Are you ready, Kiko?"

"Yes, I'm ready." We walked down the steps together, and I stood next to Lenny's chair. As I got my guitar strap fixed around my shoulder, Lenny said, "We have a new friend working with us here at Liberty Garden, and as it turns out, she is a wonderful singer and guitarist as well. She's agreed to bless us with a song before we get started tonight, so I give you, Kiko Davis."

He had never heard me play or sing, and yet he seemed to have a confidence in my talent that I was lacking myself of late, so that was a huge boost to me. I played and sang my song, and the applause was very robust. I said thank you, placed my guitar in its stand, and headed up the steps to continue doing my job with Irma.

When I was done, Lenny said, "That was wonderful, thank you so much for that, Kiko." And then he went directly into his talk.

"Have you ever found yourself arguing with someone who just won't listen to your point of view? No matter how much evidence you show them, or how many facts you present to them, they just won't even try to understand you. Most of us have spent our entire lives trying to convince other people to believe what we believe. In fact, our entire society is built upon a culture of persuasion. Over and over, on the news, in the papers, on the radio, and now on internet forums, people passionately argue their perspectives and beliefs, trying desperately to convince others that they are right, and the other is wrong. Hundreds of books have been written on the topic of persuasion. But when you argue with a fool, you're like a man trying to teach a fish how to climb a tree. You both end up frustrated, and the fish still swims away, having learned nothing. In fact, when I see two people locked in a passionate debate over some topic that neither is truly an expert in, I find it impossible to determine which is the fool and which is the informed one.

"But there is a far wiser way to deal with such madness. The world is overflowing with words. Everyone wants to be right. Everyone wants to win. Yet no one stops to ask, 'What exactly are we trying to win?' You see, if you win an argument but lose your peace, you've gained nothing of value. Sure, you may be able to claim that you won, but what thing of any value have you won? Who do you think is keeping score over such victories? The one we think of as the fool is innocent due to his ignorance.

"I say that the real fool is the one who thinks he already knows the truth. He clings to his beliefs like a drowning man clutching a plank in the ocean. When you try to take it away for the safety of a real boat, he'll fight you. Not because he's evil, but because that piece of wood is his identity. So, when you argue with him, you're not fighting over facts. You're fighting over his sense of self, and that, my friends, is a battle no one can win. Think of it this way. If you pour water into a cup that is already full, what happens – it spills over. No matter how pure the water is, the cup cannot receive it. The mind of a fool is just like that – full, closed, and noisy.

"When you speak truth into such a mind, the truth spills out. So what should one do? How do you deal with the fool without becoming foolish yourself? The secret lies not in confronting them, but in the wise man who listens, observes, and sees through the madness without stepping into it. Arguing with a fool is like dancing with a storm – you may start with balance and intention, but soon the wind takes over. You begin to shout, defend, and justify, and slowly you become swept up into the chaos you hoped to avoid. This is why the sages of old, such as Jesus, Lao Se, the Buddha, and the mystics, always taught silence as the highest reply. Abraham Lincoln once wrote, 'It is better for a man to remain silent and be thought ignorant, than to speak and remove all doubt.

"Silence does not mean agreement. It means transcendence. It says, 'I see you. I understand you. But I do not need to fight you.' Silence is not weakness – it is mastery. But silence alone is not enough. One must also know how to direct their energy. When a fool attacks you with words, with mockery, with misunderstanding, it is tempting to strike back, to correct them, to prove your intelligence. But this is precisely how the fool traps you. He drags you into his level of vibration. And once you're there, you can't win, because he has home advantage. He lives in that chaos. He feeds on reaction. The wise man, however, shifts the entire game. He does not react, he responds. And his response is often not words, but action. For example, if a fool calls you weak, you don't argue that you are strong. You simply live with quiet strength. If he mocks your peace, you do not preach about calmness; you simply remain calm. In this way, you mirror wisdom, not noise.

"The fool then finds nothing to hold on to because you have denied him the conflict he feeds on. It's beautiful, really, because when you refuse to argue, you are no longer in the same play. You've stepped off the stage entirely, and the fool is left speaking to empty air.

"Sometimes the fool is within you. Yes, inside the mind of all of us, there is a part that insists it must be right. That voice that needs to win. That ego that burns when others misunderstand you. That too is a fool. To truly never argue with a fool, you must stop arguing with yourself as well. The moment you can let your own thoughts flow without judgment, the fool loses their power. You cannot be disturbed by what you have already understood within yourself.

"There's a saying about two people trying to untie a knot in a rope – the tighter they each hold the rope, the more the knot tightens. That's exactly what happens in an argument. Both people pull harder, neither realizing that the only way to undo the knot is for one to let go.

"So, the next time you feel the urge to correct someone, to make them see your perspective, to make them understand you, pause, take a breath, ask yourself, am I speaking to enlighten, or am I speaking to be seen? Always listen to understand, but only speak to educate. If you determine that the other party does not wish to be enlightened, then just move on and let them live in their own misunderstandings. Because one comes from love and the other comes from ego and fear. One leads to clarity, the other to endless and useless debate.

"When you can do this, you begin to see fools not as enemies, but as mirrors. They reflect the parts of you still attached, still reactive. Each foolish encounter becomes a gentle lesson, saying, 'This is where you still take things too personally.' And isn't that the true gift – to use every irritation as a mirror for God-knowingness? Then even the fool becomes your teacher. Not because they are wise, but because they reveal your remaining illusions. In this way, you no longer despise the fool; you thank them quietly and walk on.

"So, what do you do? Instead of arguing, you stay still. You stay clear. You practice presence. You act from understanding, not reaction. You embody the very wisdom the fool cannot yet see. Because wisdom is not about changing others, it's about always being open to understanding, but holding on to your values, and what wisdom tells you is the truth. The fool argues to prove something. The wise person listens to understand something. And the greatest understanding of all is this, to understand that the fool and the wise are not two separate beings, but two states of the same God-consciousness, and in knowing that, the argument ends.

"Life is not a debate hall. It's a dance. And in the dance, there is no right or wrong step, only rhythm. When you argue, you lose the rhythm. When you listen, when you observe, you find yourself moving in harmony with the symphony of life. That's where wisdom lives, not in proving, not in persuading, but in perceiving. To deal with fools is to learn the art of dancing with grace and elegance. The smile when others shout, to see the absurdity of it all, and to laugh gently. Laughter is the second awakening. I don't mean mockery. True laughter is compassionate. It comes from seeing the cosmic joke that we are all pretending to know while the universe itself is laughing through us.

"So when a fool wants to argue, you might even thank them silently, for they show you the comedy of human certainty. Perhaps that's what makes the wise person so calm. They've seen the play – they've read the script. They know that every fool believes themselves to be wise, and every wise person knows themselves to be a fool. The difference is awareness, not opinion. Fools are often just louder.

"The fool senses the absence of your energy, and it unsettles them. They demand a response. They crave the heat of your attention. Do not give it to them, because attention is power, and you decide where to place it. There is no greater response to a person who wants to argue with you or debate something with you than to simply not respond. Instead of feeding their chaos, feed your stillness. That is your greatest strength. The fool cannot understand stillness because their world thrives on reaction. But your silence, your refusal to play their game, becomes a mirror so clear that it unsettles their illusion. It's like standing by a pond. Throw a stone, and the ripples disturb the reflection. But let the water rest, and soon it reflects everything perfectly – the trees, the sky, even the clouds drifting above.

"So too, with the mind. When you stop throwing stones of argument and defense, your mind becomes still enough to reflect the truth that God, rather than dogma, is showing you. And in that stillness, understanding blooms naturally.

"Jesus, confronted by the Sadducees, refused to answer their charges and stood in total silence before their tribunal, and it threw them into utter chaos. So much so that some even defected.

"You no longer need to convince anyone. The truth, like light, does not argue with darkness, it simply shines, and its very presence reveals the truth.

"'So what if the fool is harming others?' You might ask. 'Shouldn't I step in?' That depends. If he is physically harming someone, then of course. Silence is not pacifism. But you must also remember, every child of God has the right, but not always the capacity, to find and know truth in their own way and in the Father's timing. Leaving this world, still mired in foolish beliefs, is not a sin. It may be a detriment to your eternal progress, which will lead to a longer path to God-knowingness, but it is not soul-ending. The key is to respond to foolishness with clarity, kindness, and love, not ego.

"If you see a man spreading lies, you don't wrestle with him in the mud – you share your understanding of the subject, and you wash your hands clean and walk away. That's what true reaction looks like. It's effective because it's not personal. It's simply the natural movement of awareness, precise, compassionate, and free of the need to win.

"So, how do we deal with people who refuse to understand? The politicians, the parents, the skeptics. Stop trying to make people understand. Instead, be understanding. You cannot open a closed fist by force. You open it with warmth, patience, and love. Those are the only things that can make it open by itself. That's the paradox of wisdom. What you resist, persist; what you allow, transforms.

"To never argue with a fool is to trust that time and truth do the teaching. You don't have to attend every argument you are invited to. Not every comment deserves your reply. Not every noise deserves your attention. And yet, you can always remain kind. Because kindness is not an argument, it's grace. When you meet a fool head-on with grace, you are not feeding his delusion. You're demonstrating another way of being. You're showing them, without using words, that there is a peace beyond their chaos. Sometimes that silent example plants a seed for deeper than any argument could ever reach. The world does not need more clever talkers. It needs silent watchers – it needs people who can stand in the storm and not lose their center.

"You see, the more you argue, the more you become entangled in the world's drama. And the world loves to pull you in. But when you learn to stand still, truly still, you become like a mountain. The winds howl, but they cannot move you. The rain falls, but it only nourishes your roots. The fool comes and goes, and yet your peace remains untouched. Sometimes the wisest response to a fool is simply to agree, not because he's right, but because you have no interest in proving him wrong. You nod, you smile, and you let him have the last word. And in that small act, you win the only game that matters, the game of inner freedom.

"The God-knowing person does not measure victory by domination, but by detachment. They are free because they have nothing to defend. Their truth is not a possession – it's a presence. And this presence, once felt, begins to change everything around you. You no longer attract endless arguments because people learn that you won't engage with them in such activities. Fools learn that you cannot be baited, and they move on to find another target. This is not arrogance, it's evolution. Consciousness rises by refusing to descend into reaction. So when you choose peace over conflict, silence over shouting, awareness over ego, you are not avoiding the world. You are transforming it from the inside out.

"The next time you encounter a fool, the one who mocks, provokes, and misunderstands, see them not as your opponent, but as your test – as fire that reveals how still your inner water truly is. And if you find yourself stirred, reactive, and angry, good. That's your mirror. That's the universe saying, 'Ah, you still have more to learn.'

"Because every fool on your path is another invitation to deepen your own awareness. And that perhaps is their greatest gift to you. In the end, all arguments are echoes of fear. The fool argues to protect their illusion. The wise remain silent because they no longer need illusion. The fool clings to belief. The wise rest in being. So the next time you feel drawn into a quarrel, remember the urge to argue is simply the ego begging for attention, and just smile at it, breathe, and let it pass.

"Remember, the truth needs no defender. It stands timeless, untouched by noise. It does not shout, because it has already won. And if ever you doubt this path, just look at nature. The ocean never argues with the storm – it absorbs it. The tree never argues with the wind – it bends. And yet both endure – both thrive.

"Wisdom is like that. Soft enough to flow, strong enough to remain. When you live this way, the fools of the world cease to bother you. You see them as children playing with sticks, making noise in the playground of existence. You smile. You wish them well, and you keep walking quietly, freely, joyfully by.

"So never argue with a fool. The greatest wisdom is not to silence the fool, but to awaken the fool within yourself. For when you no longer need to be right, you become free. And that, my friends, is the beginning of true God-knowingness.

"Are there any questions tonight?" Lenny asked.

One woman raised her hand and asked, "So, I obviously married a fool, what do I do now?"

Everybody laughed, of course, and Lenny, without missing a beat and as seriously as a heart attack, replied, "Dear woman, he's yours now, so I suggest you either show him the better way, or stop fueling his foolishness with your own."

Everyone just looked around, not knowing whether to laugh or what, until she said with a smile, "But fueling his foolishness is one of the only true joys I get out of life. You're taking away all my joy, Lenny."

Lenny simply replied with his big smile, "Carol, find a new hobby."

Now everyone laughed, and the tension broke, and Lenny asked again, "Are there any more questions?"

There were none, so in his usual manner, he stood and said, "So let's eat then," bounded up the steps, and was the first in line to get some of Irma's goulash. As he was coming up the steps, Irma whispered to me, "Lenny is always first in line, because it says to our guest that it's okay to get in line. We found that over the years, if Lenny is not the first, people tend to hesitate. Nobody ever wants to be the first in line."

After Lenny got his goulash, he announced, "As you can see. We have a new server helping Irma cook and serve tonight, so be sure to show her how much you appreciate her music and Irma's wonderful Goulash and all the work they do to make this event happen every week." He held up a glass jar that had, Irma & Kiko, and TIPS written on it. I was no stranger to working for tips, but I had no idea how much it would amount to with just 40 people or so to contribute. I was used to drunk college kids or bachelors and bachelorettes, celebrants streaming in and out of the club all night, and tipping a buck or two each.

The night was a good one, and a lot of people stopped to tell me how much they enjoyed my song and hoped I would sing again sometime. For as long as I stayed at the Gardens, I opened every Saturday evening with a song, and many opportunities opened up for me as a result of someone hearing me at the Gardens, to do parties and corporate events in the local Austin area. I never imagined these kinds of things were even a possibility until I started getting requests, so I began posting flyers at the serving station. It wasn't a huge audience, but it led to 8 or 10 really well-paying gigs a year, which was a big bonus to my income.

By 10:00 PM, Irma and I had finished all our cleanup, and the dishwashers were loaded and running. Irma picked up the tip jar and asked, "Are you ready?"

"Yeah... I'm ready."

She began to count out all the tips, and with every new twenty-dollar bill, and even a couple of hundred-dollar bills, my jaw dropped more and more. Irma said that by the bowl count, we had 45 people present that night, and they were generous. The total was $1,140. She counted out half and handed it to me and said, "It was a good night."

I had not had tips like that since I last bartended on a New Year's Eve. "Yeah, I'd say that was a good night. Is it always like this?" I asked.

"In the summer, it usually is. Sometimes we get celebrities come and most tip even bigger."

"Celebrities?"

"Yes, especially when the big festivals are going on. Lenny has a well-known reputation, even outside of Austin, so they come."

"Like who?"

"Oh, Paul McCartney has been here once, Willy Nelson several times, Matthew McConaughey and his wife have both come, and lots of others. They are all usually very nice."

"I had no idea."

"You'll see."

Irma said goodnight and headed to her car, and as I went around the back of the house to get into my apartment, I saw my Dad and Lenny sitting on the patio, chatting and drinking some Iced tea. It was a warm evening, so I decided to go and join them. "So, daddy, what did you think about tonight?" I asked as I approached the table where they were sitting."

"It was quite something. Now I know what draws so many people here to hear Lenny speak – he's very gifted." He said as he raised his glass to Lenny. Lenny just nodded his acceptance of the compliment.

We chatted for about 15 or 20 minutes, and then I said good night. It had been a long day. "Daddy, what time do you need to be at the airport in the morning?"

"My flight departs at 11:00 AM, so I guess around 9:00 or 9:30."

"Okay, it's about a 35 or 40-minute drive from here. So I'll be ready at 8:30 if that's okay."

"That will be wonderful, Kiko, thank you," I said my goodnight to them both, and they also decided it was time to call it a night, and they rose to go inside as well.

The next morning, I picked up my dad, and he told Lenny that he was leaving me in his capable hands to keep safe. It was as if the two of them had made a kind of pact of some sort concerning me. Lenny replied that it was never a question – she will do just fine here at the Gardens. I wasn't sure how I felt about that, but it was my

Dad, and I know he was always only concerned about me being safe. He never worried about whether I could make a living or anything else, as I had shown him that I was more than capable of earning money, but he did worry about my safety, especially after Derik left. Maybe now, at least, his mind is at rest about that. Lenny offered to make us some breakfast, but we both declined.

As we were driving, he said, "I'm sorry I didn't get to see Gina on this trip."

"Yeah… did I tell you she got a promotion and is now manager over the entire restaurant?"

"No…really! That's wonderful, I'm so glad for her. If I had known that, I would have made a point of going to say hello and congratulate her."

"I'll be sure to let her know, Daddy."

We made it to the Airport at just about a quarter after nine, and we said our goodbyes at the curb. I stood there and watched him enter the terminal, and thought about the fact that Gina had not come last night. I hoped she was not upset about my living and working at the Gardens. I decided I needed to go see her, so I headed to the restaurant. I went in, and the waitress recognized me and found a place for me at the counter. I asked, "Is Gina in?"

"Yes, she's in the office doing something. I'll let her know you're here."

"Thanks."

A few minutes later, Gina came out and was so pleased that I came in to see her. I asked why I didn't see her at the Gardens last night. "I hope you're not upset that I took the job out there, Gina."

"Are you kidding, Kiko? I'm so happy for you. But this new position requires a lot of my time. I needed to get my food orders in for next week before I could leave last night, and Randy, the night chef, didn't get in until 4:30 for me to get his list. He orders for all the chefs, so I wasn't able to get there, but I really wanted to be there."

"Lenny asked me to sing a song, and it went well. I think he may want me to do it again next week. The tips were really good."

"Wow, that's great, Kiko. I promise you I have no problem with you taking that job. I wish I had spent more time listening to Lenny speak. He's so gifted."

"Yeah… last night was a really good one as well," I told her about Lenny's talk, I ate breakfast, and of course, being flush with cash in my pocket, I was sure to tip the waitress really well also. When I left, I stopped at the grocery store, realizing that when I moved in, I had no food in my fridge, and headed back home. That sounded so good, I actually had a home again, at least for the time being. I wasn't sure what might come from this new life I had embarked on, but I was looking forward to finding out.

# Chapter 8

I spent the next three years of my life living and working at the Gardens. Well, in actuality, six years. But for now, I need to skip ahead to the point where I had lived and worked at Liberty Gardens for three years. I would have expected that by then, I would have outgrown my need for the occasional existential crises in my life, but I found that I was not quite there yet.

I'll pick up my story on a Thursday morning in June 2011. A day, or weekend I should say, that I had been dreading, had finally arrived. I don't know why I was dreading it so much, because it was an occasion for joyous celebrations, but it only made me sit and stew about how my own life seemed to be stuck in a huge rut. You see, my best friend, Gina, was getting married, and I was going to be her Maid of Honor.

Now, don't get me wrong, I loved Gina, and the man she was marrying, well, he was wonderful. Gina's life over the past three years seems to have taken on fairy tale proportions. And as much as I was so happy for her, it made me examine every moment of my own life, and why, after three years, I was still working at the gardens, gigging as a musician and singer when the opportunity came open, but otherwise not much else was going on. I was doing okay financially. I mean, I wasn't getting rich, but I had a good nest egg set aside from tips and gigging, and Lenny, or the "Trust" as he liked to call it, had raised my pay every few months, and I was earning several hundred more a month than when I had started. But something was still missing, and I couldn't put my finger on it.

Let me begin here with Gina, and how her trajectory was so much, I'd like to say better, but Lenny would remind me that it was just different, not better, than my own. Gina worked as the Manager of the restaurant for one full year, and as expected, she was moved to a more important position within the small franchise group that she worked for. She was promoted to a position that put her in charge of quality and customer service for all eight restaurants and

16 fast food franchises that were owned by her company, and she was good at it. Customer reviews began to rise, and things that had been neglected for months were getting fixed. She was a rising star within the small group she worked for.

Her boss asked her to go to an industry convention in Las Vegas to give a presentation on customer service that he had been bragging about to all his fellow industry managers. It was, of course, a huge success, and she was highly complimented on the presentation. One of the attendees, a young and very handsome man who identified himself as the newly appointed CEO of a restaurant holding company, came up to her at the end of the presentation and began asking her a lot of questions. She answered them all, and he just nodded, and then their conversation became more friendly, and they went and had a drink.

The next day, the conference ended, and she went home, and he went back home too, and she thought nothing more of it for over a month. Then, a month later, her boss, the company owner, called her into a conference with several other team members, and he announced that he had had an offer to buy all the dine-in family style restaurants that were part of his portfolio, and he decided he would sell, as the offer was so good. He said they would all be informed individually how the change would affect each of them, and so Gina was left wondering what would happen to her job.

At the end of the meeting, he asked Gina to stay behind, and so she just sat there while the rest of the team filed out the door.

When they were left sitting alone at the table, He looked at Gina, and he said, "Gina, you know how much I think of you, and how proud I am of all the incredible work you've done this last year. Part of the agreement I made with the new owners of the restaurants is that I allow them to make you an offer to work directly for them. Now, you don't have to accept their offer, and if you choose to stay here, I would love you to continue working for us, but I'm sure I will not be able to match any offer they are prepared to make you, especially now that my company is suddenly one-third smaller than it was. I would never hold you back from this or any opportunity, so you need to seriously consider what they have to say. I don't know what you said to Matt Goins at that convention in Vegas, but he was certainly impressed." He slipped a piece of paper across the desk with a phone number on it and continued, "He's expecting your call."

Gina did make that call and then went in person to see Matt, who had an office in one of the downtown Austin high-rise office buildings. The Goins Group, Inc., was founded by Matthew Goins Senior in 1980. He had amassed an impressive array of restaurant properties across the western half of the US. He ran the company until just about two years ago, when he suffered a stroke that left him partially paralyzed on his left side, and simply could not endure the hectic schedule of a CEO. Matt Jr. was a trained Lawyer and litigator who had to put his personal ambitions aside for the sake of the family business, and was named the CEO and Chairman of the Board for the company. They had a portfolio of over 150 restaurants.

She sat in front of Matt Jr's desk and could not help but notice how young he looked for such an important position. He seemed to recognize how much he had to learn as well, for even though he had grown up around the business, he had hoped to become the chief counsel before he would have to inevitably take over the business, as that was always the plan, but he never imagined it would be so soon. "Gina, I bet you never thought you'd see me again?"

"Well...umm, no, I guess not."

"I didn't mean to dis you as I did, but I had a company emergency, a fire in one of our kitchens, and an employee was badly burnt trying to put it out, so I had to get out there. Then he laughed and said, "Please don't think I bought seven restaurants just to see you again," and he laughed slightly. "We were already in discussion with Owen before I even went to the convention, but after I heard your presentation, I knew we had to complete that deal."

"Oh… so all that in Vegas was a scouting trip?"

"Well, the presentation was, but the drinks, no, that was just me and you. But this is a business meeting, so I need to get to business. I want to offer you a position as our Chief Customer Experience Officer." He showed her a salary and benefits package, and she almost fell out of her chair. It was a very nice six-figure income with a matching 401(k) and a 5-year guaranteed employment contract with a golden parachute, which is typical for executive positions. How could she possibly turn that down? It was everything she had worked for since the day she entered business school.

As I'm sure you've guessed by now… yes, she did take the job… and yes, they did fall in love. I won't bore you with all the details; after all, this is not their love story, and their story is not mine to tell. But this weekend is the wedding that has caused me to, once again, question everything about my life.

The one thing that I loved about working with Lenny so much wasn't just the lectures, or the natural gardening that Irma taught me, but it was all those evenings with just me and Lenny, sitting out on the patio or at the Kitchen table, just talking. There was nothing I couldn't ask him, although there seemed to be many things I never got up the nerve to ask, because they seemed like they would be intruding on his privacy. Just last night, I asked him why I was feeling so stuck, and I wasn't able to move on from this place, even after having learned so much from Lenny. He simply responded. "Because, Kiko, you still have so much to learn here."

I knew he was right, but what was it that I was lacking? What did I have left to learn? But for the time being, these questions were going to have to wait. I had a Bachelorette party to get set up, a rehearsal dinner to attend, and a wedding and reception to boot. So I put all that aside and headed to the Downtown Omni hotel, where this wedding was going to take place, which would be my digs for the next three to four days.

The weekend was a huge success, and I can say that as of this writing, Gina and Matt are very happy and recently welcomed their first child together. My dad, Janice, and Zoe all came to the wedding. Gina was kind enough to invite them, and of course, they always liked Gina and knew how much she meant to me. Zoe was so happy to come to Austin to see me. They stayed in my apartment while I was at the hotel, and this was Zoe and Janice's first time actually meeting Irma and Lenny, as the wedding was not until Sunday, and Saturday was the rehearsal dinner, which was only for close family and the wedding party, so they had the chance to hear Lenny talk as well.

I don't know what it was about the Gardens, but Zoe, who had just turned 15, absolutely fell in love with them, and with Irma. School was out, but Suzanna was doing her in-hospital Practical Nursing experience before her final year in School, so Zoe volunteered to help Irma serve. Zoe spent the entire day with Irma, working in the Garden and preparing for the night's meal. At the end of the night, Irma, with her usual grace and kindness, shared the tips with Zoe, and Zoe was so excited. I was not there, of course, as I had other duties with the wedding Party to attend to, but my dad told me all about it. I'm not sure that Janice was as impressed with the whole Garden business as Zoe was, but she did seem to enjoy the weekend as well.

The wedding went off without an issue, and as I was talking with one of the other bridesmaids during the reception, she asked me point-blank, "Kiko, are you adopted? When you introduced me to your parents, I was a bit surprised because you don't look anything like either of them."

I was kind of taken aback by the directness of her question. It had been years, it seems, since I had even thought much about it. I couldn't remember the last time anyone asked me that question, but then again, not many people ever see me with my family since they live in Colorado. I know this girl didn't mean anything by her inquiry, but she didn't stop there. She spoke at what I like to call the speed of Texan... you know, a series of lightning-fast questions without pausing to let the other person answer.

"Do you know who your birth parents are? Have you met your birth Mother or Father?" Just a series of other, quite personal questions ending with, My cousin is adopted, but we all know who her real mother is, it's my niece from my sister. She had her at just 14, but my mom decided it would be best if my Aunt adopted her, because my Aunt didn't have any children of her own, I think her husband can't have kids or something. Do you know anything about your real family?"

She kept saying, "Real Mom," and "Real family," like I had been stolen from them or something. It was very unsettling. All night long, this girl, whom I had just met a couple of days before when she came into town for the wedding, kept asking me questions and acting as if we had some kind of spiritual bond because she had an adopted person in her family as well.

I didn't stay too late at the reception. I left as soon as Gina and Matt left. I drove back to the Gardens that night, even though I was booked at the hotel for one more night. The Gardens had become my retreat from the world, and I just felt I needed to be there. Dad and Janice wanted to stay a bit longer and dance some, so Zoe came back to the gardens with me. That night, she and I stayed up until about 2:00 AM, talking about all sorts of things. Dad and Janice stayed in the extra room up at Lenny's, but Zoe and I, for the first time in our lives, were able to just sit and talk like two grown-up sisters. And she was growing up; there was no doubt about that.

We talked about everything that girls talk about. I learned from her that she really did not have many friends back home in Denver. Janice wanted her to spend every spare hour she had, working on appointment schedules and learning the bookkeeping for the business. I had no idea she had so few opportunities to just be a kid. But Janice was always driven and wanted to make sure that she did not raise a kid who was a layabout or didn't understand the business. She was that way with me as well, just not to such an extreme, because she and I were always kind of walking on eggshells with one another, but with Zoe, Janice was free to raise her as she willed. Don't misunderstand, Janice was never mean, cruel, or harmful in any way – just a real Tiger Mom, I guess you could say, very demanding. If Zoe actually had some school project or activity to be at, Janice was all on board with that. But if she were not directly involved in School, she wanted Zoe focused on learning the business end of the business.

That may be the one weakness my dad had – he was pretty much a pushover for Janice. She was obviously the strong-willed one in their relationship, and what Janice wanted, Janice got. Sometimes I think my dad would come to visit me, just because he needed a few days away from Janice.

Zoe and I talked about boys and sex and everything girls talk about when they're alone. She asked me about my first time, "What it was like. Was I scared?" I spoke honestly and as maturely as I was capable of.

"Are you thinking of having sex, Zoe? Have you already had sex? You're so young, are you sure you're ready for this?"

"No, Kiko, I haven't had sex yet. But there's a boy at school I really like. He's so cute, and he's on the football team, and I know, well, I've heard some of the girls talking about doing it with some of the other players."

"Zoe, I can't tell you what to do, you're 15 now. God knows, no one could ever tell me what to do when I was your age. I'm sure if Dad and Janice knew we were having this conversation, they would not be happy with me. But I can tell you, Zoe, you should never have sex because some guy wants you to. That is a decision you should only make when you are ready, and only for you, and never for somebody else or to get some guy to like you. You have your entire life ahead of you, and there is no hurry to make that decision. The last thing you want is to end up with a child of some guy you need to be constantly chasing down for child support for the next 18 years of your life. Trust me, I've seen more of that in my life than I care to talk about."

"Yeah… I know you're right, Kiko." That was all she said.

We moved on to talk about other things. But I felt bad for her, so I promised her that the next summer, when she was sixteen, I would let her come and spend the entire summer with me and Irma and Lenny, here at Liberty Gardens. For some reason, she thought this was the coolest place in the world. Now I just had to tell Dad and Janice.

"We'll see," is all that Janice said."

"I think it will be good for her." My dad replied. Janice gave him the old side eye, which says, "We'll talk about it at home," but my dad looked at Zoe and said, "It sounds like a plan, provided you keep your grades up and don't need to attend summer school."

"I will, Daddy, I promise I will."

Janice was silent and just smiled politely. I was very proud of my dad for having taken a stand.

They left the next day for home, but this weekend gave me so much to think about. I knew nothing about my birth parents or why I was given up for adoption. "Who am I really?" was a question that kept running through my head. And don't even get me started on the whole sex thing.

Over the last three years, I have not had any serious dating relationships at all. One of the things I noticed after living and working with Lenny for three years at this point, was that I found it really difficult to suffer fools, and there were a lot of fools who asked me out. I usually gave them each the benefit of the doubt on a first date, but it does not take long for a fool to begin showing his colors.

Don't get me wrong, I had plenty of dates. Every once in a while, some guy at one of Lenny's talks would be brave enough to ask me out, or some executive or lawyer at a corporate event would ask me out. I guess I was a bit envious of Gina for meeting such a successful guy, so I went out with quite a few of them, but they always seemed to be middle-aged divorce men who drove red sports cars. Why red? And why sports cars? I don't get it. If you want to impress me, drive an SUV, a station wagon, or something that can be used to help me lug around my equipment and guitars to my gigs. That would impress me. I did manage to buy myself a used SUV about a year ago, so I really didn't even need that, to be honest, but the gesture would be nice.

Most of these men were only looking for one thing – to go back to the office and claim they scored with that singer from the party. Trust me, none of them ever scored. I'm no prude, but I had adopted a very strict eight-date policy before even thinking about becoming intimate, and very few of these relationships passed that test. I know that seems like a high bar for this day and age, but I was raised Catholic, so I guess some of that Catholic guilt still lingers inside.

Over the last three years, I have only had one relationship that lasted three months or longer. It was with a guy named Jeremy. He was nice, my age, and he had a really good job as a software engineer at the Apple plant in Cedar Park, about 40 miles or so from the Gardens. He came to a talk one Saturday evening and was brave enough to ask me out. He was a nice guy, good looking, polite, and treated me with respect, but a bit of a Nerd. But after nearly 15 weeks of dating, he decided that we were not suited to be with one another, because I was not into video gaming like he was. I guess I didn't understand his world, and he didn't seem to have much of a desire to understand mine either. I asked him what he thought about Lenny's talks, and he would just shrug and say, "Yeah… they're okay." But I don't think anything Lenny ever talked about registered with him.

The thing that struck me most of all when he broke up with me was how much it didn't seem to matter to me. I mean, I got dumped, you would think I would have been upset or had some flashbacks of Derik dumping me, but I had none of that, just…Oh well… was all I felt. I guess that, in and of itself, is evidence that we should not have been together.

Dating was beginning to feel like it just didn't matter anymore. Why was I even trying to put myself out there? I mean, when was the last time some guy got dressed up, did his nails, and put on make-up, or whatever the guy equivalent is, for me? They would just show up, yeah, maybe they paid for a meal or the drinks, but I was not a heavy eater, and I seldom drank more than one drink. I was beginning to just hate the whole process.

But then my brain kept telling me that the right guy is out there, and I'm way too young to give up on love. But I wasn't giving up on love, I was just tired of playing a game that didn't seem to have any end or make any difference. It's not that I was on a bunch of dating apps, trying the shotgun approach to finding someone. I had heard so many horror stories from friends who used dating apps that I just didn't want to go down that road. Of all the people I know, only one ever had any success using a dating app. I guess you could call it a success, at least they're still together. It all just seemed so futile.

But then there was this nagging feeling that I needed to do something more in my life. I was missing something, and I didn't know what. Maybe it's the adoption thing. Maybe I should try to find out more about my birth family, or at least explore the culture that I came from.

It was Monday, and my day off to do whatever I wanted, but all I wanted to do was talk to Lenny, so I went up to see what he was doing. I could see he was out in the workshop, so I took a stroll out there. He was just puttering and cleaning some tools and had his sharpening stones out for his chisels.

"Lenny, are you busy?" I asked.

"I'm never too busy for you, Kiko, you know that."

"Umm… I wanted to ask you something. It's kind of important, but if you don't have time, it can wait."

"That sounds serious. Can you meet me at the house in about thirty minutes, then I'll have all the rest of the day to talk about anything you like."

"Okay. Thank you, Lenny. Do you need any help with anything here?" Lenny had shown me a while back how to sharpen his chisels, clean his rasps, and straighten his saw blades."

"No, Kiko. I do appreciate the offer, but I'm just about done – just putting things away now."

"Okay, I'll see you in a bit." I walked up to the house, got out the iced tea pitcher from the fridge and two glasses, and sliced a lemon. Just as promised, a few minutes later, Lenny came rambling up to the house and went into the Kitchen to wash his hands, then came out and took a seat at the table.

"Okay, Kiko, I'm all yours. What is it you need to ask?"

"I'm thinking of going to try and find my birth parents."

"Oh…that is serious. Why this sudden urge to find them? In all the time you've been here, I've never heard you even once express a desire to find them."

"I don't know. This weekend, there was a girl at the wedding; she was one of the bridesmaids, and she saw me with my Dad and Janice, and she just kept asking me if I knew who my birth parents were and if I had ever wanted to go find them, and it just made me start thinking. I should know these things, right? I mean, who doesn't know these things in this day and age?"

"Only millions of children whose parents died when they were young, or who died in childbirth, or were adopted into other families from all over the world. Most of them never get the chance to know their birth parents."

"Yes, but for most of them, they at least have some record or photos or something to hang onto, so they have some sense of who they are. I have none of that. I mean, I'm Japanese, and that's what people see when they look at me, but I don't feel Japanese. My earliest memories are of Kate and Bill Davis, not anything ever remotely related to who I really am. And none of that comes even remotely close to answering the 'Why' of it all." Suddenly, I was pouring my heart out to Lenny. It was like a flood gate had opened, and a lifetime of questions and repressed emotions just came flowing out.

"I have a right to know who I am, what I am. I want to know the culture I was born into. I see pictures of Japan, and I feel nothing, but I should feel something. Sometimes it's like I just woke up in a hospital with no identity whatsoever. I feel like I'm a clone who just popped out of a bio bag full of goo, as a full-grown adult, and I have no idea who I am. Don't misunderstand, I love my adopted parents, but they can't fill this void of not knowing who I am. I need to find out something, even if it's as simple as I just wasn't wanted. My life is like looking at a wrapped Christmas gift, not knowing what's inside. The possibilities are endless, but until I open that wrapping, I'll never know for sure. I need to go and find out."

Lenny just sat there, and he listened. He didn't stop me, he didn't try to dissuade me, he just held my hand, and it all came out. Then, when I was finished pouring out my heart, he asked, "So what do you need from me, Kiko?"

"Just tell me that I'm right, or that I'm wrong, I don't care, just tell me what to do?

"Kiko, nobody can tell you what to do, and I would never even attempt to try, but I will support anything you decide to do."

"What would you do, Lenny?"

"Now…that's a very different question, but I do think I would want to know something."

"So you think I should go looking for them then?"

"I didn't say that. I said I would support whatever decision you make. I can't put myself in your shoes, Kiko. I haven't lived your life, any more than you have lived mine. Every individual's life path is totally different than every other person's. Sometimes, we get to walk the path together with people we learn to love, even if it's just for a short while. You've been feeling that you're stuck, maybe it's because you need to find these answers."

"Do you think it's time for me to leave the Gardens, Lenny?"

"These gardens are not going anywhere, Kiko, and now they are as much a part of you as you are of them. That won't ever change, and if you decide to leave for good, or just for a short time to find the answers you're looking for, we will all be here for you when you return. But I sense your path is taking you on a detour, and if it is the Father's will, it will bring you back; if not, we will still be here, knowing you are on your correct path."

"So where would I even begin, Lenny?"

"With the obvious, of course, your adopted parents. They have to have records or some kind of paperwork from your adoption."

"Oh…man, how do I even begin to ask them about that. I don't want them to think I don't love them."

"I don't think that's even a possibility, Kiko. I've never met your mother, but I do know Bill would not be even the slightest bit offended by the question."

I said, "It's just the beginning of Summer, so I'll stay until winter, when the weather gets cold, and we take our break from the talks. That should give me all the time I need."

"Don't put artificial limits or timetables on yourself, Kiko. Take whatever time you need. But I do have to ask you, are you really prepared for the answers you may find?"

"What do you mean?"

"Well, as you said, not knowing is somewhat of a Schrodinger's Box. Until you open it, every possibility is still in there. It may be the gift you were always hoping for, or it may be the curse you never expected."

"Yes…I'm ready for whatever. I mean, nothing I discover can be worse than what I've already conjured up in my own brain."

"Those sound like the last great words of a girl wishing she had never opened her box," then Lenny laughed.

I didn't reply to that last statement and just left it there. I did say, finally, "I hear you, Lenny. I'll plan on going in December and January, so I'll be here to help with all your Saturday talks." I began doing some research and making preparations that same day, but I continued to work throughout the Summer and Fall.

# Chapter 9

The summer came and went like a blur. One week just turned into the next, and all I could think about was my pending trip to Japan. But this fall was also the beginning of what I can only describe as my season of chaos. I suffered one life-shattering event after another, for what seemed like years, but in reality, it was only months – months that left me oscillating wildly between moments of great joy and the deepest sorrows I had ever experienced in my life.

After speaking with Lenny and deciding I needed to go looking for my birth parents, I called my friend Karen. We used to tend bar together, but she had stumbled upon a gig that set her up as an independent travel coordinator, with several corporate clients contracting her to make travel arrangements for their executives and employees. She worked from home and spent almost every day booking flights, hotels, tracking awards points, scheduling rental cars, whatever was needed. I had never traveled outside the country before. I didn't even have a passport at that point, so she was so kind and patient with me and just walked me through the process of submitting my application, and was able to book some great deals for me, using some discounts she had earned from some of the airlines and hotels she has relationships with. She even made sure I would have access to the executive lounges at both the Denver and Tokyo airports during my trip. By the end of October, everything was arranged, my new passport had arrived, and I knew there was no turning back now.

I had spent a good deal of my nest egg on this trip. I was going to stay for three whole weeks to learn whatever I could learn about my birth mother and the Japanese culture. I spent the next several weeks researching everything I could find about Japan and its history, but I still felt like I was just working on a school assignment or something. I didn't feel any real connection to any part of what I was learning.

But we still had the fall to get through at the Gardens, so there was a lot of work remaining to be done. Liberty Gardens had become a real home for me. Lenny had no problems with me painting my rooms to suit my taste and decorating in any way that I wanted. I began to surround myself with Japanese art and a few Japanese furniture pieces. I know it was all just cheap knock-offs. It was not made in Japan, and the mother-of-pearl was just plastic, but I thought maybe I would begin to get a better sense of the culture if I surrounded myself with some Japanese-style items. It worked a little bit, but not to any great extent.

But all of this was just a distraction from the real work at hand. The gardens needed a great deal of effort in the fall. Plants were going dormant, and it was the time we took out dead or dying foliage and began preparing everything for the Winter. The nights were getting cooler, so Lenny's lecture attendance began dropping off, usually around Thanksgiving. But until then, there were still meals to prepare, a garden to attend, and work to be done.

But the only direct memory I had of those months leading up to my trip was the day I finally got up the nerve to ask Irma a question I had been wanting to ask for three years. We were working in the vegetable garden, pulling dead plants out and preparing the garden for next spring plantings, when she expressed to me that she was concerned about Lenny, because he seemed to be getting tired faster than before. I had also noticed that he had lost just a bit of bounce in his step, but otherwise, he seemed fine to me. But since she brought up the subject of Lenny, I finally asked her, "Irma, why are you and Lenny not married? It's obvious to anybody who knows the two of you that you are completely in love with each other, so why do you two not at least live together?"

She looked at me and laughed, "Kiko, I'm surprised it's taken you so long to ask that question. Most people ask me as soon as they learn how long I've worked here."

"So, why then?"

"Of course, I love Lenny; he's the best thing that has ever happened to me, and I know his reasons for not wanting to be married or live together, but some stories are not mine to tell, and you will have to ask him about that. But I can tell you that he has been the greatest father to Suzanna that I could have ever asked for, and she absolutely adores him. We don't live together because he always wanted me to be free to date or even marry if I met someone."

"So why have you never met anyone?"

"I've had some dates. You see how many of the men who come here are not afraid to ask you out, and it was the same for me when I first came here. But I always knew that if I met someone and got married, I would have to divide my loyalties between Lenny and my husband, and that would never have been fair to either. My loyalty to Lenny is too strong, and I could never, not be here for him.

"Besides, what would that have done to Suzanna? She would have never accepted another man as a step-father when she had Lenny right here for her."

"How did they become so close? I asked"

"He's all she's ever known, but you've seen them together, especially when they go on walks through the garden together, it's such a special thing to see, and I could never have taken that away from her."

"Yeah... I've seen them together on their strolls through the garden."

"They're not just strolling; they're talking to God."

"Talking to God? I asked."

"It's all in his mind and Suzanna's as well. They walk in silence, but they both swear that they speak to God, and God speaks to them, on these walks. I remember the day it began, or at least when Suzanna began walking with him. She was about 5 years old, and we were working out here in the vegetable garden when Suzanna saw Lenny walking in the garden. As he got closer to us, she left the garden and went to him and asked 'Papa, what are you doing?' Lenny smiled that big smile of his and said, 'I'm just having a little talk with my Father in heaven, sweetheart.' 'Oh… can I talk to him too?' she said, and he took her by the hand and said, 'Of course, come with me, and I'll show you how.' The two of them have walked and talked to God every day the weather has allowed that I can remember since that day, and they became inseparable."

I had never heard that story before, and it was then that I finally understood the extraordinary bond between Lenny and Suzanna, and Irma. But I still never understood his reluctance to marry, or at least live with Irma. He always referred to Sam Eustes as his partner, and of course, being a millennial child, I had a rather millennial understanding of the term, partner. To my generation, it usually referred to domestic partners or life partners, and it always made me wonder if Lenny was perhaps Gay, but then he never did or said anything that would confirm that, so I was left to wonder in my mind and not know anything for sure, until several months later, when I returned from my trip to Japan. But that's getting ahead of my story, so I'll leave it there for now.

Lenny held his last talk for that season on the first Saturday in December. We were not scheduled to hold another one until the third Saturday of February, weather permitting. This period of rest was very much needed for Lenny. It gave him time to read and study and relax and not need to constantly produce lectures for the next week. I was preparing to leave on my trip, and I went up to let Lenny know I would be leaving in the morning. He was sitting at his desk in his office, and he had a big, blue, hard-covered book sitting out on his desk that he was reading from. I had seen him reading from it many times, but was not curious enough to ask him about it; but this time, the urge came over me.

I asked him, "Lenny, what's that book I see you reading so often?"

"It's called the Urantia Book."

"I've never heard of that. What is it?"

"I believe it's the most important book written in our lifetime, and may be for the next 50 generations," Lenny responded.

"So why have I never heard of it?"

"People find it when they are ready to find it. Since you asked, perhaps now you are ready."

"What's it about?"

"It's about everything! It's about creation and God and the structure and administration of the universe, and it contains the most detailed and, as far as I can tell, accurate account of the life of Jesus ever recorded."

"Is it some kind of secret teaching?"

"No, not at all. There is nothing secret about this book, but it is rather controversial?"

"How so?"

"It's reported to have been delivered directly by divine methods. The originators tell that the book was delivered partially by a sleeping subject who was unaware of the messages that were being spoken through him, and other papers were claimed to have been written by celestial beings and placed in a locked safe, where they would be found by the people who had been assembled to edit and arrange the papers into this book."

"So, you mean some kind of channeling thing, like Edgar Casey, or something?"

"Kind of, but more direct than that."

"So how do you know that any of that story is true?"

"Because my former partner, Sam, claimed his parents worked for years on the commission of people who assembled this book, and even alluded, but never confirmed directly, that his father may have been the sleeping subject, and I never had any reason to doubt his claims?"

He picked up the book and said, "This book is one of the very first that came off the press. Sam and I read it together many times, and it changed my life."

"I guess I should read it someday then."

"So… how did you meet Sam, Lenny?"

"I was working on a highway crew, building roads across this country. I began my working life as a carpenter, and did that work for several years, but then decided I wanted to see more of the country, and so I signed on to a highway crew to build roads. Back then, the country and the States were engaged in an all-out effort to build superhighways and roads all across the landscape, so I signed on with a company to be part of that. We were working our way across Texas, working on the very road that now sits right outside these gardens.

"We would always set up a camp several miles ahead of where we were working, and then when we reached the camp, we'd move the camp forward a few miles, and then continue to build the next section of road. One night, the crew and I were sitting out in front of a campfire, telling tall tales as men in such situations are prone to do. I drank a lot in those days, and we were all a bit drunk, and up walked a stranger I had never seen before. He just asked, as boldly as can be, 'Do any of you men have experience building houses. I'm about to build a house a few miles back up the road, I'm looking for someone who can help me.' Well, I stood up, and could barely even stagger at that point, and I blurted out, 'I can build you a house, mister.'

"He looked at me, and he just said, 'Marvelous, come with me, and I'll put you to work first thing in the morning.' I followed him to his car, and we drove to this land, and I have been here ever since."

"You're kidding… right?" You just followed him back here, and that was it?"

"Yep! I probably passed out as soon as I got back to the little campground he had set up. When I woke up in the morning, Sam showed me what he had to build his house with. He had a chainsaw, an old portable saw mill, a used John Deere tractor with a front loader and a backhoe he had bought from a local farmer, and an Airstream travel trailer that he had parked here on the land. He told me that we could buy anything else we needed. He said, 'I can pay you $700 a month.' That was all I needed to hear; the company I was working for was just paying $80 a week, so Sam's offer was much better than that."

"So how long did it take you to build this house?" I asked.

"I think it took us nearly five years to get to the point that we could move in. But then there was still a lot of other work to do. I lived downstairs in the basement apartment, and Sam lived up here, and little by little, we cleared what needed to be cleared and built what needed to be built. But Sam was not your typical person. I had never met another person like him. When I met him, I was a bitter, angry, hard person. I drank heavily. I was not afraid to start a fight if I thought someone had wronged me, and just looking at me the wrong way was sometimes enough for me to feel wronged. I was not the man you see here today, Kiko. Sam taught me things I never knew. He had a wisdom that sometimes stunned me and awed me at the same time. I don't know where it all came from. But bit by bit, I learned. And when he passed away in 1987, I was left to carry on the work he had started here. That's how I met Sam and came to be here."

"Wow...that's amazing, Lenny." I suddenly remembered why I had come up to speak with Lenny, "Oh yeah... I wanted to remind you that I'm leaving for my trip in the morning."

"So soon! I wish you the best, Kiko, and hope to see you back when you have found the answers you're looking for."

"Thank you, Lenny. I'll be back as soon as I can." I was beginning to see why Irma felt so much loyalty to Lenny, because now I was feeling guilty for leaving this place, even for a short time, but I knew he was in very safe hands with Irma and Suzanna. The next morning, I drove my car to Denver to see my dad. I brought my car because I planned to be there for a few weeks after I returned from my trip.

But now came the hard part. I had to tell both my mom and dad that I was going to Japan to find my birth mother and father, if I could. I'd not even told them I was going on this trip. I called my dad and told him I was coming to Denver for a short vacation. He was very happy to hear it, but I had not told him about the trip to Japan.

So, I arrived in Denver on a Tuesday afternoon in December, and Daddy was working. Zoe still had school for a couple of more weeks, and Janice was also at the office, so I decided to drive out to the business to see my Dad. It was nice to see the place again. Many of the guys and gals who worked for him when I was young were still there, and it was good to see so many of them. I didn't realize how much I missed that place until I was there. Of course, I had to answer all the obligatory questions about what I have been doing and how my music career is going.

It was a bit embarrassing to admit that I barely even had a music career, and now, missing the Christmas season this year, as playing at Christmas parties had become a large part of my income, I wondered if I was not available this year, would they even remember to call me next year when I was back? But this had been a good Summer for company picnics and other events, so I had done okay, but I worried that I might have done some damage to my future career by taking the season off. I also had developed a network of backup musicians I could call for these events to help accompany me, and they were also missing out on that work, which weighed heavily on my mind as well. Not that any of them could not find other gigs, as they were all capable of finding work as studio musicians or other backup gigs, but still, I felt obligated towards them, and it was difficult not to be there for the events that season.

My dad was out on a Job, and so I asked Janice for the address. It was a new construction installation, so he would be out there all day. I drove up to the construction site and walked into the large, half-completed apartment building looking for my dad. After our initial greeting, he asked, "So, Kiko, how long are you going to be here. I hope you're staying through Christmas."

My schedule actually had me spending Christmas in Tokyo, and I dreaded having to tell him that, but I guess it's easier to just rip the band-aid off in these situations, so I said, "I'm sorry, Daddy, but I'm going to be in Tokyo for Christmas."

"Tokyo, why will you be in Tokyo?"

I looked at the ground sheepishly and then just put it out there, "I'm going to see what I can find out about my birth parents."

Those words just hung quietly in the air for what seemed like an eternity, then he finally said, "Oh... I see."

I now had a tear running down my face, as I could see the hurt in his eyes, and so I quickly said. "Don't be hurt, Daddy. You know I love you, and nothing could ever change that, but this is just something I have to do."

"Oh... don't cry, sweetheart. It's okay. I understand. I always suspected this day would come. But you have to know, even if you get there, you may not be able to find much. Adoption records are always kept very private. I don't know where you would even begin."

"I've been doing some research, and I found that it is not uncommon, especially in Japan, for birth parents to allow their children to find them. I guess after World War II, so many women had to give up children for adoption that they passed a law that a mother could always specify that they gave a child the right to request to see their files if the parent gave that permission on their forms."

"Oh... I see – I guess you've been working on this for some time then."

"No, Daddy, just a few months really. But I was hoping I could find out from you what adoption agency you used so I can go and at least see if my birth mother gave permission."

"Sweetheart, I would help you if I could, but your mother has all those records. I just remember it was a Catholic agency, The Sisters of Something, and we worked with a young Nun called Sister Bonny. It happened really fast, so it just feels like a blur in my memory, but your Mom, she hoards paper records like a squirrel hoards nuts. I'm sure she still has all the documents in a box somewhere."

"A Catholic agency! Of course it was. Okay, I'll go see her tomorrow." I had read some things about how some of the Catholic agencies in Ireland had practically stolen children from their young, unwed mothers through forced adoptions, and were notorious for deliberately losing or destroying records. My mind suddenly ran towards the worst-case scenarios.

"I'm sure Zoe will be very disappointed you won't be here with us for Christmas. She was so excited when I told her you were coming to visit."

"I know, Daddy, but I promise I'll stay for a couple of weeks when I get back, and then I'll tell you all about what I discovered."

"Okay, Sweetheart. That'll be fun. I'm just about done here for today. What do you say, you and I go get some dinner together, just the two of us."

"That will be nice, Daddy." So we went to our favorite place to eat together, and we had a lovely time. I spent the night with him, Janice, and Zoe, but first thing in the morning, I left to drive to Colorado Springs to see my mom.

That night before I went to bed, I called my mom and told her I was coming to see her. It didn't go exactly as I had planned.

"Hi Mom!"

"Kiko, what a surprise to hear from you. Is everything alright?"

"Yeah, it's fine, Mom. I'm at Daddy's, and I just wanted to drive down to see you tomorrow if that's okay?"

"Oh... tomorrow... umm...well, yes, I guess that will be fine. Are you sure everything is okay?" This was the first time since I had left her house to go and live with my dad that I had ever gone to see her at her house. I guess I should have suspected she would be suspicious that something was up. "Yeah... Mom, everything is okay, but I was just wanting to see you, and I need to talk with you about something." That certainly didn't help. Now she knew I was coming for something other than to just visit, and I would leave her hanging all night before she knew what. She probably thought I was coming to tell her I was getting married, or pregnant, or something, but what I had to ask, I really felt I needed to do it face-to-face, so I left her hanging on that bit of information.

So the next morning, I drove to Colorado Springs and arrived at her place at around 10:30. She had called in and taken the day off so she could be there when I arrived and came out to greet me. As we hugged, standing out in the yard, the neighbor, Mrs. Warner, came over and asked, "Is that Kiko, I see? My word, young lady. Look at how you've grown. It must be 15 years since we've seen you here in the old neighborhood.

"Hi, Mrs. Warner, it's nice to see you, " I replied as we hugged. "It's not quite 15 years, but it's getting close for sure.

"So, where are you living now?" I'm sure my mom had told her several times, but you know how people are, they ask redundant questions just to fill the empty air.

"I'm living in Austin, TX. Still playing music and just going along to get along. You know how it is?"

"Oh, how wonderful. You should see my Ricky, he's in the Air Force now, you know, a Pilot. He's so handsome in his uniform. He's stationed in Idaho, though, but he's married and has two children, so I love going to see them."

"Yeah, I'll bet he is handsome in his uniform; he was always good-looking," I said. Ricky and I were the same age and in school together, and yes, I did have a crush on him, until I abruptly moved to Denver."

Finally, my mom stepped in and said, "Well, it's good to see you, Sheran, but it is pretty cold out here, and Kiko is not used to damp cold anymore, so I think we need to get inside."

"Oh yes, of course. It was so nice to see you, Kiko."

"You too, Mrs. Warner. Tell Ricky I said hello. I'm amazed she still lives next door; didn't you tell me she's a widow now?" I said to my mom as we went inside.

"Yes, Fred died in a flight accident in Afghanistan about 6 years ago. But she had his insurance from the Air Force and his pension, and she works out at the base as well, so she's doing okay."

"That's good to know." I took off my coat, and we sat at the kitchen table. "Wow, the place has hardly changed in all these years, Mom."

"Yes, I know. But the club takes a lot of my time these days, and I really have never been big on redecorating anyway. It's comfortable, and that's all that matters to me." She has always been somewhat of a workaholic, so I understood the need to just have someplace comfortable and familiar to come home to every night. "Oh… I hope you don't mind, I told my friend, Don, that you were coming to town, and he offered to take us to dinner at the club tonight."

"Umm…yeah, okay, that'll be nice."

"So, Kiko, what did you want to talk to me about? You kind of just left me hanging to wonder last night on the phone."

"Oh, yeah. I wanted to ask you about my adoption."

"Your adoption, what do you want to know about your adoption?"

I took a deep breath and just put it out there. "I'm on my way to Japan, Mom. I want to see if I can find anything out about my birth mother. I also don't really know anything about Japan, and I want to learn more about where I come from."

"Oh…okay, I guess it's only natural that you would have some curiosity. Okay, yeah, that's good. I'm happy you want to know more about where you came from."

"Really, you're okay with it."

"Kiko, I know you well enough to know it wouldn't matter if I were okay with it or not – you've obviously made up your mind to go looking, so all I can do is support you." She smiled then added, "I'd like to say you inherited your tenacity from me, but we both know that's not possible, so you must have come from some very determined people. Yes, I'll support you in any way I can."

"Good, Mom, because I was wondering if you still have all of my adoption papers. Daddy said you should still have them."

"Oh…yeah, of course, I have them in a box of records in the attic up above the Garage, I'm sure."

It was just then that I noticed that my mom's eyes seemed to be very yellowish, and so was her skin tone. She looked thin and didn't seem to have the energy that I remembered. She always had beautiful Irish green eyes and that gorgeous red hair, and it was beginning to go grey and not quite as shiny as it once was. I asked her, "Mom, are you okay? You seem a bit tired."

"Umm… I'm okay, Kiko. In fact, I thought maybe that was why you called me. I wouldn't have put it past Don to call you and spill the beans on my condition."

"Condition, what condition?"

"I've been diagnosed with Liver failure, Sweetheart. Now, I'm okay, I'm doing well, and the doctor tells me as long as I stop drinking alcohol and take my meds, I should be okay for a long time, but ultimately, I could need a liver transplant. But we're still a long way from that point, so this is not something you should be worrying about."

"Not worry, Mom, how can you tell me not to worry?" I began to cry. Despite all our differences, the thought that I might lose her was something I was not even prepared to think about. We sat at the table that afternoon, and we talked in ways we had never talked before. For the first time in a long time, I felt Kathrine "Kate" Louise Griffin was my mother. After a short time, I crawled up into the attic and pulled down the box of papers my Mom had marked, Kiko. And we went through it together. It was full of old photos I had never seen, of me as an infant and a little girl. Every award I had ever won, every picture I ever drew for her, every bit of my childhood was stored in that box, and yes, every record of my adoption. Then we found it, the name and address of the adoption agency. The Sister of the Sacred Heart adoption agency and home for Unwed Mothers. The name of the nun who handled my adoption was on the document. Her name, just as Daddy had remembered, was Sister Bonny. "Oh… I remember her." Mom said, "She seemed so young to be a Nun, couldn't have been more than 20 years old or so. She was so kind to us."

"Well, I'm sure she's not still there. Can I take this with me? It had a date and case number on it. That may help them locate my file?"

"Of course, Kiko. This is all yours. I was just hanging on to it in case you ever wanted any of it." But I could see she was really keeping it for herself.

"I'll take the rest with me the next time I come, okay. I have to go back to Denver tomorrow, so I can prepare for my flight to Tokyo on Friday."

"Oh, so soon, well, you'll have to come and spend some more time when you get back."

"I will, Mom, I promise."

That night we went to the Officer's club to meet her newest, and she says most serious relationship she has had in many years, Donald Howe. Don, as he likes to be called, was a retired Air Force fighter pilot who now worked at the Cadet flight training school as a civilian instructor. He was about 6 feet tall, slim, with dark hair and graying temples, and a perfect smile. He looked like a cover model from GQ magazine. I was impressed. He was very handsome, but also a very friendly and kind man. "Kiko, it is so nice to meet you. I've heard so much about you. Your mother brags about you and your wonderful musical talents endlessly."

"Thank you, Mr. Howe."

"No, No, No…it's Don, just Don."

"Okay, Don. It's nice to meet you as well. I've heard equally nice things about you."

We had a lovely evening together, and we danced some to the music that was playing. I was even asked to dance by a couple of very young and handsome officers who were in the club that night. I could see he was absolutely head over heels about my Mom, and I was so glad to see my mom in what seemed to be a very healthy relationship in her life. Overall, it was the most wonderful time I could ever remember having with my mother. I was so glad we had spent that time together. But I needed to remain focused on the task at hand, so after saying our good-byes in the morning, I headed back to Denver for my final packing to prepare for three weeks in Japan.

Daddy said to me that night, "Be sure to pack long johns. It can get bitterly cold in Japan this time of year. The worst chest cold I ever had was in Japan after spending an afternoon working outside on an aircraft with the wind blowing in on me in the wet cold on the ramp in Yokota. It can really sneak up on you – be prepared for anything."

"Okay, Daddy, I will be." The next morning, Daddy took me to Denver International for a Non-stop flight to Tokyo. I arrived three hours before my flight, so thank God, Karen had thought to make sure I had access to the executive lounge at my terminal; it really made waiting much easier than any I had ever had before.

# Chapter 10

I boarded my flight and found, to my surprise and delight, that Karen had used some points or other coupons to allow her to upgrade me to Business class for my flight to Tokyo. She didn't tell me this, but I know I hadn't paid for it, or she would have said something, so I told myself I would have to do something special for her when I got home to Austin, to say thank you.

I had an Aisle seat, and my seatmate was a very nice lady, but a bit chatty for someone I was going to have to sit next to for the next twelve and a half hours. She was a Geneticist, traveling to Tokyo for a conference on some new procedure for gene splicing, whatever that means. She was very excited about what she did and even showed me some video simulations on her laptop to try and explain what it was all about, and I just nodded my head as if I understood and then tried to crawl into my own little world, but she just kept talking and asking me questions about what I did and why I was going to Japan.

I didn't know what to tell her. I didn't want to say that I was a singer and musician, because then I would have to explain why she had never heard of me. My experience was that any time I told people I was a singer or musician, the next question was always, "Oh, what have you done? Have I ever heard anything you sang?" I didn't like answering that question. It always made me feel like a failure, so I decided I would borrow Irma's life for the duration of the flight, and I told her I was a natural gardener, going to Japan to learn some new gardening techniques from a Japanese expert on gardening. I just made it all up as I went along. I felt kind of bad about it, but at least I knew enough to sound somewhat literate on the topic. In reality, all I knew was to plant this, pull that, till this area, and hoe these weeds before they take over the area. But I managed to surprise myself with how much of what Irma had taught me had actually taken root in my brain, and was able to at least sound like I knew what I was talking about.

I realized on the flight how little I knew about so many other things. I really had lived somewhat of a cloistered life at the gardens. It kind of made me wonder what else I may be missing out on and if perhaps it was time for me to think about finally leaving, but what would I do, and where would I go? It had been nice to be home in Denver, and I would like to maybe be closer to my mom, now that we had finally grown to a place where we actually liked each other. I would like to be there for her now that she's ill, but that's something I was going to have to figure out at a later time.

After about 40 minutes in the air, the in-flight movie began, so I put on my headphones while my seatmate just stared into her computer screen and typed furiously on something she was working on, and we just sat in peace for most of the rest of the flight. Every once in a while, there would be a break between one movie and the next, or when I was not just listening to music on my phone, and she would chat me up again for a few minutes, then the movie would begin again, or I would close my eyes, and it was quiet until the next interlude. I never realized how hard it is to just sit and do nothing for a full twelve hours at a time. It was awful, but I got through it.

Our flight arrived in Tokyo on time, and I passed through customs and collected my bags. I was booked at the Tokyo Hilton and was able to catch the Hotel bus from the airport directly to the hotel. *That was easy, I thought… this is going to be a breeze.* Boy, was I wrong. The first hurdle I faced was that everyone kept wanting to talk to me in Japanese. Everywhere I went, I found myself having to tell people, "English, I only speak English," only to see a really confused look on their face. But after a couple of days, I figured it out. I bought a T-shirt that said, "I Love Seoul." People just assumed I was Korean after that.

The train announcements were all in Japanese, but the signs were in both English and Japanese, so that at least made it possible to get on the right train; it was getting off at the right stop that could be difficult – the announcements all came so fast.

On my third day in Japan, I decided it was time to try to go to Yokota on the train, but I was very unsure of myself, so I took a chance and went to the concierge at the hotel to get some assistance. I had observed her from a distance for some time and noticed as she helped other hotel guests that she seemed to speak English quite well, so I went up to her and asked, "Can you help me figure out how to take the train to Yokota?"

She smiled and said, "I saw you sitting there and watching me, so I wondered if you would come and ask me a question. My name is Noa. How can I help you?"

She looked to be about my age and was very attractive, dressed in her hotel uniform, perfectly pressed and fitted, hair perfectly styled, looking like a little Barbie Doll or something. I, on the other hand, was wearing three layers of clothing, and my hair was its usual mess with my electric blue bangs hanging down over my eyes.

I said, "I'm sorry, I know I'm Japanese, but I grew up in the US, and I have no idea how to speak Japanese, and it seems every time I try to ask someone for help, they try to speak to me in Japanese, and they get very confused when I tell them I don't speak Japanese."

"That's okay, it happens more than you might think." Her English was very good, but obviously, as a second language, "What is your name?"

"I am Kiko."

She smiled and said, "That is beautiful. I hope it is true."

I didn't understand what she meant, and she did not explain. I later found out that all Japanese names have meanings. But just then, I didn't know enough to ask her what my name meant. She asked me if I would be spending the night or returning the same day. She said she could book me a hotel room if I needed.

I asked, "How far is it?"

"40 Kilometers, about 1.5 hours on the train. Lots of stops."

"No, I can return later the same day."

"Okay, I will book a round trip for today."

So, she helped me book my ticket to Yokota and explained to me where I needed to go and that the train would stop at Yokota, as it was the end of the line for that train. I followed her instructions, and it went exactly as she said.

I had the documents from the adoption agency that my mom had given me, and they had the address for the agency written on the top, in both Japanese, or Kanji as I learned it is called, and in English, so all I had to do was show it to a taxi driver, and he would be able to take me directly there.

As I rode the train, I noticed the variety of people who were on it with me. It was mid-morning, so the train was not packed, but it was busy. I had been warned about trying to take the train during the morning and evening rush hours, so I tried to avoid that. I figured my business at the adoption agency should not take more than an hour or so. I watched the people as we rode. Some men were dressed in suits and ties, and the women in business attire, others in school uniforms, while some dressed like me. I felt oddly comfortable being in a crowded space where everyone looked like me. For the first time in my life, I did not stand out in the crowd. I enjoyed the ride and just stared out the window. I notice that on the trains, people don't look directly at each other. They all seemed to avoid eye contact as best they could. I wondered, *How do men and women meet on the trains when they won't even look at each other? Maybe they just don't, I don't know.* It seemed like a waste of opportunity to me, but then, who was I to judge, living my life at the gardens and barely dating at all over the last few years.

The train ride was pleasant, and I enjoyed the scenery as it whizzed by. In about one hour and 40 minutes, we arrived at the station in Yokota. I went out to the taxi stand, and I showed the address to the taxi driver. He looked at me kind of oddly, perhaps he thought I was going to adopt or maybe give up a child for adoption, who knows, but he just said, "Hi, which is Yes, in Japanese," and he took me to the address. It was a rather nondescript-looking building with double glass doors, as most office buildings would have. But to my surprise, it still had the sign, in English and Japanese, Sisters of the Sacred Heart Adoption Center. It no longer said anything about Unwed Mothers, but maybe that wasn't necessary anyway.

I entered the lobby and stood there, but the lobby was empty. Then a lady came walking down the hall towards me. I looked around and saw a video camera up in the corner, pointing towards the doors, so I guess she saw me come in. The lady was wearing a blue and white Nun's habit, but no headdress, just short dark hair. She was Japanese and looked to be in her 40s or early 50s. She spoke to me in Japanese at first, and in a very sympathetic tone, as if she knew I was there to seek help with an unwanted pregnancy.

"I speak English," I said, and her tone changed slightly, as if she knew what I was there to ask her. "Yes, how may I help you?"

I smiled at her, and I said, "My name is Kiko Davis, and I was adopted at this agency 27 years ago."

I showed her that paper I had with me, and suddenly she smiled and said, "Yes, I remember you. Wow, you have grown up to be so beautiful. I'm sister Bonny, I was the one who helped your parents with your adoption."

I was shocked; it was the same Nun who had helped my mom and dad with my adoption, and after all these years, she was still there. "Umm…I want to know if my birth mother left permission for me to know who she is or to contact her, in my file."

"I see… I will have to check. I remember your mother. She had such beautiful red hair. That made a very deep impression on my mind. I hope your parents are well."

"Yes, they are both doing well." I didn't see any point in going into the whole divorce thing or any other details of my life; I just let her think that everything was as it was when I was adopted.

"Well, I will have to go and pull the file and look to see if she left permission. It was not unusual back when this adoption was made. Come with me, and have a seat while I go and look for the file."

She took me to an office area and sat me in front of a desk, "This might take a few minutes," she said."

I sat there and looked around. One other Nun was sitting at a desk, talking with another couple, but they were not speaking English, so I wasn't sure what they were saying. After about 15 minutes, Sister Bonny came back in, and she was carrying a file in her hand. I thought, *this must be good, right?*

She sat at her desk, and she looked at the file. She said, "Hmm, yes, this is unusual, but I remember this girl. She was one of the students at the Catholic Girls' School in Yokohama. A very sweet young girl."

"Oh...is that good?" I asked.

"Yes, and no," she replied. "Because she was so young at the time of her pregnancy, she was not allowed to return to school afterwards, so I don't know what became of her after she left here. But she did permit us to give the child this, if you ever came to enquire about her."

She handed me a business card. It was written in Kanji, and it had the name lined through and another name written underneath it, like someone was using another person's card. "What does it say?" I asked.

She wrote the English translation of what was written. It was the name and address of a jewelry store in Tokyo, and the president's name was scratched out, and the name Koharu Meiko was written in. "What is this?"

It is the name and address of a business in Tokyo. That's all I can say. I don't know anything else. I guess you will have to go there to discover more. I wish I had more to tell you, but this is all I am allowed to say."

"Oh...well...okay then. Thank you for this."

Before we said our good-byes, she asked me, "Are you married, Kiko? Do you have children?"

"No, I'm not yet married, and I have no children."

"Have you ever thought about adopting a child. I believe the best adoptive parents are those who were adopted themselves."

"Oh... really... I've never even considered that."

"That is why I do this work. I grew up in a Catholic Orphanage, and I have made it my life's work to find parents for children who, for whatever reason, find themselves in need of a loving home."

"I see. That's very noble of you; you should be very proud of the work you do here. You most certainly found me a wonderful family."

"If you ever consider adopting, I hope you will contact us here at this agency."

"Okay, I will be sure to give it some consideration," I said as I left the building. I went outside and found a taxi, and went straight back to the train station. On the way, we passed the main gate to the US Airbase at Yokota, the place where I had spent the first two years of my life. I tried to imagine my mom and dad living in this place, but couldn't really get a very vivid image of it in my mind.

I boarded a train back to Tokyo and just sat there, staring at that business card, not knowing what I would find, or even what I would say to anyone when I got there.

It was nearly 6:00 PM when I returned to the hotel. I wanted to go talk to Noa to see if she could tell me anything more about the card, but a man was sitting at the concierge desk, so I decided to wait until morning. I ate at the hotel that night, as they served American-style food there, and I didn't feel like going out in the cold in search of an American franchise restaurant, so I stayed in and went up to my room early.

As I was sitting in my room, it dawned on me that maybe the business listed on the card has a website. Such things didn't exist when the card was made, so there was no web address on it, but surely, I thought, if it is still open, they must now have a website. I opened my Laptop and began to search, and there it was, Meiko Fine Jewelry, Tokyo, Japan. It was written in Kanji, but at the top of the screen were tabs for other languages, one of which was English. I clicked it, and the screen shifted to a full English version.

It was beautifully done, with vivid pictures of glistening gemstones and incredible settings of rings, necklaces, pendants, watches, and earrings. On the banner running across the top was a tab that read, About Us, so I clicked on it. It said that Meiko Fine Jewelry was founded in 1872, and had been the official Jeweler to the Imperial family for 6 generations. I wasn't sure what that meant, but then it said, "The company is now run by Koharu Meiko, a direct descendant of the founder. Koharu is considered one of the foremost experts in all of Japan on the quality and art of gemstone setting and valuation." My heart jumped out of my chest. There it was, the name on the card. Koharu Meiko. Is that her? Is that my mother? I could hardly believe what I was seeing. Her name was underscored with a blue line, indicating it was a link, so I held my breath and clicked on it. There, staring out at me from the screen was her picture, and I felt like I was looking into my own eyes. It was unsettling, so I quickly closed the lid on my laptop, as if I had stumbled on some great secret that was never meant to be revealed.

*It can't possibly be so easy*, I thought. Surely there has to be more to the story than this. Nobody finds their birth parents this fast. This is supposed to take weeks or months, I had been told over and over, sometimes even needing to petition courts for records. But I had been at this for just a week, and now I think I have already found her. *This can't possibly be!*

It was a very restless night. I tossed and turned all night. I doubt if I even had 15 or 20 minutes of continuous sleep. I finally got up and showered at around 6:00 AM and went down to the lobby to eat breakfast. As I exited the elevators, I saw Noa sitting at the concierge desk. I wondered what her working hours were, if she was here this early. I thought that maybe I would see her sometime after breakfast, but this was as good a time as any to go talk to her, before she got too busy with requests from other guests. I walked over and said, "Good morning, Noa."

"Oh...Kiko, how was your visit to Yokota?"

"It was good, Noa. I accomplished what I had intended to do."

"I'm very happy for you. Can I help you find something today?"

"Umm...I need some advice, if that's okay?"

"Yes, of course."

I showed her the business card, and I said, "I need to go to this place today. How would you recommend that I go there?"

She looked at the card very intently, like she was reading tea leaves or something. "Oh, very nice card. This person is very important... the best cardstock." It was like she was reading the quality of the ink and the paper more than looking at the content on the card itself. She asked, "Do you want to buy jewelry. This place is very expensive. You see this symbol on the top of the card; it means that it has an Imperial Warrant. That means they are the official jewelers of the imperial family, very prestigious."

"I know, I saw something on their website last night."

"There are less expensive jewelers I can help you find, if you would like?"

"No, thank you, Noa, I need to go to this place. It is part of why I came here."

"Okay, you could walk if you like. It's only about 12 blocks, or you can take a taxi; it is not far." She pulled out a map of the Tokyo shopping district that was given to guests and showed me where we are, and how to get to the place I am going. She was so kind, but she never pried into my personal business. That was part of her training, I suppose. I thanked her and then went into the restaurant in search of some breakfast. They had the most incredible buffet set up, so I was well fed for the rest of the day.

I spent the entire morning giving myself a pep talk to get myself prepared to walk into that store, and practiced over and over again what I would say. I decided to walk. It was sunny outside, even though the temperature was very cold. I thought I needed the invigoration of a nice cold walk to prepare myself for what I was about to do. It took me nearly an hour to find the street I was looking for, and the store was right there on the corner. It was a large storefront with huge window displays. Jewelry, high-end watches, and all kinds of beautiful items on display and for sale. I stood outside looking through the windows for about 10 minutes before finally working up the courage to go in. I looked around and saw no sign of Koharu, so I summoned the courage to approach a young girl at the counter. She, of course, began to speak to me in Japanese, and then I said, "I only speak English."

All of the people working at the counters were wearing meticulously fitted uniforms and had perfect hair and polished shoes. I kind of felt like I had stepped into an episode of The Twilight Zone or something, then the girl said, "My apologies, how may I serve you today?"

I handed her the business card, and I replied, "I am looking for Koharu Meiko."

"Oh…umm, okay, I will see if she is available."

The girl disappeared through a door behind the store walls. At one point, I saw someone peek out from behind the window in the door to the back end of the store and look at me, and then disappear. *Oh my god,* I thought, *what have I done?* I should not have come to her place of business. I was sure I was breaking a thousand protocols of the Japanese culture. It seemed like I was standing there for an hour or more, but I'm sure it was just a few minutes. The girl came back out, and she handed me a piece of paper with an address written on it in English and Kanji, and said, "Madam Koharu has requested that you come to this address tomorrow at 2:00 PM. She said she will see you then."

"Oh… okay, that will be fine. Please tell her I will see her then." I was disappointed, but also highly encouraged at the same time. Maybe she was not my mother, but she knew who she was. Maybe she was just a go-between or something. The anxiety was killing me, and I thought my heart was going to explode, but I'd waited this long; surely I could wait one more day.

I spent the rest of that day just walking around the Tokyo shopping district. I figured as long as I had the Map that Noa had given me, I might as well get acquainted with Tokyo. This was the first time in my life that I had ever just explored, without an agenda or specific location I was trying to find. Even after years in Austin, I can't say I ever just explored. I mean, I knew all the places that I used to hang out, or where events were held, as Derik and I had been to all of them at one time or another, but to just say, "Okay, let's go see what's out there," I had never been that adventurous.

Walking around Tokyo was true joy. I found I was never afraid or felt unsafe. I never felt like I stood out in a crowd. It was amazing. Tokyo was unlike anything I had ever experienced before. The stores were a mix of large chains and small mom-and-pop vendors, all strung together in one tight little community. The police were all kind and helpful; most spoke some level of English, so if I had a question, I could just ask a traffic cop. Crossing the streets did take some getting used to, though. The lights would all change to red at once, for every direction, and the crosswalk signal would come on, and everybody would cross in every direction all at once – some even diagonally, across the center of the intersection. Food vendors were everywhere. You could get a bowl of noodles with an egg in it or a piece of beef or chicken in it. I quickly learned to ask, "How much?" in Japanese. I swear that when I began to ask for a price in Japanese, vendors charged me less than they did if I only used English, although I probably couldn't prove that. I was surprised to learn that the Japanese refer to Japan as Nippon. I didn't ask why.

Other than my initial disappointment at the jewelry store, it was a wonderful day. I finally made it back to the hotel at about 4:30 and saw Noa still sitting at her Concierge desk. I couldn't wait to go and tell her about my day. I showed her the address I had been given at the store and told her, "I have to go to this place tomorrow."

"Okay." She searched her computer and then looked up at me and said, "This place is about twenty kilometers away." She looked confused and said, "This is a very exclusive part of Tokyo, only the most wealthy people live here, big homes and lots of land." She laughed and added, "Old money."

"Oh…alright, well it's just a business thing," I said.

"Okay," she replied with her typical customer service smile." My feet were sore, and I had learned, as cold as the days are in December in Tokyo, the nights are even colder, so I just stayed in that night, watched some Japanese TV, which was a bit crazy to watch, and I just looked at the city lights out of my 10th-floor window. I was fast asleep by 10:30 that night.

When the morning came, I went down to eat breakfast at the buffet – it came with the room after all, and I had learned that eating out in Tokyo was not cheap. When I got off the elevator, Noa was sitting at her desk. I wondered, *how many hours a week does she work?*" I decided to go and ask her. I walked over to the desk, and I said, "Good morning, Noa. Do you mind me asking, how many hours a week do you work?"

"Hours… per week?" I'm not sure she understood why I would be asking such a question. "Umm…My work day begins at 5:00 AM and ends at 5:00 PM, when the nightshift Concierge comes to replace me."

"Twelve hours a day, and on Saturday?" I replied.

"Hi, it is typical of a salaried position in Japan."

"Wow!" I said, "In America, we work 8 hours a day and only 5 days a week." She did not reply, just nodded as if she understood, but it didn't seem to register any alarms to her. "Okay, I will go eat now," I said after a few awkward moments of looking at each other.

As I turned to leave, she said, "You must leave here by 1:00 to meet your appointment. Come and see me, and I will give the Taxi driver instructions."

"Okay, thank you, Noa. I will see you then."

When I returned to my room, I began looking through all the clothes I had brought to see if I could find something appropriate for going to this appointment. I was more concerned with packing warm clothes than I was with anything fancy or formal. I did bring one decent dress, so I decided that I would have to wear a dress. I had seen many women on the streets wearing dresses despite the cold, so I figured I could tolerate it for at least one afternoon. Besides, I was going to be in a Taxi, and then inside a home, presumably, if Noa's assessment of the address was correct. The next few hours leading up to the taxi ride were excruciating. My mind raced as it began to run through every possible scenario it could imagine. *Would she be kind or cold? Would she accept that I am her daughter, or would she question it or be angry that I had even come looking for her? And what if she were married and had other children?* Oh God, I hadn't even considered that before now. Do I have other half-siblings out there, besides Zoe, some that I actually shared some genetic material with? I was suddenly reminded of my conversation with Lenny and his Schrodinger's Box thing. I was standing in front of the box and about two hours away from opening the lid. Once I did, I would have to live with whatever I found inside. I questioned if I was prepared for that moment, but it was here nonetheless, and I had put this entire situation in motion on my own.

The hour had finally come. I put on my heavy coat, and I took the elevator down to the lobby. I walked up to Noa, and I said, "Hello, Noa, I'm ready for my taxi."

She smiled and replied, "Come with me, Kiko, I have your taxi waiting." She took me out front to a waiting cab and said, "This is my cousin, Yuito, he will take you to where you are going and be sure to bring you back. I gave him a voucher from the hotel, so you will not have to pay him directly."

"Oh.. that's so nice, Noa, thank you so much for that."

I climbed into the back of the Taxi and just sat in silence for the next 50 minutes while Yuito skillfully weaved his way through the heavy Tokyo traffic, until we seemed to leave the district of downtown and got more into the, I guess you would call them, suburbs. But the homes were as Noa had described, Large. *This was surely the Beverly Hills equivalent of Tokyo*, I thought to myself. Then, we pulled up in front of a fenced-in property with a gate in front.

Yuito turned and said in broken English, "This is your address. I wait here."

"Oh, okay, thank you. He came around and opened my door, and I got out. I stood in front of the gate for a moment, not sure what to do, then I heard the sound of the lock buzz and click to open. I pushed on the handle, and the gate opened.

# Chapter 11

As I opened the gate, I was standing at the head of a gray granite stone path, which was about 100 to 120 feet long. It was absolutely beautiful. A wonderful Japanese Garden stretched from the front gateway to the steps leading up to the house. There was a pond on both sides of the walk, with carp swimming in it, and steam rising from the water, indicating that it was heated to keep it from freezing in the cold winter air. About halfway to the house stood an arched wooden bridge to allow a small stream that connected the ponds on either side. I instinctively took out my phone and began taking pictures, thinking to myself, *Irma has got to see this*. It was like looking at something out of a landscape magazine.

As I approached the house, there were three wooden steps leading up to the covered porch with beautiful scrollwork carved into the ends of the beams that held up the roof. I raised my hand to grab a knocker on the door, but before I could reach it, the door opened. An older Japanese woman simply motioned for me to come in, and then motioned to a small seat, and indicated that I should remove my shoes. As I did, she presented me with a beautiful pair of hand-embroidered silk slippers and simply said with a thick accent, "Please."

I slipped them on, and she motioned for me to follow her. I was escorted into a room, which I can only describe as a ceremonial tea room. As we walked through the house, it appeared very modern. The furniture was all western-style couches and chairs, with a large dining table. But this room looked very traditional. There was a small table set in the center with a tea service setting on the table. The older woman said, "Lady Mieko will be with you shortly," and turned and left the room.

I was nearly breathless at that point. My heart was pounding, and I could hardly see straight. I thought for a moment I would pass out. The woman did not ask me to sit at the table, so I stood. While I waited, I noticed all the things that were hanging on the walls. There was a series of formal-looking photographic portraits with what appeared to be Husbands and Wives posing for the camera. The names underneath were all written in Kanji, but the dates were standard numbers as we use. The first was 1875, then 1896, 1921, 1947, and 1968, and the last was her, Koharu Mieko, dated 2003. They changed from very old Sepia-type to black & white to full color in the last two photos.

On the wall hung a beautifully mounted Samurai sword and a Koto, a long, traditional, 13-stringed instrument used to play classical Japanese music. I had read an article about them when I was doing my research for this trip. It did not look new; like it had been well played for quite some time. Then I saw her. She walked into the room wearing a gorgeous coral colored silk dress, form-fitting, and slippers like I was wearing. She stopped and closed the sliding doors behind her.

We both stood there for a few seconds, just staring at each other, not in a menacing way, but like we were both looking into mirrors, trying to find something familiar. Then, finally, she broke the silence and held out her hand and said, "I am Koharu. What may I call you?"

"I'm Kiko, Kiko Davis." I somehow managed to squeak out.

She motioned to the table, "Please, sit." I was surprised as her English was quite good. "May I offer you some Tea?"

"Umm...tea...yes, thank you."

Koharu poured us both some tea, but more in an English-style tea service, rather than a Japanese-style tea ceremony, which I had seen in some videos and movies.

She looked at me, and she reached over to touch my hand, and then she said, "In this room, when the doors are closed, you may ask me any question and say anything to me that you wish to say. We have both waited for this day for many years. Now is the time to understand."

I almost started to cry, but I managed to keep my emotions in check. So I said, "Then let's begin with the obvious – why did you give me up for adoption?"

"I was 15 when you were born, out of wedlock, of course. My family, as you can see, is a very traditional Japanese family, with very high status in Japanese ceremonial culture. Having a child out of wedlock would have brought great shame on my family. My mother was raised Catholic, so termination was never even a consideration, so she chose for me to give up my child for adoption."

"Your mother chose for you?"

"Yes, that is the Japanese way. I do not believe that my father ever even knew I had had a child."

"Who is my father?" I asked. Her eyes sank to the floor.

"I was afraid you would ask that question. Are you sure you want to know this?"

"Yes, I'm sure. I've waited a long time to learn this, so I am prepared for whatever you tell me."

"I am so sorry to tell you that your father died before you were born. His name was Ao… Ao Tanaka. He was so handsome and so sweet. We both attended the Catholic school in Yokohama. He was what we called 'a towny,' not a boarding student, but someone who lived in the city. He was not even Catholic, but his mother believed the school was the best private school in the city. We were very much in love, or as much as teenagers can be. But we were naive and idealistic, which is never a good thing for two strong-headed teenagers. We both wanted to live our own lives, but our families had already mapped out our lives for us, and we were both determined to set out on our own. Ao's father had been an Architect, but died when Ao was just eight. His mother insisted that he was going to be an architect also, but he just wanted to do something with his hands. He was very artistic. And my life was predetermined from the moment I was born. We both wanted to live our own lives, not someone else's.

"When I became pregnant, the Sisters found out – one of the girls in the dormitory had told them. Ao and I wanted to run away. We thought we could just get on a plane and go to New Zealand, Australia, or even America. We did not think things through very well – we thought it would be so simple. When the Sister Superior called my mother to tell her of my situation, my mother immediately had me transferred to the home for unwed mothers in Yokota. I didn't even get to say goodbye to him.

"I was finally able to get word to him through a friend at school, and I waited weeks for him to come and get me, but week after week, he did not come. I thought he had abandoned me. After about 5 weeks, I received a letter from my friend, who told me that when Ao learned where I was, he stole his mother's car and was driving to Yokota to find me. He was only 15 and not a good driver, and it was late and raining. He was in an accident and died. Two weeks after she buried her son, his mother took her own life at her husband's grave. Having lost both her husband and only son, she could not go on.

"I was so shocked by what had happened, when my mother told me that we would put you up for adoption, I was just empty. I had no more will of my own, so I just said, 'Okay.' I just gave up. I thought, if I could not live my own life, then maybe I could give that gift to you."

By now, we both had tears in our eyes, and I could see that it was painful for her to talk about this, so I decided I knew what I needed to know, and the two of us both stood up and just hugged. She held me so long and so tight I thought she would suffocate me. I think that was the first time she had ever allowed herself to just mourn for Ao's loss.

Then I asked, "Why did you name me, Kiko?"

"She looked at me funny, and began to say, "I did not..." and a sudden look of realization came over her face, and she said, "Is your adopted mother the red-haired girl?"

"Yes, she has red hair. Her name is Katherine, Katherine Louise Griffin-Davis." I said as if I was chastising her for not using her proper name, but then realized, *how would she even know that*, but it was out there, nonetheless. "I'm sorry, that sounded much harsher than I intended. But I recently found out that she is ill, and I suppose that leaves me just a bit touchy on the subject of her."

"I apologize. I am very sorry to hear that she is ill. May I ask what kind of Illness she has?"

"Her liver is failing, and she may need a transplant."

"I see, I hope she will be well."

"I'm sure she will be, but thank you for your concern."

"To answer your question, when you were born, and while you were waiting to go to your adoptive home, I was allowed to go and see you in the nursery once every day. I could not hold you or even feed you – the Sisters were very strict about that. They wanted no bonding between us. On the day you moved to your new home, I was standing in front of the nursery window when a woman with red hair came up beside me. I simply said to her, as I turned to leave, 'She is Kiko.' Kiko in Japanese means, 'Happy Child.' You always had such a big smile on your face and looked so happy in your crib. That is all I said to her. Perhaps she misunderstood."

I almost had to laugh, "So for my entire life, my name has been a misunderstanding? My mother always told me that you had named me, Kiko, and she thought she was honoring you and my culture by keeping that name."

Again, Koharu reached out and took my hand, and she said, "It is a beautiful name, and I am very honored that she heard what I said." Koharu added, "Now it is my turn to ask. "Are you still, Kiko…a Happy Child?"

"Yes… I suppose I am, for the most part. I won't lie to you, Koharu, my mother and I have always had some tension between us, but I have the best father I could ever have asked for. But my mother and I had just gotten to a place where I think we really liked and accepted each other, and then this news of her illness came."

Koharu smiled, "That is always the way it is between mothers and daughters, especially strong-willed mothers with strong-willed daughters. It was the same between my mother and me. So, Kiko, have you lived the life you wanted to live, what do you do?"

I was unsure if I should tell her that I was a singer, but then I decided that this was not the time for pretense. "I'm a singer and a musician, and I also work as a gardener in a place called Liberty Gardens. I live in Texas. Gardening is very rewarding work – a way to really connect with nature, and music just seems to be part of my soul. I love to play my guitar and sing."

"A Gardener and a Singer, how wonderful." She responded.

I took out my cell phone and showed her a video of me playing at Liberty Gardens, taken at our last meeting for this year. "This is me. I play a lot of corporate events and parties. I used to play in nightclubs a lot, but I found that these corporate events pay better."

She watched the video and had a huge smile on her face as it played. "You are very talented, Kiko."

I pointed to the Koto hanging on the wall, and I asked her, "Do you play?"

"No, that belonged to my mother. If you inherited your musical talent from my family, it would have been from her. She was very accomplished at playing the Koto. I am afraid music is a gift that has eluded me for some reason."

I had never considered the possibility that my voice and love for music might have been inherited, but perhaps there was something to what she said. From that point on, we seemed just to be talking like two girls. I told her about my life at Liberty Gardens, and about my relationship with Derik and how he had left me, and about Lenny and Irma at the gardens and how they had changed my outlook and understanding of life. At one point, I asked her, "Where did you learn to speak English so well?"

"After you were born, I was not permitted to return to the school in Yokohama, so my mother arranged for me to attend an all-girls boarding school in England. So that is where I completed high school, and then after, it had become tradition in my family to send heir to the family business to Central Saint Martins, Royal College of Art in London to learn jewelry design and gemology, and then I did a two-year apprenticeship at Garrard, one of the most prestigious jewelers in all of England. I lived in England for nearly eight years; it was a wonderful place to live. If it had been up to me, I would have stayed there, but when I was 24 years old, my father died of a sudden heart attack. Two men showed up at my flat from the Japanese embassy one night. They said that my father had died. That Lady Mieko had requested my immediate return. There was a diplomatic flight leaving in two hours, and I was to be on it. That was the end of my life as an independent person. From that moment on, I became Lady Mieko, Jeweler to the Imperial family, and that is how it has been ever since."

"Wow, I…I honestly don't even know what to say about that. Why did you like England so much?"

"It was the only place I have ever been allowed to just be Koharu, rather than the daughter of Asahi Mieko. When I was still in school, I would come home for a few weeks between terms, but I would immediately be required to go to work in the family business. And as the daughter of the CEO, I was not allowed to mix or mingle with the other workers, so here, I never really had the chance to make friends or go out to just have fun. In London, I had friends, and was allowed to just be Koharu."

"So, are you married? Do you have other children?"

"No, I am afraid not. Japan is a very patriarchal society. If I had married, I would have been expected to take a back seat to my husband and his career and turn control of the family business over to him or other managers. I could never do that. I had given up too much for family honor already. I was not going to give that up as well."

I pointed to the pictures on the walls and asked, "And these, are they your ancestors?"

"Yes, and yours as well. Come, I will show you." We walked over to the pictures, and she explained the entire family history, beginning with the first, "This is Haruto Mieko. He was the first. He was the swordsmith to the Emperor of Japan in the mid-nineteenth century. Not the swords for war, mind you, but ceremonial swords that the Emperor would give as gifts and awards at special ceremonial events to the Western diplomats who would come to visit. When Japan began to open up to the West, the Emperor and Empress would often receive wonderful gifts from other nations as diplomatic gestures, and they became very fond of Western-style jewelry. Haruto was very savvy, so he decided to send his eldest son, Nagi," and she moved to the next photo, "to England to apprentice with Garrard, to learn the art of making Western-style jewelry. When he returned, he brought a beautiful diamond and sapphire brooch which he had made for the Empress, and the Emperor was very impressed, so he named Haruto and his sons as the official Jewelers to the Imperial family. That is how we became the official Jewelers to the Emperor." Then she continued down the line, This is Haru Mieko, and next is Sora Mieko, and then Minato Mieko, my father, Asahi Mieko, and me."

I asked, and the women in these photos?"

"They are just wives. I know that sounds harsh from Western perspectives, but wives in those times were just ceremonial. They had much power within the home, but outside, none."

"What are their names?"

"The first is Rina, Nanami, Aya, Hina, Miyu, and my mother, Rin. As many times as I have shown these to guests, you are the very first to ever ask the names of the wives." She then showed me the sword hanging on the wall and said, "This is the very last Sword made by Haruto. It should really be in a museum, but I have not been able to bring myself to donate it for some reason."

We continued to talk and ask each other questions for nearly two hours. I finally stood and said, "Thank you so much for talking to me and answering my questions, Koharu. You have been so very kind. I know you did not have to do this."

"Kiko, there has not been a day in my life that I have not thought about you. You have brought great pleasure to me today. You also did not have to do this. Thank you for being Kiko, a happy child. It brings me great joy and happiness to know this. To know that you have had the freedom to live your own life, and not one bound by duty and Family Honor, lets me know that I made the right decisions to let you be adopted."

As I was getting ready to leave, she asked, "May I have your address so I can write to you from time to time?"

"Umm... yes, of course." I gave her my address, and I even showed her how to follow me on Facebook. She walked me out to the waiting taxi that had been dutifully sitting right where it had left me over 2 hours ago. She said something in Japanese to the driver, and he responded in kind. I didn't understand what. I got in, and we drove off. I didn't know what to expect when or if I ever met my birth mother, but I don't think that it could possibly have gone better than it did.

Yuito, my taxi driver, carefully weaved his way through the busy Tokyo traffic once again, returning me to the Hilton Hotel where I was staying. I thanked him, but did not tip him, as I had learned during my stay that service workers such as Yuito are not usually tipped, as they consider it a sign of disrespect. In Japan, workers consistently perform at their best, and their fees are set at a rate that appropriately compensates them for their work. As a result, the Western habit of tipping is generally not understood or appreciated. This was a difficult lesson for someone like me who grew up in a culture and profession where I had mostly lived on the tipping generosity of customers as a gig musician and bartender.

I was excited to tell Noa about my trip, but by the time we made it back to the Hotel, it was already after 5:00 PM, and the night shift Concierge was at the desk rather than Noa. The sky was clear that evening, so I decided to take a stroll to see what I might find nearby to eat. I found a noodle shop and ordered some Ramen. It had been such a mixed day of stress and happiness that I felt completely spent by the time I had finished eating, so I returned to my room and just stayed in that night. My mind was still racing a thousand miles an hour with all I had learned. I sent the Photos of Koharu's garden to Irma, but didn't give any specific details about where I had seen them, and by 9:30 that night, I was fast asleep.

The next morning, I woke up and went down to get breakfast and saw a sign on the Concierge desk that read, "No Concierge on Sunday, please see the front desk for assistance." I was disappointed, but *I could figure out what to do with myself, I'm sure*, I told myself. Tokyo was a beautiful city, full of bustling crowds and shops everywhere. I went out and just strolled the shops and bought Christmas gifts for all my friends and family. It was a lot of fun to buy a gift for each one of them, one by one, just finding something that I thought each one would enjoy. We were just one week away from Christmas, and even though Japan was primarily a Shinto culture, they do love to celebrate Christmas. Not as a religious celebration like in America, but mainly as a season of national celebration, with even more commercialism than in the US, if that's possible. The streets and shops were all beautifully decorated, and gift bargains were in every store. It was a great time to be looking for gifts for friends and family. When I returned to the hotel, I was loaded down with bags and unsure how I would get it all in my suitcase to take it home. It was an expensive day, but so much fun.

I had scheduled three weeks for this trip, and I was just barely one week into it. I still had a lot to learn about Japan, but I was unsure at the time where to even begin. I knew that Noa would be able to direct me to some local museums and sites.

The first thing on Monday morning, I went to speak with her. "Good morning, Noa."

"Oh...Kiko, how was your meeting on Saturday?"

"It was very good, thank you, and please thank, Yuito, for me again. He made the trip very safe and very enjoyable for me."

"That is wonderful for me to know. I will tell him how satisfied you were."

"Noa, my official business in Tokyo has been completed much earlier than I had planned, and I find I have two full weeks to myself to just explore and learn about the Japanese culture and society. Can you recommend some places for me to go see and ways I can better experience the Japanese culture?"

"Yes, of course. There is much for you to do here, and most everything you can do in a day, and then return here every night. I will put together a list of things for you, and you just tell me which ones you want to do, and I will schedule them for you."

"Thank you, that's so kind." I went to eat breakfast, and when I returned, she had a list of about twenty popular tourist sights and places to go. I looked at it, and then I said to her, "These all look like so much fun, but then I drew close to her, are there things that are not just tourist places. You know, I really want to understand what the people of Japan do, not just what they want us westerners to see."

I could see in her eyes she understood what I meant and her eyes darted back and forth like she was looking to make sure no one was watching us, then she said, "I will give you one activity from this list every day," and then she looked around again, "every evening at 6:00 PM, meet me at the noodle shop across the street, and I will show you the real Tokyo."

So from Monday to Friday, for the next two weeks, I took a tour to some attractions with other guests from the hotel, and then at 6 o'clock every evening, I would meet Noa, and she would show me the real Tokyo.

I had a great deal of fun on the scheduled tours with my fellow hotel guests. They were from many countries, but still quite a lot of Americans, and they were all so nice to me. I told people that I was born in Japan, but raised in America, without going into specifics, and that I had come to explore my heritage, and they loved that. If I happened to tell someone that I was a singer, they all wanted to follow me on Facebook or other social media sites. I had taken to having my performances at the Gardens videoed, and I would post them on various social media sites, and so I was slowly building followers. But they were crude, with very little editing. Even so, I probably gained another 50 or 60 followers during this trip. That was all great fun.

But every evening, I would meet Noa, and she would show me the other side of Tokyo, and boy, did she show me. The first night we met, at the noodle shop, I said, "Should we eat here, before we go.

Noa said, very seriously, "No, not here…come."

She took me off the main street, down a smaller street, to an even smaller street. She turned into a street vendor, and we sat at a counter just off the side walk. She ordered for the two of us. Remember when I said before that I thought I was charged less when I used just a few Japanese words that I had picked up? Well, I was correct, but had no idea to what extent. A noodle bowl with beef that would easily cost 1500¥ at a main street vendor costs about 500¥ in one of these small shops. This is where the rank and file Japanese worker eats, you know, the shop girls and the taxi drivers and the people who had to live on a minimal wage in a city built for wealthy foreign tourists. This is where the workers live, love, and play. And the food was so good. Nothing out of a box or can, everything was fresh and handmade. What a difference from what I had grown used to.

We ate, talked, and learned more about each other. I discovered that Noa was college-educated and spoke Japanese, English, and French fluently, and passable Swiss and German, which is how she got the job as a concierge at a big hotel like the Tokyo Hilton. It was considered a prestigious job, and she was very grateful to have it, but it was a stressful job. There was never a day as a concierge that she was not required to be constantly smiling and friendly – no bad days allowed. 12-hour days, six days a week, but it did pay well, and Noa was hoping to soon get into a management position, which is what she went to school to learn, Hotel Management.

I told her about my life in America, and how I worked as a singer and worked at Liberty Gardens. She asked me, "So what business did you have in Tokyo?"

I still was not comfortable talking about my adoption, as I felt that might lead her to make the connection between Koharu and me, which might betray Koharu's trust, so I just said, "I came to look at some Japanese Gardens, to do some research. The place I went on Saturday was a home that had appeared in a landscape magazine, and the owner was kind enough to show it to me and explain the philosophy behind the concept of Japanese Gardening. I was so grateful to her; she was very helpful to me."

"So why did you go to the jewelry store?"

"My trip to Yokota was to see an expert. He arranged for me to meet the owner of the garden I was interested in, who happens to work at that store. She was in a meeting but asked me to come to her home the next day so I could see it for myself."

That seemed to satisfy her curiosity, as she did not bring it up again. Our next stop that night was the most surprising one of all. We walked for about 15 minutes through the streets, up one and down another, until we came to a small movie theater. Outside in the line were about 100 to 150 people waiting, some dressed as we were, others dressed in large pompadour hair styles, and the girls in Poodle skirts and the boys in suits with thin ties. The marquee was in Kanji, so I didn't know what was going on until I saw the poster on the wall. It was a movie poster for Elvis' Viva Las Vegas, and next to it another one for Girls, Girls, Girls – a double feature that night.

Now, I of course know Elvis – I'm very familiar with his music, but I don't think I had ever seen an Elvis movie up to that point in my life. This was the wildest thing I had ever experienced. Not the movie so much, but the people. Every song was a sing-along, and there was room at the front of the theater to dance. Moviegoers sang along, acted out the parts, cheered, and had the time of their lives. I had no idea that Elvis was such a beloved figure and cultural icon in Japan, but we had so much fun. We danced, and we sang, and the movie plot or dialogue didn't matter; all that mattered was the music and the dancing.

I had only experienced something like that once in my life, when a friend convinced Derik and me to go to a Rocky Mountain Horror Picture Show midnight showing many years ago, and I didn't really get it. It seemed silly to me, but this, this was on a different level. Noa told me that this theater is just Elvis movies, all the time. It just shows every movie on a rotating schedule, and people come back over and over to watch their favorite shows. Even the one movie where Elvis doesn't sing, Love Me Tender, will pack the house. It was not a huge theater, only about 300 seats or so, but it was packed most every night.

After that night, the routine was the same – eat at a local mom and pop stall somewhere, and then off to some local entertainment venue for music and dancing, and some drinking as well, but not too much for either of us – we always kept our wits about us. We went to karaoke bars and nightclubs of every variety. We even got up to sing karaoke ourselves, sometimes solo, sometimes together, at several of them. One night, we went to a place that had a live trio of Japanese singer/musicians, who sang old folk songs from the 50s and 60s, you know, Peter, Paul, and Mary, and Kingston Trio and such, and they were so good. They even let me come up and sing a song with them.

These were absolutely the most wonderful two weeks. We had a lot of fun, and the food, it is so incredible. There is nothing like homemade food from an 80-year-old grandmother who has been in the same spot on the same corner for 40 years.

American fast food is also very big in Japan, but of all the American franchises in Japan, there is nothing quite like Kentucky Fried Chicken. The Japanese take their KFC to a new level. You know in America, how some people love to go to a Chinese restaurant on Christmas, well, in Japan, KFC is the go-to food for the Christmas meal. Some places had a 30-minute line, all the way out the door, to serve the needs of all the customers wanting KFC.

I ate my Christmas meal at the hotel, since they put on a wonderful full American-style meal for the guests at a reasonable price. It was a good chance to mingle with many of the people I had met on my day trips, and it was good fun as well.

I can't express how much it meant to me to see this side of Japan. Oh... I saw all the tourist sites, museums, and the day trip to Mount Fuji and all that, but the nightlife, or real, rank in file Japanese nightlife, that was wonderful. Finally, my last Friday arrived. I knew I needed to rest on Saturday, as my flight was on Sunday, the day after New Year's day. I wanted to do something really nice for Noa. So I spent the day shopping. I struggled with what gift I could give her that would not get me in hot water, either with the Hotel or by violating some cultural taboo, so I finally found the perfect gift.

On New Year's Eve night, I took her to a really nice sit-down American-style Italian restaurant. Yeah...I know that sounds weird, but they do exist in Tokyo. There are Olive Gardens in Japan, and although maybe not the most authentic Italian food, they are a true, authentic American-type dining experience. She had never been to a real sit-down American-style restaurant before, and I wanted to give her a little experience of something American – something from my culture. I also bought a beautiful picture frame, two actually, one for each of us, and found a copy shop that could print out pictures someone had taken of us singing Karaoke in a bar that specialized in American country music. We were wearing cowboy hats and singing together. When I gave it to her, she almost cried. "It is the most beautiful memory of us that you could have given me," she said. After Dinner, we stayed up to watch the Fireworks at Midnight. That was our last night together in Tokyo.

Noa and I remain friends to this day, and I am happy to tell you, she did receive a promotion to management and then a year later, was hired to work at the Hilton Hotel in Sydney, Australia. She met a man there. His name is Nicholas Soto. He is half Japanese and half Australian. They are married and have decided to build their lives together in Australia. Noa still works for the Hilton Hotel. I am so happy for her. She keeps asking me to come and visit her, so that is another trip I will be sure to take someday.

I had to buy an extra piece of luggage to take home all the things I had bought, even though I knew that was going to cost me extra on my flight home, but I decided, I may never get to Japan again, so why not? On Sunday morning, when I was preparing to check out to go to the airport, I went to the front desk, and the clerk handed me my bill, but at the bottom it said "PAID."

"Paid?" I asked her. I was confused. Who would have paid my hotel bill? "Are you sure?"

"Yes, ma'am, it has been paid." She assured me.

At first, I thought *maybe Noa had worked some hotel magic, but no, that could not be; she valued her job too much to try anything like that*. But then I thought, *Lenny... I'll bet Lenny contacted Karen and had the Trust pay for my Hotel*. I felt a bit angry at that thought. This was an expensive trip for sure, but I had been saving for a long time and could well afford it.

I said, "May I ask who paid my bill?"

She looked up my bill on the computer, and she replied, "It was placed on a card belonging to a Koharu Mieko." Koharu, that must have been what she asked the taxi driver – what hotel was I staying at? I couldn't believe she had done that. I wasn't sure what to do, but then Lenny's voice rang out in my head, *Never reject the generosity of another, for to do so would be a rejection of them, more than of the gift.*

*I will have to send her a note of thanks when I get home,* I thought. My flight home was uneventful, mostly just a repeat of the flight over, but when I arrived in Denver, very tired and ready for a few days of rest and recuperation, I turned on my phone and found a message from a number I did not recognize. I didn't listen to it right away. My dad and Zoe were waiting for me at the baggage claim. It was about 10:00 AM, and I just wanted to get to Dad's house and tell my dad what I discovered. I know he's dying to know, as he texted me at least once every day to make sure I was okay. I also had gifts to deliver. But most of all, I wanted to get home to Liberty Gardens. Despite how successful my search had been, it left me still with a lot of questions and confusion about who I am, which I just didn't think anyone, but Lenny, could help me sort through.

We finally made it to the house, and my phone rang again – it was that same number as on the message.

# Chapter 12

I looked at my phone and decided to answer. "Hello?"

"Kiko, it's Grandpa Kellen, sweetheart. Are you still in Japan?"

"Grandpa? No, Grandpa, I just got home this morning." In all the years since I had left home, neither my Grandpa nor Grandma has ever called me directly. Grandma Evelynn passed about three years ago, and Grandpa Kellen has lived a quiet life in Colorado Springs, just a few blocks from my mom, ever since. I always got my news about them, and they about me, through my mom, so hearing his voice raised an immediate alarm. "Is everything okay, Grandpa?"

"No, sweetheart. I had to put your mom in the hospital last night. She asked me not to call you until you got home from your trip, and I tried to wait, but I think you need to come down to see her. Her condition is worse than she has been letting on to any of us."

"Okay, Grandpa, I'll be there first thing tomorrow morning."

"Okay, Kiko, I look forward to seeing you."

"Yeah… me too, Grandpa. Text me the hospital name so I can pull it up on my phone."

"Okay, I will."

My dad asked, "Is everything okay?"

"No, mom's in the hospital. Her condition has gotten worse. I need to get there. I told him I'd be there in the morning."

"Okay, I took the liberty of having new snow tires put on your car while you were gone. I didn't want you to make the drive back to Austin without some good snow tires, so you should be good to drive down the mountain without any problems.

"Really, Daddy, you're always so good to me." I spent the rest of the day doing laundry and telling my Dad, Zoe, and Janice about meeting Koharu and all the fun I had exploring Tokyo. I gave them the gifts I had bought for them. Even Janice seemed to really appreciate the watch I gave her. In all the years my dad had been married to her, my Christmas gifts for her had been pretty benign things you might pick up for people when you have no idea what else to get them, you know, perfume or scented candles.

But this time, she saw that I really put some thought into it, and I think she truly appreciated that. But my mind had already moved on to my mom and her condition. I could hardly wait to get to Colorado Springs to see her. I left Denver at 8:00 the next morning, and by 10:00, I was walking into the hospital. I took the elevators to the third floor and found my mom's room. Grandpa Kellen and Don Howe were there, sitting with her. She looked very drawn and had a distinct jaundice-yellow tint to her skin. It took all I had not to burst into tears. After greeting Don and Grandpa, they both made an excuse to leave the room for a while, and left the two of us alone to talk.

My mom just looked at me and padded the bed and said, "Come, sit and tell me all about your trip. Did you find what you were looking for?"

She genuinely wanted to know how it all went. I told her all about it, about meeting Koharu, and her family business, and my name mix-up – we both had a bit of a laugh about that. But it didn't matter, I think I loved my name more now than I ever had in my life. I told her about my father dying before I was even born, and about Noa, and our nighttime carousing, and what great fun we both had. But when I had finally finished telling her everything I had to tell, I said, "So now, tell me about you. Why didn't you tell me that you were so sick?"

"I didn't want to worry you. I guess by the time I finally stopped drinking, it was too late, the damage had been done, and it has finally caught up with me. I'm sorry, Kiko, that I will probably not be here to see you get married and have children." We were both now is full crying mode. "But I love you so much, and I have caused so much pain in your life."

"No, don't talk like that. You can get a transplant or some experimental something. There has to be something they can do!"

"I'm sorry, sweetheart, the medical boards that select transplant recipients don't look very favorably on alcoholics who have destroyed their livers of their own accord. I'm not just saying that. Those were the words of my doctor when she explained the seriousness of my condition yesterday. Harsh, I know, but the truth is often that way." She said these words with that furious stoicism the Griffins were all so well known for.

"That's not fair, you're barely 50 years old."

She took my hand and said, "Don't say that. God is never unfair, sweetheart. You know what the Bible says, 'we reap what we sow.' I'm okay with it. I'm prepared for whatever happens from here on out. You need to be prepared, too. I don't want you to worry about anything. I've put all my affairs in order, and Daddy has all my papers and my power of attorney to take care of everything."

All I could do at that moment was just cry. I lay with her in the bed for almost an hour, and I just cried. When I was finally able to sit up again, my mom was asleep, so I left the room to find Grandpa sitting in the hall.

"Don had to leave for work. He said he'll be back later this evening." Grandpa said.

"You didn't need to stay out here. You could have come in."

"No, you and your Mom needed the time together. So she tells me you've been in Japan. How was that?"

"It was wonderful. I found all the answers I was looking for, and now I'm okay."

"I'm glad to hear that, sweetheart," was all he said. He was never one to talk much, always just quiet and kind. In fact, I was never quite sure what he thought about me – if he was happy for me to be his granddaughter or if he just thought about me as the kid his daughter had adopted. He always held his cards close to his chest, and it was difficult for me to read him.

As we were sitting there, Mom's doctor came to look in on her, and she had a hospital administrator with her. She didn't know me, but she recognized my Grandpa and came over to us. She looked at me kind of oddly, not sure she should say anything about my mom's condition in front of me, so I said, "I'm Kiko, Katherine's daughter."

"Oh… It's good you're both here then. I have to be honest; there isn't much we can do for her at this point except keep her comfortable and out of pain. We need to consider sending her into Hospice care sometime soon."

"Really, there's nothing that can be done?" I asked.

"No, her liver has nearly completely stopped functioning now. I don't want to give you false hope for a recovery or even being able to go home. She needs round-the-clock care at this point, but she could last for weeks, maybe even a month or a little more, so what she needs now is just observation and comfortable surroundings. Hospice is the best place for that, not an intensive care unit. This is Ms. Terrel. She can help you make the proper arrangements for getting her moved."

"Thank you, Doctor," Grandpa said. And the Doctor went into my mom's room to check on her, while Grandpa and I spoke with the lady from the hospital. Two days later, we transferred my mom to a hospice that was just a couple of miles from her home, so Grandpa or I could be there with her most of the time.

The next two weeks were so hard. Grandpa insisted that I stay with him at his house rather than at my mom's house, which turned out to be a nice thing. In the evening, after Mom had kicked us out of her room for the night, usually around 6:00 PM, when Don would come to visit her, we would go by Mom's house for a bit and try to make sure things were in order.

Grandpa said to me one night, "Your mom left everything to you, but the house still has five years left on the Mortgage, and she took out a second mortgage a few years ago to replace the roof and all the mechanicals, so it's actually in good shape. I'll contact a realtor to see about getting it on the market when the time comes to sell. I don't know how much will be left after that, and she has some life insurance through her employer as well – that will also go to you. You need to find anything you want to keep and take it home with you." He spoke so matter-of-factly, but for some reason, that's kind of what I needed to hear at that moment, just plain cool logic. But about the third day, as I was in my mom's room looking through her jewelry box to see if there was anything I needed to take or if it was all just costume stuff, I suddenly heard a loud crash of breaking glass in the kitchen. I ran to see what it was, and Grandpa Kellen was standing there with a smashed bottle of Vodka laying on the floor. He had found it hidden inside a plastic pitcher in the cupboard. He looked at me, and he just broke. "That damn devil juice," he shouted, and he began to cry. Then I began to cry, and we just cried together, hugging each other, standing in the middle of the kitchen. It was like a lifetime of emotions just came pouring out of him.

We didn't know if it was a new bottle or one she had bought before she stopped drinking, and just forgot it was there. I cleaned up the mess and took him home, and that night we sat up looking at old 8mm home movies he had taken of my mom when she was growing up. I had never seen them before. He had them digitized and put on a CD a few years ago. I never even imagined that my mom had been a young girl before, but there she was at 5, at 8, and at her first junior high dance, her senior prom, and her high School graduation.

It's funny how we never imagine that our parents were once as young as we are. With each new scene, Grandpa would narrate the circumstance and tell me about her at that age and about a life before me, before my dad, that I never knew she had. After that, my Grandpa and I grew very close to each other. A few years after Mom passed, he sold his house and moved to a retirement community in Pheonix Arizona, to be nearer my uncle Gregory and his kids, but I make a point of calling him at least once a month now.

My mom stayed in the Hospice for just two weeks and four days. I was on my way to the Hospice that morning when my phone rang, and it was the Nurse telling me that she had just passed. I had to pull my car over, and I cried for nearly 10 minutes before I could continue on my way. She had prearranged all her funeral details, and it was a lovely affair. We had her memorial service in the evening, and the next day, we held a traditional Catholic Mass and graveside service. My dad came with Zoe, and to my surprise, Irma came as well. She flew into Denver the night before and stayed with Dad and Janice. She said, "I told Lenny that one of us needed to be here for you, and he agreed," and that was so nice.

Mom's funeral was a veritable who's who of military officers and their wives and people she knew from the civilian workforce at both the air base and the Officers Academy. I had no idea how many of them knew my mom and loved her. There were Generals and Colonels and retired officers of all ranks from the surrounding community there to say goodbye. Many of them spoke and had such wonderful things to say about her. As I sat there and listened, a tremendous sense of guilt came over me for never allowing myself to know that side of her. The base commander, Brigadier General Collins, talked about how hard she fought for the funding to renovate the ballroom of the officers' club, to turn it into something that had become the envy of every officers' club on every military base of all the uniformed services. He announced that they would be renaming the ballroom at the club in honor of my Mom, to the Kate Griffin-Davis Ballroom, and revealed a plaque that would be placed at the entrance of the ballroom to honor her. I was so proud of her at that moment.

The next few days were just a blur. Grandpa and I spent some time getting the house ready for a realtor to begin showing it. All of my Mom's personal items were either donated or otherwise removed from the house. On the day the Goodwill came to pick up all her furniture and boxes of clothing, I had a real sense of, *Is this it? Is this really all that's left of any of us when we die, just old furniture and a few boxes of discarded belongings*? It was a very upsetting thought.

A week after the funeral, Grandpa and I had done all we could, so I knew it was time for me to go home. I drove to Denver to say goodbye to my dad, Janice, and Zoe, and I reminded Zoe, "Don't forget, you're coming to spend the summer with me this year."

She was so happy I remembered our agreement and said, "Of course I won't forget. It's going to be so much fun."

I drove back to Austin the next morning. I took it slow. There was a lot of snow in the mountains of Colorado and all the way to Amarillo. It wasn't until I was as far south as Lubbock that I left all the snow behind me. I took three full days to make the drive, stopping frequently and ensuring I was in a safe hotel by around 5:00 each night. Finally, about 5:30, on the third night, I arrived back at Liberty Gardens, and I had never been so happy to see that place in my life.

# Chapter 13

After just two weeks at home, we held our first event at the Gardens for that year. I opened with a song, Lenny spoke, we served chili as the weather was still a bit cool, the evening's events ended, and Irma and I cleaned up for the night. When we had finished, Irma said goodnight to Lenny and me and headed home. I sat down at the kitchen table for a moment before going down to my own apartment, but said nothing. I had been fairly quiet since returning from my trip to Japan and the loss of my mom. Lenny could sense that I wanted to talk, but he was never one to force me to talk about something before I was ready.

As we sat at the table, he finally said. "Kiko, you've been very quiet for the last two weeks since you came home. I know you've said that it was a nice trip, and your birth mother was even very kind to you, but I sense there is much more to the story than what you're telling. Now, you can hang onto whatever it is until your dying breath if you like, or you can come out with it and figure out what to do with it. Either way, you know I'm here to listen."

"You're right, Lenny, and yes, I'm ready to talk about it."

Lenny took a deep breath. He knew what I had learned was upsetting, but he was unsure of what I was about to tell him. I proceeded to tell him what Koharu Meiko had told me about my biological father, my adoption, and the name, Kiko, that my adopted mother had given me.

I just poured it all out to him, "I'm just... I just feel so lost, Lenny. I don't know how to deal with all of this information, all of these feelings, all at once. I found my birth mother, but then lost the only person I ever knew as my mother within weeks. I'm so conflicted. It seems one set of feelings makes me feel guilty for having the other feelings. Liking Koharu makes me feel guilty for not knowing Katherine better, and mourning Ao makes me feel guilty for loving my dad. I had the best father in the world in Bill

Davis, but I have such a deep sense of loss for the father I never even got to meet.

"I was going to be a successful singer. I was going to be with the man I loved and thought we would be together forever. And now, I don't know who I am." By this time, tears were streaming down my face.

Lenny, so resolute and steadfast, said, "Who told you that you should not feel all these things at the same time, Kiko. It's okay to feel all of this at once, to be conflicted about these feelings. They are all real and legitimate feelings, and you have the right to experience every one of them. There should be no shame, no guilt to any of that." He just held my hand, and he said, "I know that if Ao could look down and see you today, how grateful he would be that you had Bill Davis to raise you as his daughter. And I'm sure that Koharu feels the same about Katherine.

"I know you're right, Lenny, but when I was at my Mom's funeral, listening to all the wonderful things people had to say about her, I felt so guilty for not seeing that side of her. She was so accomplished at her job – worked so hard for that club, to make a place that all the officers could be proud of. I mean, you should have seen it, Lenny. Everyone from Generals to cadets, to retired officers from all over the country sent flowers to her funeral. She was so loved. But for some reason, I was never able to get past the single moment of that morning when we had our biggest blowout. Why was I never able to get past that moment to see her for the wonderful person she was?"

"It was a dramatic moment for you, Kiko, one that no doubt has informed every moment of your life since, but did you ever stop to think of how dramatic that moment was for Katherine as well. Just as you were never able to move past that moment, she also was stuck in that moment. The realization of the jeopardy that she might have put you in. Why do you think she never fought to keep you there, never complained when she had to drive to Denver to see you, or fly out here to Texas? Who knows what effects that moment had on the rest of her life, having to live with that moment playing over and over in her head as well."

"I...I never thought of it like that, I guess."

"We never do. But that's because we allow ourselves to live in the past or some fictitious future that only exists in our heads. I'm going to let you in on something I learned a long time ago. It may sound harsh. Are you ready to hear it?"

I looked up at him and nodded yes.

"Everything they told you about how life is supposed to work is a lie, Kiko. Success, happiness, love, all the things we're supposed to want, all the things we're supposed to chase after, all the things we're supposed to feel, we got it all wrong.

"I was just 21, standing on the beach on the Island of Iwo Jima, soaking wet from having just waded ashore from a troop carrier, what we called a gator boat. My friend Jimmy, a young private who had just been assigned to my platoon, was standing beside me. He was only 18, and seconds before a bullet tore through me, I saw one go right through his head. Three seconds later, I was lying on a beach covered in blood. Jimmy had said to me, "Everything happens for a reason, Sarge," and I'm sure he truly believed that, but I have never found a reason for what happened to us that day.

I was in the hospital for 28 weeks, and that was the end of the war for me. People came to me during my recovery, friends, family, visitors who came to comfort wounded soldiers, and over and over, they kept saying, "Stay strong, Marine." I heard that so many times, but none of those platitudes could change the fact that the life I had all mapped out just a few months before was now not even a possibility, and I was in deep mourning and sorrow over that, and the image of that bullet hitting Jimmy, I couldn't get it out of my head. I didn't know how, or even if, I was going to survive that. It was worse than any wound I could have suffered. "I had lost men before; I was stationed at Ewa in Hawaii when the Japanese attacked

Pearl Harbor, and I lost many close friends that day, so losses were expected. But I had never experienced anything like what happened to Jimmy on the beach that day.

After Ewa, I was told, 'Buck up, Marine, this is war,' like grief was something I was supposed to fix or ignore, but I didn't know how to fix that kind of grief."

"I'm so sorry, Lenny, I never knew that. Wait, Iwo Jima, wasn't that World War II? Lenny, how old are you?" I asked.

"I turned 93 on my last birthday, but don't get me off track. Anyway, it was all a long time ago, and I came to terms with it all. However, I have come to realize that the entire framework we use for understanding what life is supposed to be is fundamentally flawed. I began to realize that my life, most of it anyway, wasn't mine at all. It was someone else's plan that I had bought into."

"What do you mean?" I asked.

"I was engaged to my high school sweetheart at the age of 20, because that's just what the plan was for every young man when I was growing up – get married, have children, and become a farmer. That's what I knew; that was the plan laid out before me, and I never questioned it. Then, when I saw that it was inevitable that war was coming, I didn't question that either. I joined the Marines because that's just what was expected of young men. But that bullet changed everything for me. It tore through my groin, making sure I would never have children, and inadvertently destroyed all desire to live someone else's plans for my life. I guess you can say, in some macabre way, it was a good thing. Without that bullet, I would not be sitting here with you tonight. The one thing I learned from that day was to question everything. I lived before I questioned everything, and then again, after I learned to question everything, and I can tell you, questioning everything was scary, but it was also a huge awakening."

"How so?"

"Kiko, the fact that you are now beginning to ask these questions, struggling over these conflicting feelings, suggests that you also are ready to stop living someone else's version of your life and start figuring out what your version looks like."

"How do I do that, Lenny?"

"I started by digging through all the ideas I had about life that weren't actually mine. I asked myself, where did they come from? Soul-archaeology, I call it. Digging down through all the layers of beliefs to see what's underneath. I discovered that most of what we call reality is just agreed-upon fiction. At some point, we all decided that certain things are true, and then we just stopped questioning them. But I discovered that when I dug beneath all my beliefs, I found that they were built mostly on other people's fears. The events that led up to that moment with you and your mom, what do you think led Katherine to that moment – fear, fear of being alone, fear of being labeled a failure as a wife, fear of not being enough for your dad, all that fear played over and over in her head.

"You talk of wanting to be a successful musician, Kiko, but what does success mean to you? Really think about it. Is it money? Is it fame? Is it having a big house or a nice car, or people fawning over you?"

"I don't know, I just thought that if I played and sang well enough, success would just happen, but I've never really tried to define what form that success would take," I replied

"Before I was wounded, I thought success meant accumulation, you know, collecting things, achievements, possessions, experiences, having the biggest farm in all of Indiana that never ceased to expand, that was the dream anyway. But here's what I figured out. That's not success. That's fear. Fear that I was not enough. Fear that I'll run out of something. Fear that if I stop accumulating, I'll disappear somehow. But now I believe that real success was actually letting go. Now, for me anyway, success is being okay with whatever I have today. Being okay with who I am, not needing more all the time. Being content today. I stopped living in the past and waiting for some future time, and learned to become happy with today.

"I don't know how to do that, Lenny," I said.

"It may sound difficult, Kiko, because I know you are truly hurting right now. But I came to understand a great deal of idea-crushing things when I began digging. We're supposed to be obsessed with security, right? We think if we can just control enough variables, plan enough scenarios, save enough money, and build enough walls, we'll be safe. But no kingdom that ever surrounded itself with walls has ever been safe from an enemy – the enemy will just use those walls to keep them prisoner within them.

"I learned when I lost everything I thought my future depended on, that I can't control anything. Not really. Death comes when it comes. Accidents happen. People leave. The universe doesn't care about our plans.

"I was raised to believe that security comes from control. But now I believe it actually comes from accepting impermanence. When you accept that everything is temporary and illusory, you stop trying to hold on to it so tightly. That's when I found peace. When I was deprived of the opportunity to ever have a child, I tried to control my grief. I tried to process it the right way. Tried to make it mean something. But that kind of grief isn't controllable. That loss wasn't manageable. It just was.

"And my concept of love I had all so backwards as well. Before I was even out of the hospital, I wrote my fiancé a letter and told her I was not going to hold her to any obligation she had to me and that I would not be returning to Indiana when I was released from the hospital. I wished her well and told her to go out and pursue the life she always wanted with someone else who could provide that to her.

"You see, our dream, which we had shared for years together, was to have a farm and lots of children, and I knew that was never going to happen now. But I discovered as I sorted through all the layers of my life and desires, that that was really her dream; I was just a silly boy in love, and I wanted it because she wanted it.

"I figured out that love meant possession. 'I love you, and you're mine, and if you love me, I'm yours.' 'We belong to each other.' 'We complete each other.' All that stuff. But now I realize that kind of love is actually just fear wearing a disguise. Fear of being alone, fear of not being chosen, fear that love will run out if you don't hold on to it tight enough.

"But I know now that real love means complete release. I learned that if I truly loved her, then I wanted her to be free, even from me. She wrote to me and said it didn't matter, that we could be together anyway, but that is just what everyone expected her to say. I knew what was really in her heart and what she truly desired for her life, and I could never give her that. Why would I have deprived her of her heart's desires, just to be with me? I was so broken at that time. That would have been very selfish of me, and she would have developed great resentment over time. And I was right, she married our classmate from high school, and they had eight children together and a very successful farm. Love isn't about keeping someone. It's about celebrating them exactly as they are."

"That's hard, Lenny. That goes against everything I've ever been taught about relationships." I replied. "I was taught that we were supposed to fight for love, endure hardship for the person you love, sacrifice for them, and them for me."

"I know, Kiko. But in that kind of relationship, if you examine it closely, you find that only one partner does the sacrificing; endures the hardship. You can't truly love until you find and know yourself."

"I hear that constantly," I said. "But what if the self I'm trying to find isn't real either? What if it's just another story I inherited? I've spent years trying to figure out who I am. Like, there is some true authentic version of me hiding under all the roles and personas and expectations, and somehow, I just haven't stumbled onto the right persona. But the more I look, the more lost I feel."

"You will never find your true self until you let go of all the masks you have put on to please other people. All the stories you've told yourself about who you are, all the identities you've collected - Singer, songwriter, waitress, bartender, bookkeeper, daughter, girlfriend, and now orphan, what if they're just in the way, masking the real you?

"When everything in my life collapsed, when I lost every possibility that I thought the future had in store for me, all my identities fell apart too. I wasn't the respected and seasoned Sergeant; I had tremendous guilt over not saving Jimmy. I had appointed myself as his protector. He was 5 years younger than me, so I looked at him as if he were my little brother. I looked at all of them in that way, all the 18, 19, and 20-year-old Jimmys in my platoon. I told myself that the bullet that killed him should have killed me instead, but that was just the story I had written in my head.

"I also wasn't ever going to be the father I thought I was going to be. I was never going to be the husband, the provider, the successful farmer, the guy who had it all figured out. And you know what was left when all of that was gone? Just me, just this consciousness, experiencing whatever was happening that moment. No story about it, no identity wrapped around it, just being. That was scary as hell. But it was also freeing.

"When everything else was gone, I saw what was actually real. What's real doesn't need all these stories and identities and plans for security. Once I lost all those identities that others had created for me, and that I had bought into, I was able to begin learning who I truly was. I started asking what I wanted, what was important to me?

"But that didn't all happen overnight. I bummed around for over a decade, angry, bitter, hard drinking, fighting, working all day in the hot sun, living as a day laborer or road man, drinking all night, day after day, until I met Sam Eustes. Sam was the one who helped me truly understand these things."

I sat silent for a moment and then asked, "What if all those things I feel have passed me by, the music career, the husband, the children, all of it, are what I truly want, Lenny?"

"Then you haven't lost anything, Kiko; they are just delayed until you're ready for them. But here's something else I started noticing, Kiko. Most of my suffering, aside from the physical pain, wasn't actually coming from what happened to me. It was coming from what I thought should have happened instead."

"What do you mean?"

"When Jimmy died, the fact of his death wasn't what was hurting me. It was all the stories I had about it running around in my head. He was too young. It's so unfair. This shouldn't have happened. I should have been able to save him.

"But who says he was too young? Not one of us is ever guaranteed a single day in this mortal existence. Who decided what he had left to give? Scarred by the horrors of war, he may have lived a horrible life afterwards, so many of us have been haunted the rest of our lives by what we did and saw during those days in war. Who wrote the rule that this shouldn't have happened? It's been happening since the beginning of humanity. I made all that stuff up in my head, or I inherited those rules from somewhere, from some programming about how life is supposed to work.

"Your pain isn't from what happened. It's from believing lies about what should have happened. Maybe that sounds cold, Kiko. It's not meant to be. When you first came here, I told you I would never lie to you and would be completely frank about what I believed, so here is what I have come to know. My suffering was coming from my false beliefs, and when I learned that, I understood that maybe I didn't have to suffer as much as I was.

"We all get taught all these lies, you know, like really fundamental lies about how reality works. Time, for instance. I was taught to live in the past and for the future. Always regretting things that had already happened and worrying about things that haven't yet happened. But you know what? Life only exists right now. This moment, that's it. The past, that's just memory. And those memories aren't even reliable.

"I remember Jimmy so much differently now than I did all those years ago when we were on that beach together. My memories of Mary keep changing, too. So, if our memories keep changing, how real are they?"

"That's true," I added, "even now, when I think of Derik, the only thing that comes to mind is that day he walked out the door, but I know we had such good times as well, I just can't seem to find them."

"Exactly, Kiko, and in time, all you will remember are those happy times."

"Do you really think so? It doesn't feel like that now."

"Think of it like a cut on the finger. When it happens, it hurts so bad. But it slowly covers over with a scab, and every time you look at it, you remember that pain, but eventually, the scab falls off, and it heals into a slight, barely noticeable scar. Every once in a while, you get a glimpse of the scar, and you remember, but all you can remember is how your mother cleaned the cut, kissed your finger, wrapped it up, and made sure it was always clean and healing, and now that scar is a reminder of a beautiful moment in your life.

"And the future, it doesn't really exist. It's just imagination, projection, fantasy, probability, possibilities, mostly based on fear, if I'm honest. But right now... right now is real. This breath, this heartbeat, this conversation we're having, this is the only place where life actually happens.

"They taught us to live everywhere except where we actually are. We're obsessed with trying to control outcomes. Like if you just work hard enough, plan enough, want it bad enough, you can make things turn out the way you want them to. But there is no guarantee of any of that. Life is full of uncertainties that cannot be predicted or controlled. Jimmy's death taught me that. We did everything right – train, drill, practice, but what is that saying, 'The best laid plans of mice and men.' You may do everything right and still not get what you want in life. But that doesn't mean you give up, you just keep putting one foot in front of the other, every day, day after day, and see where life takes you. You just let each moment be the best moment it can be, and let life take you to places you never imagined it would.

"The very idea of the future has something disingenuous in it. To live for the future is an indefinite postponement of life. We are all told, 'we do this today, for a better tomorrow, for our children's future.' There's always a five-year plan that things will be better than what we have now. Our notions of the great society are based on a futurist's approach to life.

"You go through your entire education, from kindergarten through university, and finally, you become a graduate because you were told you don't have a future if you don't have an education.

"But when you've graduated, you find that you're still looking to the future before you can finally become successful. So you follow all the rules, and finally, your status grows, and your wealth grows, and you become the president of the corporation or a great leader in some movement, and you still end up with a funny feeling that you have been cheated.

"You've climbed the stairway and reached the top, but then there's nowhere else to go. Since you've never been taught to live in the present, you don't know what to do. So you do one of two things, you keep chasing the illusive "Future" and grow your wealth and the company's influence and your fame in the world, but still, in the end, you feel like you have so much more to do to reach the illusive future you so longed for, or, you just retire and shed all the responsibility that has been placed on your shoulders and finally pursue your dreams and aspirations of becoming an artist or a writer or just gardening. And so you retire and continue chasing that future time that always seems to be just out of your grasp.

"In the end, you will die, as we all must at some point, and you still feel cheated, because the "future" that you were promised never seemed to come for you. It was always just one more deal, one more painting, one more Grammy-winning song, or prize-winning flower away. You feel cheated because you were never taught to live for the present; you were taught all your life that happiness was always in the future.

"We don't teach living for today to our children because it's thought of as being feckless and irresponsible. 'It's everybody's duty to contribute to a better future,' we are told, because if you don't do that, you become a nuisance. You become aggressive, you'll become a thief, a dredge on society, or you become a power maniac who's trying to organize society to suit their own needs and desires, all because they haven't learned the very simple art of living in the present moment.

"It doesn't take much energy to maintain a human life. If you consider what you need to eat, what you need to wear, and how much housing you need to survive, it comes down to something quite simple, and the simpler your life is, the more you can enjoy something as mundane as watching a spider build a web. But if you sit and watch a spider build a web, and you say, 'Wow, look at that!' everyone thinks you're crazy, because you're just sitting there watching a spider build a web. 'Can't you find something more important to do?' they will say.

"So we have a mentality that does not value watching a spider build a web. If you do these things, they will say, 'You are of no value.' You're not even considered human unless you're changing things, unless you're interfering, unless something is happening and some great operation is taking place, and you're busy with it, then you're not contributing, or you're 'lazy,' a 'good for nothing,' because you are not working for the future.

"With every new advancement in technology, we just accept it, but never bother to ask why we need it. Take the automobile, for example. They've been around for a hundred years now and have been a great benefit to mankind. Modern cars are marvelous machines. They're filled with electric gadgets and computer controls of all kinds, but at the same time, all that wiz-bang stuff made cars so expensive that to own one, you need to get yourself trapped in a never-ending cycle of debt, because as soon as you get one paid off, it's in such poor shape and so expensive to repair, that you might as well just go out and buy a new one. Is that really progress? What was wrong with a car that just drove and worked well on simple mechanical systems? It performed its stated function perfectly well.

"By putting our focus on the future, we achieved initial success. We can destroy diseases, we can keep people alive, but in the end, we get the atomic bomb and the ability to destroy it all with the press of a button. We promise ourselves that good things are going to happen, promising, promising, promising. So you see, Kiko, the future is really just an illusion.

"Consider a simple tree. When most people look at a tree, they see the utility it has to offer – the board feet of lumber they can harvest from it, the shade it provides, and the warmth it will bring in the fireplace. Those are all things we are taught to see in the tree when we look at it. But if you take a small child and sit them in front of the tree, all they see is the tree, its beauty, its enormity, the wondrous nature of the tree. It's not until we have educated the wonder out of the child that they begin to see the tree purely for its utility. When you start to see what's in front of you, you begin to see the world in an entirely different way. You see the wholeness of everything. You see yourself as part of the whole, instead of something separate from it. You live in the present, instead of the past or the future, just this moment, because this moment is really the only thing that truly exists. The past is just a present memory, the future is just a present possibility, and the present is the only thing that is real.

"So, where does all that leave you, Kiko. Now you have opened that box and seen what's inside. What does any of that have to do with who Kiko Davis is? You learned a few names, heard a few stories about your birth parents, a bit about genetic ancestry, but none of that can change who you are – sitting here, in my kitchen tonight. You are a product of your actual day-to-day experiences, all given to you by Bill and Katherine Davis, not of the stories you have made up in your mind of the past that should have been or a future you are missing out on. The only person who gets to decide who Kiko Davis is – is Kiko Davis.

"We're constantly told that happiness is just around the corner; just get that promotion or find that relationship, buy that thing, reach that goal, then you'll finally feel complete – then you'll finally be enough. But what nobody mentions is that you've probably already achieved goals you once thought would make you happy. Remember when you believed that if you were just able to move away from home, live with Derik, and play your music, you would be happy? Well, you've already done all of that, and did it make you happy, Kiko?

"No, not really, Lenny," I replied.

"Of course not, because you believed the lie. After a brief moment of satisfaction, the wanting started all over again. The goalpost moved. The finish line disappeared. This isn't a flaw in you. This is the setup. We're living in a system designed to keep us perpetually dissatisfied, perpetually seeking, perpetually wanting, because satisfied people don't make good consumers. People at peace don't desperately scroll through social media. People who feel complete don't obsessively chase status, and we end up trapped in what feels like a maze with no exit. We're stressed, anxious, overwhelmed, and we don't even know why. We achieve things and feel empty. We get what we want and still feel incomplete. We try to fix ourselves with self-help books, motivational videos, and productivity gains, but nothing seems to create lasting change. Why? Because we're trying to solve the wrong problem.

"The real problem isn't that you're not successful enough, not disciplined enough, not positive enough. The real problem, Kiko, is that we've been hypnotized into believing we're separate from life itself. We've been conditioned to see ourselves as an isolated ego that needs to constantly fight, strive, and prove itself in a hostile world. And from that perspective, nothing will ever be enough. No achievement will ever satisfy you. No external validation will ever fill the void."

"I apologize, Kiko, I seem to have gone into a bit of a tangent – one of the hazards of me being me, I'm afraid, but my point is, we have all been mistaught how to look at the world and our circumstances.

"Then what do I do now, Lenny? How do I put all that stuff behind me and just live for the moment?"

Lenny just smiled and said, "You've already made the best choice you could by choosing to return here after your trip to Japan and just listening and serving others who also come to listen, and soon, very soon, I expect, it will all begin to come into focus for you, Kiko, because you are now asking all the right questions. I have confidence that you'll figure it out, Kiko."

When we were finished talking, I went down to my apartment, and I slept so well that night, like a thousand-pound weight had been lifted off my shoulders.

# Chapter 14

The next two days, I had all to myself. I ran Lenny's words over and over in my head, especially "Question Everything." I was sitting in my apartment, picking something on a little Ukulele that I had picked up somewhere, and had been teaching myself to play for about a year, and all I could do was to keep asking myself, *why?*"

"Why do I sing the songs that I sing? Why is music so important to me?" I've seen my videos, and technically, they are perfect. Perfect pitch, perfectly timed, but one look at my face, and I don't look like I'm having any fun at all. I remembered all the fun I had in Japan, singing Karaoke with Noa, doing a song with that folk trio, and singing and dancing to old Elvis movies. I wondered why I never have that much fun with music when I'm singing here at the Gardens or in front of an audience. "What was I afraid of? Who am I singing for?"

I opened my phone and took a look at the playlist in my music app. When I'm out working in the gardens, my earphones are always in, and music is constantly playing in my head. I had 712 songs in my playlist, and it was the most eclectic mix of music and genres imaginable. Songs written from the 1940s all the way to current pop phenoms like Adel. Ballads by deep storytellers like Gordon Lightfoot, Roger Whitaker, and Marty Robbins, to silly tunes like the Irish Rovers Unicorn song and Bobby Russell's Saturday Morning Confusion. Yet, I didn't play any of them live. It's like I was afraid just to have fun when I sang. I saw a song in the playlist, an old one, called 'Let's Talk Dirty in Hawaiian.' I loved that song, yet I have never tried to play it. Written by John Prine in the 1980s, it begins, "I packed my bags and bought myself a ticket, for the land of the tall palm trees." I decided I was going to learn that song on my Ukelele, which is how John played it, and perform it at next Saturday's event. I practiced it every chance I got that week, but never told Lenny or Irma what I was planning. I was afraid they would disapprove.

The week went by quickly, as it was still technically winter, and we had done all we could to prepare the gardens for spring, so there wasn't much for us to do. Irma had a few winter vegetables growing, but most of the plants were still dormant or just beginning to emerge. Saturday came, and I was so nervous. Would they like this playful side of me, or reject it? I didn't know. Maybe the song was too bawdy for some people? Most were pretty open-minded and tended to like to laugh, so I thought they would take it in good humor, as it was intended.

Saturday evening came, and there I stood at the top of the steps, waiting for Lenny to come out so I could walk him down and do my song before he spoke. When Lenny arrived, he looked at the Ukelele in my hand, and he said, "Well, this is different. I don't think you've ever played the Ukelele for us before. What a treat." We walked down the steps, Lenny took his seat, and I walked over to my mic. I looked out and saw we had a pretty good crowd that night, 40 to 50, I would say. I closed my eyes, took a deep breath, and said, "I thought I'd try something a little bit different tonight." I began to play, and the faces in the audience just lit up. Several people were familiar with the song, and they were singing the chorus along with me, and the more they sang, the more animated I became with the song. Lenny was just laughing and clapping, and when I was done, I received the biggest ovation I had ever received, at least at the Gardens. I was so relieved, and that felt so liberating to sing what I felt like singing, as silly as it was, and not so concerned with the structure and perfect pitch of the song. I felt like I did those nights in Japan, singing Karaoke with Noa.

When I was done, I did a slight curtsey and began to walk back up the step, but before I could, Lenny grabbed my arm and whispered to me, "Now that was the genuine Kiko." I went up and took up my place with Irma, behind the serving counter, sat and listened to Lenny deliver his talk.

He began, "Have you noticed that the masks you have been wearing for decades, suddenly seem to be dropping off one by one. The games everyone is playing around you have become painfully obvious. The life you built with such effort has begun to feel like a prison made of other people's expectations. You are not imagining this. You are waking up! This awakening comes slowly at first, an inevitable shedding, a letting go of everything that is not truly you. This does not happen in one dramatic leap, but gradually. Piece by piece, mask by mask, until one day you look back and wonder how you ever lived any other way."

I don't know if the talk we had had just a week before had brought him to deliver this talk, on this night, but I felt like he was talking directly to me once again. He talked for nearly 25 minutes that night. Point after point, every word struck me as if he were speaking only to me, and every word was absolutely spot on. I was changing. I didn't know in what ways or how any of this would change my life, but I just knew my life was changing. I was looking for the real Kiko Davis, and bit by bit, I was beginning to emerge, like a butterfly from a cocoon.

But little did I know that those changes would begin in earnest that very night. After Lenny's talk, I went down and walked him back up the steps as had become our routine. Irma and I were serving as we always do, and as people came up to be served, they all said how much they enjoyed my song and wished I'd do more playful songs like that. "It was so much fun," they would say.

Carol, a regular at the Saturday events, came up to be served, and she had a young man with her. He was cute, maybe my age or possibly a year or two younger. He smiled at me and complimented me on my song as well, but didn't say anything else. When Carol and he went to sit, I asked Irma, "Who is that with Carol?"

"Oh…that's Tommy, her son. He used to come here with her almost every week when he was a teenager, but I think he went in the Navy or something, so it's been eight or nine years since he's been here."

"Oh…okay. He's cute!"

"Yeah, he is." Irma responded, "Suzanna had such a huge crush on him when she was young."

I laughed, "Yeah, I remember being that young myself."

About thirty minutes later, as things were beginning to kind of wind down for the night, Irma and I were starting our cleaning routine, and Tommy came up to Irma and, with a huge smile, said, "Miss Irma, I'm so glad to see you."

Irma gave him a big hug and responded, "You too, Tommy. Look how tall you've gotten. Are you home from the service now?"

"Yeah, I actually got out several years ago, but I joined the Austin Fire Department, so I'm usually working Saturday nights, but I happened to be off today, and Mom said she was coming here tonight, so I thought I'd join her. I always enjoyed listening to Lenny speak. So how's Suzanna? I'll bet she's all grown up now."

"Yes, she's at college, studying nursing. She has one more year, then she will be an RN."

"Wow…that's wonderful." He then looked at me and said, "So, I guess you're the new Suzanna."

"Umm… I guess I am. At least I try to be. I'm Kiko."

"Hi, Kiko, I'm Tom. I loved your song, you're very talented."

"Thank you."

"So, Kiko, is there a Mr. Kiko, or a significant other Kiko?"

I felt flustered at the directness of his question, but managed to stammer out, "No, Tom, there is not, at least not at the moment."

"Okay, so what would it take for me to get you to go out on a date with me, Kiko?"

His tone was playful, but sweet, so I tried to be playful too. It was not my usual manner, but I was starting to like this new me – it felt right. "Well, I don't know, maybe an actual request for a date and a willingness to pick me up and drop me off afterward. That usually seems to work for a first date."

"Oh...okay, you like the direct approach, I see. Okay, would you go out with me?"

"Sure, Tom," I said, and then just looked at him in silence for a few seconds, then followed up and said, "So, did you have a specific day or time in mind, Tom?"

"Umm. Oh yeah, umm, I'm off on Thursdays, would Thursday be okay? Say, 6:30."

"Alright, then, Thursday at 6:30. You can pick me up here."

"Here? You live here at the Gardens?"

"I do, right out there underneath that tree." And I pointed to the big oak tree close to Lenny's house.

He looked out at the tree I was pointing to and then back at me, confused, and I laughed. "I live in the apartment beneath Lenny's house."

"There's an apartment under Lenny's house?"

"There is, and I live there."

"Okay, umm, can I have your phone number, you know, just in case I get called in to work or something? Firefighters are always on standby, even on our days off, I'm afraid."

"Yeah, sure." I gave him my number and asked, "So what do you think we might do on this date, Tom?"

He looked at me sheepishly and replied, "Oh... I don't know, maybe we'll just talk dirty in Hawaiian. The ship I was on in the Navy was stationed at Pearl Harbor, so I've gotten pretty good at it." I couldn't help but laugh out loud. Even Irma, who was hard to make laugh, had to laugh at that." Tom and I went out, and we continued dating for over two years.

But that was just the beginning of the changes that the next year brought into my life. About 4 weeks after that, I got a phone call from my Grandpa Kellen. "Hi, Grandpa, how are you? Is everything okay?"

"I'm fine, Kiko. I just wanted to call and let you know your mom's house went under contract today. It should be in escrow in about 5 days, and then another 40 or so days until it closes. That will allow me to finalize and settle up all your Mom's estate, so hopefully in about 40 days or so, you should have a nice little check in the mail."

"Oh…that's so wonderful, Grandpa. I can't thank you enough for taking care of all that for me. I love you, Grandpa."

"I love you too, Kiko. I'll talk to you again in a week or so and let you know how things are going."

"Okay, bye, Grandpa." I didn't really know what he meant by nice little check. I mean, there was still some mortgage left to pay off, and a second for all the upgrades she had done, so I wasn't expecting much. I thought $10k would be a huge boon, but I wasn't really expecting anything. I was trying to follow Lenny's advice and not project what the future might hold.

But just two weeks after that, Lenny called me up to the house one afternoon. "There's a FedEx delivery for you that you need to sign for, Kiko."

"Okay, thank you, Lenny." I signed the iPad and took the package. It was just a standard document envelope, you know, the cardboard kind that FedEx uses. As soon as the door closed, I tore it open to see what was inside. I thought maybe Grandpa had sent me something I needed to sign, but instead it was another envelope. It was addressed from the Civil Service Employee Life Insurance Company. I had completely forgotten that Grandpa had told me that Mom had some life insurance and I was named her beneficiary. I opened it and looked at the check and almost fainted. It was for $250k. The attached letter had all the details, stating that my Mom had insurance for 2x her base salary. I couldn't believe it. I just screamed, and Lenny and Irma both came running into the room. I showed them the check, and I was crying so hard I could hardly even speak.

When I had finally calmed down enough to talk, I had to call my Dad, and he was just as stunned as I was. I had never even imagined that I would see that many numbers on a single check in my life. Later that day, Lenny handed me a slip of paper with a name, Andie Hall, and a phone number. "This is the investment manager for Liberty Garden's trust. She can help you find a safe place for that money until you figure out what to do with it." I called her the next day, and then went to see her a couple of days later. We put the money into a money market for the time being, knowing I still had more money coming from my mom's house, so at least it was safe for the short term.

Six weeks later, my check arrived from Grandpa Kellen. Once again, I was stunned. After everything was settled on the house, plus the sale of my mom's car and closing her checking and savings accounts, and some pay she was due for unused annual leave, another $217,000 check. In a matter of just a few weeks, I went from earning about $23.00 an hour with a few thousand in my checking account, after my trip to Japan, to sitting on over $465k in cash. I didn't go wild or anything, but I did buy a new SUV, and I splurged and bought a couple of new guitars I had had my eyes on, but the rest just went into a brokerage account for growth, until I figured out what else to do.

The spring came, and Irma and Lenny and I just kept on holding events every Saturday. The gardens that year were spectacular. So much color and so much beauty. I was so proud of Irma. All the work she put into that place year after year was all for these few weeks when everything seemed to come alive all at once. It was such a wonderful place to be in Spring and early Summer.

Tom and I continued seeing each other. He was a really nice guy, probably the nicest I had ever dated since being alone. But he was a firefighter and had irregular hours, you know, the 24 on and 48 off kind of schedule, and he had another job he worked on his off days. When he was in the Navy, he was something called a Machinist

Mate. He learned how to use metal lathes and all kinds of machine tools, so he worked for a friend who owned a machine shop that did machining of all kinds. It was kind of fascinating work. I once watched him make a thing out of nothing but a thick steel bar. That was almost like magic watching it take shape. We found what time we could together. Neither of us was in a hurry to get involved.

June came, and so did Zoe. I wasn't sure I was ready to try to corral a 16-year-old for the entire Summer, but I thought I had some resources now, so we could take a few trips around Texas and see the sights and do all the tourist things, but Zoe had plans of her own. From the moment she arrived, all she wanted to do was work in the gardens with Irma and me. She absolutely loved learning about everything gardening related, and she was a natural. She would sit in the apartment at night and read books and articles and learn new things every day. I never saw a 16-year-old so fascinated with the whole natural gardening world. After a few weeks, I just let her go and do what she seemed to love doing, and she and Irma became joined at the hip. She did do one thing for me, though.

I had struggled to gain any real traction with my videos on various online platforms, but Zoe, it turns out, was an absolute whiz at it. She and her friends seemed to know instinctively how to make videos, post videos, get likes, followers, and subscribers. She took to the internet like a fish to water. She began videoing all my performances on Saturday, and even some extra stuff we did during the week. She downloaded some editing software, added graphics, and made them look like a real pro had made them.

I began to earn followers, and with followers, some sponsors. We discovered that YouTube had figured out how to identify song copyright holders and automatically pay out royalties from earnings, and the sponsor money on top of that was all mine. I wasn't making big money back then, but I was building a following. This led to inquiries about my availability and some higher-paying gigs. I even got an invitation to SXSW that year, the big Austin music festival. I also began getting calls from some of the Clubs in Downtown that had refused me before, but suddenly wanted me to come to perform for actual pay, not just tips. But still, I loved the Gardens and was not yet ready to give up my work there. That was 2012, and it was the most wonderful year of my life, up to that time.

But then came 2013, and even more incredible changes. Just one year and 2 months after I had completed my trip to Japan and met my birth mother, Lenny and I were sitting out on his patio one Monday afternoon when his doorbell rang. I went in to see who it was and found a man in a suit and tie standing at the door, with a big box sitting at his feet.

"Hello, can I help you?"

"I hope so, I'm looking for a Kiko Davis."

"Yes, that's me."

"Ahh...Miss Davis. My name is Jeffery Whitman." He handed me a business card that read, Jeffery Whitman, Bank of America, Investment and Trust Division. "I have something I need to deliver to you and also have some paperwork I need to complete with you."

I had no idea what this was about. I thought that maybe it was something from my Mom's estate that Grandpa had not told me about, or wasn't aware of until now. "Oh...okay... umm... come in."

He stretched out his hand to hand me his valise and asked, "Would you mind?"

"No, of course not." I took the valise, and he bent down to pick up the box. "You can just set that on the coffee table, I suppose."

"Wonderful. I'm here to inform you that a trust has been established in your name with the Bank of America. I believe if you open the box, you will find a letter explaining everything."

By now, Lenny was also standing in the house and pulled out his pocket knife to cut the box open. As we opened the box, we saw the most beautiful jade and mother-of-pearl inlay on the top of a wooden chest that was obviously a handmade Japanese chest of some sort. It took both of us to lift it out of the packaging, but when we got it out, it was stunning. Lenny and I just looked at each other until he said, "It's yours, open it." So I opened it, and inside was the most stunningly beautiful hand-embroidered silk kimono I had ever seen. Sitting on top was a handwritten letter on beautiful handmade paper that was simply addressed to Kiko. I opened it and saw it was from Koharu.

This is what it said. *"My dearest Kiko, your visit to me last year had a profound effect on me. Seeing you and the wonderful life you have built for yourself, so free of obligations and duty, gave me the courage to do something I had been wanting to do for a long time. The Cartier Company had been trying to buy my family business for some time, but I was always afraid to sell, because it had been in my family for so long. But meeting you gave me the courage to write a letter to the Imperial family and ask permission to be relieved from our Imperial Warrant, so I could sell the business. The Emperor summoned me to the Palace, and I thought I was in for serious chastisement, but he and the Empress were so kind. They invited me to tea, and he spoke of how he wished he could do the same sometimes. He permitted me to sell the business and was very pleased to know that it would go to such an impressive brand as Cartier.*

*"I never told anyone this before, but when I lived in London, all those years ago, I had become a British Citizen, so I decided to also sell my home and all my holdings in Japan and relocate to London. I have recently acquired a position at Central Saint Martins, Royal College of Art in London, as an Associate Professor of Gemology and Jewelry Design. Thank you for giving me the courage to do this.*

*As you can imagine, the sale of my, our, family business brought me a great deal of wealth, so I thought that I would share some of it with you. I established a trust in your name. It will not make you instantly rich, but hopefully can allow you the freedom to live a life in the pursuit of happiness.*

*"The Kimono is a gift for you – part of the Trust. It has been in my family for over 150 years, handed down from mother to daughter for six generations. You are the seventh to own this kimono. If you look carefully, down in the hem, you will find the names of each maternal ancestor who had owned and worn this kimono. I hope you like it and can someday pass it to a daughter of your own.*

*Below is my new address. I hope we can keep in touch. With all my Love, Koharu Meiko.*

After I read the letter, Mr. Whitman said, "That kimono is worth almost as much as this house. It is museum quality, so be very careful with it. Well, we just have a little bit of business to conclude, and then I can be out of your hair. The trust is for the amount of $150k per year for life. You can designate how you wish to receive that money. You can take one lump sum annually on this date in perpetuity, or you can designate that quarterly or monthly payments be made in appropriate amounts. The trust itself is considered an inheritance and falls below the threshold for tax burden, but you will need to pay taxes on any amount the trust earns in interest or dividends each year. The Trustee, the Bank, will make sure that those taxes are paid as part of our fiduciary responsibility. So, if you can just sign this document here and provide me with the routing and account numbers for where you want your money deposited, you should receive your first payment in about 10 days. Just call the number on that card if you have any questions or need anything at all regarding the Trust, and I, or one of our Trust managers, will be happy to help you in any way that we can."

I was in shock. I couldn't even muster a response, other than. "I'll find you a blank check with my account information on it." He was all so matter-of-fact and businesslike, yet he had just changed my life in a way that he could not have possibly imagined, or maybe he could. Even Lenny seemed to be at a loss for words, and he was never at a loss for words. I, of course, immediately wrote to Koharu and thanked her for the gift and told her how much her gift of the kimono meant to me, how special it is, and how I will cherish it all my life. We did not talk much the rest of that year; it wasn't until the following year that she and I began to really build a relationship.

Even with this newfound wealth, I continued to live at the gardens for most of that year. My music videos were picking up steam. Even from Denver, Zoe continued to do all my posting and finding sponsors and such. I told her, before she left for home, that I would pay her 10 percent of all my income for her work, and that was all the motivation she needed. At first, Janice was a bit put out that she was spending all her time on a project for me, instead of working in the office after school, but then she began to see how much money Zoe was bringing in, more than five-hundred dollars a month, well, she changed her tune pretty quickly.

A few months after I had received the Trust from Koharu, and with all the cash I had sitting in my brokerage account, I decided I needed to consider buying a house. I wasn't in a hurry, thought I'd just take my time to look around, but I knew I had no reason to keep living in that one-bedroom apartment under Lenny, even though it was mine for as long as I wanted to stay there. But Susanna was about to graduate, and I thought it would be nice for her to have a place of her own to begin her new life with, so I was beginning the process of looking.

Then one Saturday evening, one of the Saturday regulars, whose name is Jema, came up to me and said, "Kiko, Lenny tells me you might be interested in buying a house."

"Umm.. yeah... I'm just beginning to look around." I thought *Oh no, she's a real estate agent or something and she wants my business.* But instead, she surprised me.

"I work in the distressed property division of a local bank, and I have something you might be interested in."

"Oh... really... okay... tell me about it."

"Well, it's been vacant for about two years. It went through some kind of criminal seizure, but that is all cleared up now, and it has been released to the bank as a foreclosed property. I just had the inspection completed, and, mechanically, it's in really good condition, but it does need a lot of work inside and outside as well. The bank has put me in charge of getting it off our books. I could just put it up for auction, 'as is,' but we could be leaving a lot of money on the table if we did, or I could spend the money to make it marketable and sell it through a traditional sale, but that will take time and money. Lenny says you're pretty handy with tools and not afraid of hard work, so maybe this is a project you might want to take on."

"Um... Okay...maybe? I mean, I'd have to see it."

"Yeah, of course. How about tomorrow? I have the key, and we can go to see it tomorrow. It's really just about three miles from here, not far at all."

"Oh...okay... yeah, tomorrow will work, I can take a look at least." She gave me the address, and so the next day, I went to meet her. I called Tom and asked if he'd go with me. He was also pretty handy and knew construction as well, as his dad owned a small construction company, and Tom had been swinging a hammer for his dad since he was a teenager.

Tom and I went to the address, and she was right, the outside definitely needed help. It was stained an ugly brown, and the landscaping looked like it had not been touched in years. But that was all within my capability and means. As Tom and I waited for Jema, we looked around a bit. It was not a huge lot, not what you would consider acreage, but fair-sized, nonetheless. The back patio looked out over the hill country vistas, and that was nice. Along the north side of the house was a stairway going down about 12 to 15 feet to a door, and Tom said, "Oh, look, there's a basement of some kind."

"Oh, yeah." But just as we were about to explore it, Jema drove up, so we went to greet her. I introduced Tom, and we went inside. The first words out of my mouth were, "Wow, needs work is an understatement, Jema."

"Yeah, it does look a bit worse than the photos the inspector sent me."

'But it's big," Tom said. "Open. How many bedrooms?"

"Jema looked at the folder she had in her hand, "Umm… four bedrooms, two and a half baths, and an office, a three-car garage, a living room, dining room, a kitchen, basic stuff, it seems. No appliances, they've all been removed."

We went upstairs and looked at the master suite, and it was quite large with a large walk-in closet and a fairly nice bathroom, maybe a bit out of date, but passable.

"Where's the basement door?" Tom asked.

"Oh…yeah… there is a basement. That's really unusual for around here."

"Why are there so many holes in the walls?" I asked."

"I think whatever legal trouble the previous owner was in required law enforcement to look for hidden assets like cash or even drugs."

"You mean this was a drug house?"

"No, it's not like that, not quite so dramatic, maybe a stash house for cash or money laundering or something, but whatever may have been here, the police have long ago found and taken away."

"So, where's the basement entry? I want to see the basement," Tom said.

"Oh, Umm, okay, it looks like from this photo, it's, huh, it's behind the bookshelves in the office. There seems to be a secret door of some kind. See." She showed Tom the picture, and it showed the bookshelf, revealing a staircase. We walked into the office, and Tom looked at the picture and fiddled around with the molding on the shelving, and the bookcase popped open.

"Oh, there it is, just move this molding to the right about two inches," Tom said.

We walked downstairs and revealed a full basement, about 1300 square feet, totally unfinished. There was the door leading to the outside, "It has proper Egress, as long as you don't add bedrooms," Tom said, but otherwise, it was a total blank slate.

All I could say was, "WOW, this could be a wonderful space for my studio, for making my music and videos. This is incredible!" Tom just nodded.

So now I had to ask the obvious question, and I was afraid I might not like the answer: "So how much does the bank want for this place?"

Jema took a breath and said, "Well, Umm, the bank really just wants to be made whole. This place has about $72k left on the mortgage, and we have some money we've spent on some legal fees and two years of back taxes, and all in all, I think I can convince the bank to let this place go for about $85k in a cash sale. Or, we can look at a mortgage, but you would have to qualify for that."

She must have heard from Lenny or Irma about my inheritance from my mom, but I had not told anyone except Lenny, Irma, my dad, and Tom about the trust, and I know none of them had said anything to anyone either. But Jema must have suspected I had the cash from my inheritance available to do this deal.

Tom just looked at me and said, "It's not that much work. I can help when I'm available."

I held out my hand and said, "You got a deal. Cash it is. What do you need to get started?"

Just $500 down in earnest money will get the paperwork started, and we should be able to get the ball rolling first thing tomorrow."

22 days later, I signed the papers and handed over a cashier's check for the entire amount. That's how I became the owner of this beat-up old house that needed so much work but has so much potential.

# Chapter 15

My dad couldn't believe that I had bought this house without him looking at it first, but I assured him that Tom was there, and he had been around construction his whole life as well. "He thought it was a great bargain," I insisted.

I think Daddy was hurt that I didn't ask him about it first, so he quickly said, "I'm coming out to see you, I need to see this bargain of yours."

"Really, Daddy, you don't need to do that. I'll send you some videos and tell you all about it in the videos."

"That will be great, Kiko, but I still want to see it for myself. I'm coming out, I'll be there next week sometime."

Now I was a little hurt that he didn't trust me, but I soon found out that there was more behind his rush to come and see me.

Regardless of all that, I had a lot of work to do to make this place livable, and I still had work to do at the Gardens with Irma – I was not going to leave her high and dry. Spring in the Gardens is a busy time. We get the most visitors to Lenny's talks in the Spring. So, between the house, the gardens, and Lenny's talks, I was as busy as I can ever remember. Tom and I spent almost every Sunday and Monday patching holes in the walls of the house and making plans for the basement studio.

My Dad arrived on Wednesday of the week following our phone call and showed up at my apartment with a very sheepish look on his face.

"Hi, Kiko."

"Daddy!"

"I'm so sorry, I know I sounded a bit pushy on the phone, but good news, I came bearing gifts."

"Oh… well then… you're welcome here anytime. What did you bring me?" I could never stay mad at him for long, and he knew that.

"You need to come out to the truck to see it."

We walked out to his truck, and he pulled back a tarp covering some cargo and said, "My housewarming gift for you."

At first, I was unsure what it was, just a bunch of boxes of some sort. "Daddy, what is it?"

"You said you wanted to turn your basement into a recording studio. Well... I did some research and discovered that the best acoustic flooring for a recording studio is a hardwood floor – Oak to be specific. I remembered, my friend Fred, you remember Fred Dryer, Right?"

"Yeah, Mr. Dryer, the flooring guy. He used to work on all those really big homes up in Aspen and Telluride."

"Yeah, that's him. Well, he told me that he had ordered over 6000 square feet of Oak Hardwood flooring for a project he was doing, and at the last minute, the customer changed their mind and asked for something different. So I called him to see if he had any left, and he did, so I bought 2000 square feet, at a great price by the way, and I thought I would give it to you as a housewarming gift."

"Oh, my god, Daddy, I don't believe you did that for me! How wonderful!"

"So, when can I see this house of yours?"

"Right now, I guess, just let me go and tell Irma that I'm going to show you the house."

So I took my dad to the new house, and of course, right away, he was concerned. "Why are there so many holes in these walls?" he asked.

I had to tell him about the circumstances that led to the house being so cheap, but he just said, "Oh... okay then. It's all fixable."

"I still have a lot of work to do, and I need to buy all the appliances and all that stuff, but I should be ready to move in by the time Zoe gets here for the summer and Suzanna graduates."

As soon as I mentioned Zoe, I could immediately tell that something was wrong. At first, I thought maybe she had changed her mind. I mean, she's only 17, so she's allowed to change her mind, I suppose. But then he said, "I have something I need to tell you, Kiko. Here, let's take a seat on the stairs."

We sat on the steps of the stairs, and he said, "Janice and I are separated, Kiko."

"Separated, what does that mean, separated. Did you move out?"

"No, sweetheart. Janice moved out."

"What… when… how come you didn't tell me?"

"It's only been about a month now. But I'm not sure she's going to let Zoe come here this summer. She thinks you're a bad influence on her."

"Bad influence! How am I a bad influence?"

"You know, Janice has always wanted Zoe to go to college and study business and take over the business someday. But every time Zoe comes and spends time here, all she can talk about is making videos and working in the Gardens with Irma."

"Well, yeah, I always wanted Zoe to go to college too, but she has a mind of her own, and she wants what she wants. You can't blame me for that."

"I don't blame you, sweetheart, you know that. If anything, I blame Janice. She's always pushed you girls into the business too hard and at too young an age."

"So, is that what this separation is about – me and Zoe?"

"No, I wish it were that simple."

"Well, what then, Daddy – spill it."

He hesitated and stammered a bit, and then finally came out with it, "Janice has left me for another man."

"What! Who! When!…. I don't understand. Who's she left you for?"

"No one you know, sweetheart, just somebody she met. I don't know him… well, I do know who he is. He's a customer of ours, a developer who builds condos and apartment buildings. We've done lots of work for him in the past."

"So, some rich asshole then! How long has she been seeing this man?"

"Umm... about two years or so, she says."

"Two Years! Did you know or suspect anything?"

"No, not really. I mean, she's gotten really good at bidding projects, so I just kind of let her take over that function, and that means she spends a lot of time out of the office, so I never suspected anything was going on. Maybe I'm too trusting, or just oblivious."

"Don't say that, Daddy. Trusting is a sign of a good heart, and you have the most beautiful heart I know. So what does this mean for you, Daddy – for the business?"

"I'm not completely sure yet. Janice and I have been married for 18 years now, and we built that business together. As a result, it may need to be liquidated, or one of us can buy out the other, or we could continue running it together. Who knows? At this point, everything is uncertain."

"Please tell me you won't keep running that business with her. Not after this."

"Well... that's definitely the least likely scenario, but if we can't find a buyer or one or the other can't find the financing to buy the other out, it could happen, at least for a while. And to tell you the truth, Kiko, I won't even attempt to take on that much debt to buy her out. I'm afraid I'd be paying that off for the rest of my life. But she doesn't seem to have any issues with taking on the debt, so we'll just have to see what happens."

"How much would it cost to buy her out?"

"I don't know. We have 52 trucks now, and 110 employees, and we did nearly $15M in revenue last year."

"Really! I had no idea the business had grown that big."

"Yeah, and even I have to admit, Janice has been a big part of that. She's relentless when it comes to bidding on ever bigger and bigger jobs. But the bottom line is, she may not let Zoe come back out here this summer.

I laughed out loud, "Does she really think she can keep Zoe from doing what Zoe wants to do? That girl will hitchhike out on her own if you try to tell her no. Wait – I just spoke with Zoe last week, and she didn't say anything to me about this. Have you two told her?"

"Yes, of course we did, but I asked her not to say anything until I could come and talk to you in person, so she managed to keep it to herself."

"Well, Daddy. I'm disappointed, but what can I do? You know I love you, and I'll always stand by you, no matter what."

"I know, sweetheart, and I love you too. It'll all be okay, I'm sure of that."

"So what will you do if you have to give up the business? That place is your life."

"I don't know, if Zoe comes out here when she graduates, maybe I'll come too. Maybe it's time for a change?"

"Hmm... Change is a good thing. I've been thinking that maybe it's time for me to make some changes as well."

"Oh – what kind of changes?"

"Nothing big or dramatic, but you know, with the house now, and if I can get this studio built, maybe it's time to go back to concentrating on my music again. I mean, my videos are beginning to gain some traction, and if I can improve on them and improve the sound, then I might have something here. A lot of artist are producing their own music now, you know, they're taking back control. There are so many ways to get music out there now, not like before, when you had to have agents and managers and record companies, each taking large percentages from you. Now, you just have to produce a video and post it, or post your own music on iTunes or Spotify. Besides, if Zoe comes out here to work with Irma, she won't need me there to help. I mean, I love the gardens, but it's been over five-years now. Lenny always said I would know when it was time to move on, and I'm beginning to get that itch, and now with the money from Koharu and Mom's inheritance, it's no longer a matter of me needing the job."

"I was never sure why you stayed there so long to begin with," Daddy said.

"Yeah, I know, but when Derik left me, and then I got blackballed from the clubs for wanting to do the right thing, it really did a number on me. And that's not to mention that six-years working in the clubs as a singer and bartender, fending off drunks every night, it took its toll. I just felt so empty and so dirty, like I had sold my soul. But coming to Liberty Gardens, well, Lenny made me feel heard, and working with Irma made me feel clean again, like I had made atonement or something. I know that sounds crazy, like spending all day with my hands in the dirt could make me feel clean, but somehow, it did."

"I understand that. I'm glad you found that place. It's been good for you, Kiko. You have really come into your own in these past five years. Not to mention you met Tom there. So, how are things going with Tom?"

"They're going quite well, thank you, and that's why we won't talk about it. I don't want to jinx it. I promised Lenny we would come and have dinner with him and Irma tonight, and those boxes aren't going to unload themselves. We'd better get a move on."

"Yes, Ma'am!"

We took some time to unload the boxes of flooring in the back of his truck and put them in the basement, and then we returned to my apartment. We had dinner with Lenny and Irma that night at Lenny's, and Daddy and Lenny spent all the next day together in the workshop, doing whatever they do. They really seem to like spending time together. Daddy left on Friday to get home. He didn't want to leave Zoe alone any longer than necessary, as he was afraid Janice would move her out of the house and in with her if he left Zoe unattended for too long.

The rest of the Spring was wonderful, and at the end of May, Zoe came. Janice tried to convince her to stay and come work in the business that summer, but Zoe had made up her mind, and this is what she wanted, so I suppose Janice knew if she tried to force the issue, she would push Zoe away even more than she already had. It wasn't hard for me to see so much of Katherine and me in their relationship as well, and that was painful to watch, given how much I loved and respected Katherine at the end of her life and regretted all those years of being distant. But try to tell that to an angry, hurt, and confused teenager, and they just won't see it.

Dad and Janice figured out the equitable split of the business. It seems that the development company that Janice's new man owned saw the business as a good opportunity, and the entire business as an investment. Janice, it seems, had presented his Board of Directors with a presentation on how she could turn the business into a national home services company with franchises all around the country, offering monthly service contracts for businesses and homeowners, which was the current business model, and they saw it as an opportunity to enter a growing industry. They paid my Dad and Janice both a hefty sum and then installed Janice as the new President of the services company – Daddy was left very well off, but out.

Daddy had committed to Zoe to stay in Colorado and in the same house for the remainder of her senior year of high school, and Janice agreed to that, so at least that was a good thing. The summer went by like a whirl. I don't remember many specifics; it seemed to come and go so fast. Zoe and I had lots of fun, and Zoe continued working and learning with Irma, and doing my videos in the evening. I gave up my pay at the gardens to her for the summer, as I was grateful to have the time to spend on my house. I had finally gotten to a place that I felt comfortable moving in, and Zoe stayed with me.

Suzanna graduated in May and was hired by a large hospital on the South side of Austin, so the commute from the Gardens was quite easy. She was now living in the Apartment, and everything was well. We had developed a bit of a family: Lenny, Irma, Suzanna, Zoe, and me. We ate meals together a lot and spent almost every Saturday evening together. It was a good time, and I have such fond memories of that summer with the five of us all together.

My music studio was now developing as well. Tom's dad had seen to it that the flooring was laid properly. We built a bathroom and a separate control room for the mixing board and voice booths for vocal recording. I knew that if I was going to build a real studio, I needed to visit my old friend Mark, the owner of Rondo Studios in Austin, to truly understand everything that was needed acoustically and electronically. So, Tom and I drove out there one day to meet with him. He seemed so happy to see me.

"Kiko, where have you been. I see your videos occasionally, and they're great. I miss not having you around here."

"Awe… thank you, Mark. I miss not being here too."

"So what brings you here, looking to book some time in one of the studios?"

"Umm… No, not quite." I introduced him to Tom and told him about my coming into some money when my Mom passed, and that I had bought a house. "I want to turn the basement into a real, usable studio, and we need to kind of get some professional advice, if that would be okay," I said shyly.

"Oh…yeah…that would be fine. Congratulations on that, I mean the house, of course, not your Mom passing, that was terrible."

"I understand."

"Yeah… come on, let me give you the grand tour. We've done some major upgrades over the last year or two. The need to keep up with the bigger studios is never-ending, but so far, we're holding our own."

"That's good to know."

"Yeah... we just upgraded to these new 24 Track tape recorders last year. It's all the rage, although I don't know why so many producers insist on them. Most never use all the tracks."

Tom asked, "So you still use tape, not digital?"

" No! Professional recording is always done on magnetic tape. You can't get anything better for sound reproduction, especially if you're going to press vinyl or some sort of distributable medium."

"So...what did you do with the old 16 Tracks you used to have?" I asked.

"I sold one on eBay a few months ago, but I still have three others sitting in my storage room, as back-up, just in case I need them for something."

"And they all still work?"

"Yeah, they work great."

"Would you consider letting any of them go?"

"Umm... I could be persuaded, for the right price."

"And what would that price be?" I said, fully prepared to dicker a bit.

"I have a TASCAM MS-16 that I paid about $5k for just six years ago. But for you, Kiko, I could let it go for $2k."

I half-jokingly and half-seriously said, "Let me get my checkbook."

"Okay then, it's a deal."

We continued our tour, and Tom asked a thousand questions about everything from studio acoustics to how the control board was set up. But as Mark and I were talking, the engineer in the booth, Jared, slipped Tom his phone number and whispered, "I can come set all that up for you." Tom just smiled at him and said, "We'll be in touch."

Mark sent his assistant, a girl called Betsy, to wheel out the machine and take my check. As we were leaving, she followed us out the door, I suppose to help load the tape machine, but as soon as we were out of the building, she said, "Kiko, I don't know if you remember me, but when I was at UT, I used to listen to you play on Sixth Street all the time."

I looked at her and said, "Oh yeah, your hair was different back then, but I remember you."

She smiled with a slight laugh, "Yeah, I got rid of the purple." She handed me a phone number and said, "I really like your music. I've seen all your videos. I think you're super talented. So… umm… I play drums and any kind of percussion, and if you are ever looking for someone to back you up, I'd love to come play with you. Mark lets me sit in as session drummer sometimes, if he needs someone at the last minute. I majored in Music at UT. I was in the marching band, and I've done just about every kind of percussion, but mostly I just love playing a drum kit. I've been in a couple of bands too. And I also do all the booking and scheduling for set musicians for Mark, so if you're ever looking for set musicians, I can help you find the best in town."

The desperation in her voice was noticeable, but I was very sympathetic. I know how hard it is for female musicians to be taken seriously. "Okay, Betsy, I'll keep you in mind. Thank you for giving me your number. We'll talk again later."

"Thank you, Kiko."

I knew that if I was serious about doing some real recording, I was going to need backup musicians, but my conversation with Betsy started me thinking seriously about something I had been tossing around in my head for some time. *Maybe now is the time to really embrace it*, I thought.

I still had Derik's old mixing board, and it was more than adequate for a 16-track recording system, so I knew that I was now well on the way to having a real, professional-level recording studio of my own – a place where I could do what I wanted to do, for the first time in my life.

I waited about two weeks, and then I called Betsy. She came to meet me one day at the house, and we had a lovely talk. I told her what I wanted to do, and she was all onboard with it. You see, what I wanted was to put together an all-female backup band. Basically, just girls who loved music as much as I did, and wanted to come and just have fun making the kind of music that we liked, that made us happy, and even made us laugh from time to time. "I don't even want to get back to the place where I'm not having fun with my music. I don't want to make people just tap a toe; I want to make them smile, and even laugh out loud at the silliness of some songs or maybe even just the performance."

"I think I know exactly what you're talking about, and I know some really great musicians and back-up singers who are exactly what you're looking for." Over the next few weeks, Betsy brought me five girls, well, women actually. They ranged from age 22 to 38. The first, of course, was Betsy herself. She was 25 and could play anything that you could bang with a stick. Then there was Ronda. Ronda was a 38-year-old mother of three teenagers and a full-time music teacher in the Austin ISD. She was a keyboard wizard and a pretty good vocalist herself, but preferred not to be a lead vocalist – she even offered to bring in the full upright Steinway that she had purchased from the school district when it was replaced with a concert-style piano, if we could figure out how to get it down into the basement. Next was Laura. She was 28 years old and married, but was a working studio musician, one of the best bass guitar players in Austin. She had had a really bad experience when working as a backup bass player for a well-known country singer, who made her travel on a bus for six weeks with him and five other people. The experience had left such a bad impression on her that she had settled for a life as a studio session player rather than a live band musician.

Next came 26-year-old Rachel. Rachel was the most versatile musician among us. She could play fiddle or violin, regular, slide or steel guitar, mandolin, and banjo, and was a pretty good vocalist in her own right. She began playing with her family in a family band at the age of 5 and has continued to play ever since. She was married very young and divorced by the time she was 23. But she loved music and was willing to play whenever she could get the opportunity. Last, but not least, was Sany. Sany played a beautiful lead, rhythm, or classical guitar. This girl could play Classical Gas or Malaguena as if it were just flowing off her fingers like water one minute and then Stairway to Heaven or While My Guitar Gently Weeps the next. Sany was 32, single, born in Thailand, and migrated with her parents to the US when she was just 4 years old. She was probably most like me. She turned to music as a solace when she was a teenager living through some very difficult times while her parents struggled to run a small family-owned Thai restaurant.

Together, we made a very different and eclectic group of girls. We all had different tastes in music and skill levels, but the more we played together, the more we learned that we all loved to make each other laugh. Sany especially. She was very quiet by nature, but she loved to show up wearing outfits that made the rest of us just bust out laughing, and she would just say, "What, I woke up feeling like a cat today, so my cat woman outfit just felt right this morning." She inspired the rest of us to just let our inner child out to play anytime the mood struck. By the end of fall that year, I had a wonderful group of gals whom I had dubbed "The Strange Girls," all ready to make beautiful music together.

Meanwhile, we had reached the end of another season at the Gardens. I knew that this was likely my last full year at the Gardens, as by June of the next year, Zoe would be here full-time working with Irma. We had come to the last talk for the season. It was the second Saturday in December. There was a big crowd that night, all of the Strange Girls were there, which was very unusual, and Carol and Tom's dad had even come, and there seemed to be a lot of people I hadn't seen before. I asked Irma if this was a special occasion. I had been very busy the last few months, so I thought maybe I had missed a memo or something.

Lenny's age was finally beginning to show, as he needed more help getting up and down the steps to the speaking floor, but his voice was still strong, and his mind was as sharp as it had ever been. As was our normal routine, I met him at the top of the steps and held his arm as we walked down the steps. He took his seat, and I went to open the evening with a song. The audience was very receptive to my song and applauded vigorously. I stood from my stool and turned towards Lenny and saw Tom standing at the edge of the speaking floor. He was dressed in his full dress Fireman's uniform and looked so handsome. I thought that maybe he had come down to help me and Lenny walk back up the steps.

When I saw him, I said, "Tom, this is a surprise. What are you doing here? You look great in your uniform, by the way."

He didn't say a word. He just went down on one knee, pulled a box out of his pocket, and said, "Kiko Davis, will you marry me?"

Oh My God! I was so totally unprepared and unsuspecting that he was going to do this. I just threw my arms around his neck and said, "Yes! Yes! Yes!" It was then that I realized who all these extra people were. They were all Tom's firefighting friends and his friends for the machinist shop. He gave me a beautiful engagement ring. Suzanna, of course, had my dad and Zoe on the phone on a video call.

Lenny did not speak that night. He said we had a much more wonderful thing to come together to celebrate instead. Irma, obviously, was briefed that this was going to happen, as she pulled out a big congratulations cake for everyone to share in. Suzanna helped Irma serve that night as people just wanted to congratulate Tom and me, and that was informally, the last night I officially worked at the Gardens. It was not my last night at the Gardens, however, but I'll talk about that in a bit. That night was such a special night. I had seen Lenny perform several wedding ceremonies at the gardens, so I knew he had a state license to do so. I made him promise me to perform Tom's and my wedding sometime in the coming months. And that is how Tom and I stopped dating, and began our life as fiancés and eventually husband and wife.

# Chapter 16

It didn't take Tom and I long to set a date in August of the next year as a wedding day. Meanwhile, there was a lot of planning to do and a few special tasks that I alone had to take care of. In February of 2014, I flew to London to see Koharu for the first time since meeting in Tokyo two years before. We had exchanged some letters since then, just polite notes mostly, and she sent a lovely congratulations card when she saw my engagement announcement on Facebook, but I felt that this was something I needed to do in person. I didn't tell her I was coming to London, as I was only going to be there for two days, so I didn't want her to make any fuss over my visit. After arriving and checking into my hotel, I took a taxi to Central Saint Martins, Royal College of Art.

I enquired of a gentleman at the front gate where I could find her office or classroom, and he directed me to her office. Her office door was open. She was sitting behind her desk, looking very professor-like, with a stack of papers on the desk. I quietly said, "Uhhumm," as I stood there for a second, and she looked up and saw me. The look on her face turned to one of instant joy.

"Kiko! I'm so happy to see you. Why didn't you tell me you were coming? Please come in and sit."

"I came to give you something, Koharu."

"Oh! What have you come to give me?" I handed her an invitation to my wedding and thought she was going to break out in tears.

"You want me at your wedding?"

"Of course I want you there, Koharu. It wouldn't feel right if you were not there. Besides, who else is going to make sure I have my kimono properly worn? No one else would even know how to begin wrapping me correctly."

"You're going to wear your kimono, how lovely. You will make such a beautiful bride."

"I hope so."

"So, how long are you in London for? We must go out and celebrate. Where are you staying? You can stay with me. I have three bedrooms in my flat."

"Thank you, Koharu, but I wouldn't dream of imposing on such short notice. I've already checked into my hotel, and I leave tomorrow afternoon at 5:00. I just came to deliver this to you. I was afraid that if I mailed it, you might think I was just being polite, but I really do want you there."

"How about your father? Are you sure he won't mind me being there?"

"He's very much looking forward to meeting you."

"And his wife, I will have to bring her a gift."

"Umm, that won't be necessary. My dad and his wife have divorced."

"I'm so sorry to hear that."

"It's all okay. They both seem to be dealing with it quite well, actually. Anyway, next time, I'll let you know before I come, and I can stay with you then, and we can plan some things to do together.

"That will be wonderful. But if tonight is all we have, you must have dinner with me. I belong to a wonderful supper club. I think you will enjoy it immensely."

"Thank you, that will be very nice. I don't want to keep you, though, you look like you have a lot of papers to work on."

"Yes…student essays about why they want to be in the jewelry business. I need to assess their motivations for being here. It's an important part of how I teach."

"I understand. Okay then, I'll see you this evening."

"I'll pick you up at your hotel promptly at 7:00."

"Okay, I'll see you then."

Koharu looked so relaxed in that environment, not at all like when I met her in Tokyo. Her hair was down, and she had glasses on and was wearing a simple blouse and tan trousers with sneakers. I think this new life of hers really appeals to her.

She arrived at the hotel promptly at 7:00. I got in the taxi, and we drove to a private club in downtown London. As we were driving, she took my hand and looked like a frightened child afraid to ask for an extra cookie. She said, "Would you be embarrassed if I introduced you as my Daughter?"

"Of course not! I'd be hurt if you didn't." That seemed to make her most happy.

The club was located in a building that did not look like anything very special, just old granite, but well-maintained. We approached a large wooden door. There was a polished brass sign adjacent to the entrance that simply read, "The Occidental Club." She scanned a card, and the door unlocked. We went in, and I saw something that looked right out of Victorian England. A beautiful red carpet, custom-woven no doubt, with a one-of-a-kind pattern. Wood paneling was everywhere. The wait staff were all in formal wear. A small string ensemble was playing at the front of the dining room. A woman checked our coats.

The Maître D' said to her, "Madam Mieko, how nice to see you again."

"Thank you, Jeffry. This is my daughter, Kiko. She is here visiting me from America."

"Oh! All the way from across the pond. Welcome, Kiko. We are so happy to have you here. Please don't hesitate to ask any staff member if there is anything at all we can do for you. Madam Mieko, I have your table ready right over here."

I had never seen this kind of posh anywhere outside of a movie. But it was nice. The dining was definitely five-star. The meal was lovely, and Koharu and I seemed to talk with a level of comfort that I had only experienced with close friends. At one point, Koharu had to excuse herself to go to the powder room, and as I watched her walk across the floor, it was like watching an angel glide across a cloud. She moved with such grace and elegance. I was not the only one who noticed either. Almost every eye was drawn to her as she moved past table after table. I couldn't help but think, *I have got to learn to walk like that.*

After dinner, we moved into what was called the Blue Room. As we crossed the threshold, the carpet changed from red to an incredible royal blue, with the same pattern as the red carpet, just color morphed into blue shades. This room was for relaxing and talking, and some people were playing games like bridge and other card games. As we walked to a small seating area across the room, people greeted Koharu, and she would introduce me. She was so proud to be able to say, "This is my daughter, visiting from America." I wished I had booked more time there, if for nothing else but to give Koharu the chance to introduce me to people. She just seemed so happy to be able to say those words.

It was a lovely evening, although I will say, a bit highbrow for me, but it was a great opportunity to see how the other side lives. I got flashes of seeing myself bringing my children here someday to visit Grandma Koharu, and what pleasure she will take in that. But I had so many other things to attend to back home, so I had to stick to my schedule. She dropped me off at my hotel at about 11:30, and I got some badly needed sleep to make up for the jet lag. I departed for the States the next day. I had scheduled my return flight to go through Denver, as I had one more bit of business to take care of.

I arrived at Denver International, and my dad picked me up. The next day, I borrowed his car and drove out to the location of the business where Janice now served as President. The place had changed quite a bit, and Janice had a secretary sitting out in front of her office like a guard dog. I gave her my name and asked to see Janice.

"Is she expecting you, Ma'am?"

"No, but if she's available, I think she'll see me."

The secretary picked up the phone and told Janice I was waiting to see her. "You can go in, Ma'am," she said as she pointed to Janice's office door.

I entered the office and looked around. She stood and said, "Kiko, I'm surprised to see you here. Is everything okay? Is Bill okay?"

"Yeah, he's fine. You've made some changes around here," I said.

Janice was obviously in defensive mode. "Yeah, a few. Do you need something, Kiko?"

I imagine she was expecting me to just let loose on her, but I had no bitterness in me. Lenny had taught me that such emotions only harm us, not the people we are bitter towards. "I came to deliver this to you, Janice." I handed her an invitation to my wedding.

"You're inviting me to your wedding, Kiko? That's very nice of you. I really didn't expect you to do that."

"Janice, I can't excuse what you did to my dad, but he's a big boy, and he seems to be weathering the situation just fine. But you've been part of my life since I was 10 years old. I couldn't not invite you."

"Thank you, Kiko. I'm not so sure Bill, and right now even Zoe, would want me there, however."

"Well, it's not their wedding, it's mine, and I get to invite whomever I want. Besides, I want to show Zoe that carrying grudges and hatred around is no way to live one's life. I remember how much I regretted keeping Katherine at a distance all those years, and how much I missed out on knowing her. I got to see the real Kate during those last few weeks of her life, and I discovered what a talented, capable, and strong woman she was. I don't want Zoe to make that same mistake."

"Really, you think I'm strong and capable?"

"Janice, we all know that this business would not be half of what it is without you. Even daddy admits that."

"Thank you, Kiko. I'll... I'll think about what's best for you when it comes to attending or not. I'm very proud of you, Kiko. You have grown into such a lovely young woman. I have to admit, I had my concerns, but you really have made me see what a wonderful person you are."

"Okay, then, I'll let you get back to work." As I turned to leave, I added, "It is a plus-one invitation, if you want to bring someone."

"Thank you, that's very kind."

When I got back to my dad's, I told him what I had done, and he just hugged me and told me how proud he was of me. Two days later, I flew home to Austin.

The Strange Girls and I had been doing some really neat things in the nearly complete studio, and our YouTube numbers were beginning to climb. It turns out that Sany was also pretty good at doing Videos, and I could tell that Zoe was kind of over the whole video phase of her life. She was in her last semester at high school and had other things that she wanted to spend her time on, especially with what was happening with Daddy and Janice. So I think she was relieved that I had someone else willing to edit and post all our videos.

Finally, the time came for Lenny to begin his discourses once again. I was no longer working in the garden with Irma daily, but I still came every Saturday to help with the Saturday meal and still did a song to open Lenny's talks every Saturday night. Now, however, Laura or Ronda would come to sing and play with me, or maybe both if they could make it. They both began to come to Lenny's discourses when they could and enjoyed it almost as much as I did. It was nice to have some friends there – to know that I had introduced Lenny's teachings to someone else. Passing this along made me feel like my time there was now complete – like I had fulfilled my purpose there or a sacred duty of some sort. Not that I would ever just move on and never go back, but it made me feel less compelled to attend every talk myself once Tom and I were married, and I was no longer needed to help Irma.

Spring went by so fast, and it seems that before I could even get my bearings, I was flying back to Denver to Zoe's high school graduation. It was a wonderful time, and I was so happy for her. High school graduation is such an important rite of passage into adulthood in American culture, and I was so happy to see Zoe reach that milestone. She was planning on coming back with me to Austin. She didn't want to waste any time after graduation to move. I couldn't condemn her for that, as I was also so anxious to get out on my own at that age. I just wanted her to slow down a bit and allow herself to see through my experiences how so many of those teenage dreams will change over the coming years. But then that's the way with experiences, they can only truly be appreciated by the experiencer.

No matter how you try to convince someone to see life through your eyes, it's simply not possible. Every person must develop wisdom through their own experiences. Gees, listen to me, I sound like Lenny now.

Anyways, plans were progressing, and I soon discovered why Zoe was in such a hurry to relocate to Austin, and if you're guessing a boy, well, you got that right. More on that later.

Daddy had put their house up for sale in Colorado and was also planning to move to Austin as soon as the sale closed, having finished all his other affairs there. Janice was living in Castle Rock with her new man or fiancé or whatever he was, I wasn't quite sure, but he had a big, beautiful house in Castle Rock, so she just signed the house that she and Daddy had over to Daddy – a consolation prize, I suppose, and was getting on with this new life she had built for herself. I was at least glad to see that she and Zoe were on speaking terms now.

Zoe had her own car, a big Ford Explorer, not new, but not very old either, that Daddy and Janice had gone together to get her for graduation, and she wanted to bring it to Austin, so she and I drove it back to Austin from Denver together.

Tom and I were living together now, and we had the entire upstairs of the house to ourselves, but Zoe and Daddy, at least for a short time, would be staying in the downstairs rooms, or so I had planned. Zoe, it seems, had plans of her own. She had not been here three weeks when a boy, or young man, I should say, showed up at the front door one day. I answered the door, and he was standing there, looking shy. "Is Zoe home?"

I recognized him from somewhere, but couldn't quite figure out where I knew him from. "Umm…yeah, she's here. Let me go get her. Come in, please."

As he entered that house, he held out his hand and said, "I'm Josh."

"Hi, Josh, I'm Kiko."

"I know who you are. I watch all your videos, they're great."

"Thank you, we work very hard to make them entertaining."

"I know you from the Nursery also." He blurted out. "Millers Nursery, you used to come with Miss Irma."

"Oh!" I suddenly realized where I recognized him from. "Yeah, I remember. Well, look at you, all grown up."

"Yeah, that's where I met Zoe, too, last summer when she would come with Miss Irma. That's how we became friends."

"Okay, I'll go and get Zoe."

I knocked on Zoe's door and found her getting dressed for a date.

"So, Little Miss Zoe, when were you planning on telling me about Josh?"

"Is he here? Please don't get mad, it's just a date."

"Zoe, you're 18, you don't need my permission to date. I just wish you had told me that you and Josh were a thing."

"I'm sorry, Kiko. Don't be mad. I just didn't want everyone to think that I was coming out here just for a boy. It's not like that. I really love doing the work with Irma, but Josh and I met last summer, and we just hit it off. He's into the whole natural gardening thing like I am, so we just had a lot to talk about, so we've kept in touch.

"Zoe, it's fine, you have nothing to apologize for. That's one of the great things about being an adult, Zoe, you get to live your life."

Meanwhile, Tom had been studying for months for his engineer's exam. In the world of Firefighting, earning your engineer's certificate is a big deal. Passing that exam qualified Tom to be able to drive the big Fire Trucks and operate all the equipment. The day he passed his exam, he was like a five-year-old who had just unwrapped the best toy in the world on Christmas morning. He was simply giddy over the prospect of being able to drive and operate the trucks, and it opened up more opportunities for him at the department. Tom wants to become a fire Captain someday, and maybe even a Battalion Chief, and this was a huge step in that direction.

Daddy didn't make it to Texas until around Mid-July. The wedding was fast approaching, and there was so much to do. We had planned on a fairly simple wedding ceremony at Liberty Gardens, with fewer than 100 guests, but still, there were so many details to take care of. I ended up hiring an event planner, not to create an elaborate wedding, but just to help organize everything. He turned out to be a real godsend. Just calm, cool, and collected in the midst of a chaotic situation. His company had put on everything from huge weddings to small business conferences, and it was easy to see why he came so highly recommended. He took care of everything, from the photographer to the catering, flowers, cushions for the seating at the oratorium, and everything you can imagine.

When he learned I was going to wear my kimono, he at first wanted to make it a totally Japanese-themed wedding, but I had to put a damper on that. I explained the significance of the kimono and why I was wearing it, but I believed trying too hard to embrace that part of me would be disingenuous. Once he understood that what I was going for was simplicity, grace, and elegance, then he knew exactly what needed to be done, and he hit that mark right on the head. It was lovely.

The Strange Girls all offered to perform, but I didn't want them working at my wedding – I wanted them to just come and celebrate and enjoy themselves like everyone else, so we just hired a Disk Jockey.

The day Koharu arrived at the airport, two days before the wedding, I went to pick her up. She looked so nervous to meet everyone, but everyone else was so excited to be able to meet her. I kept saying, "Don't be nervous, everyone will love you." We arrived at the house, and right before we entered, she stopped for a second, straightened her dress, and took a deep breath before I opened the door. As I opened the door, Tom, Zoe, and my dad were all standing there. I introduced each one, and when I introduced my dad, she took his hand with both of hers and just began to cry and say, over and over again, "Thank you, thank you, thank you. You have raised such a wonderful daughter. I cannot thank you enough."

By then, we were all in tears, but my dad just wrapped her up in his big ole grizzly bear arms and replied, "Thank you for allowing me to have her in my life. She's been such a blessing to me." And the two just held in embrace for a long time.

The following night was the rehearsal dinner, and Koharu got to meet Lenny and Irma, and Tom's parents. My wedding party was small, just Gina, Zoe, and Tom, who had only his best man, Gregg Foster, the guy who owned the machine shop that Tom worked at when not on firefighting duty. The rehearsal dinner was simple, Italian food at a local place in town.

The day of the wedding, as we were in the apartment below Lenny's, dressing for the ceremony, Koharu said, "I understand that there is a tradition here about the bride having something Old and something New and something Borrowed and something Blue, so I brought you a gift to go with your kimono, so together they represent both something old and something new." She gave me a jewelry case with the most stunning brooch I have ever seen. It was a cherry blossom tree, with tiny rubies for the cherries and pink jade for the blossoms, and the tree was made of twisted gold braiding that was amazing. She gave Gina and Zoe each a box containing earrings for Zoe and a necklace with a single cherry blossom to Gina, and she said, It is a matching set, and now you must always remain sisters, so you can borrow from each other.

We were all in tears. Then Koharu added, "I designed them, but I had my best student make them. I think she deserves an A+ for these. What do you think?" Koharu then took such care and precision in wrapping me in the kimono. It was like watching an artist at work. I had never felt so beautiful, and so Japanese, in all my life.

The rest of the day was fabulous and went off without a hitch. The food was wonderful and the cake stunning. Lenny even wore a suit and tie for the occasion. I began to notice something, however, that caught me a little by surprise; I guess it should not have, but I noticed my dad and Irma sitting very close to one another, and I think I even saw them holding hands at one point. I didn't say anything; I didn't want to jinx that, but wow, what a great turn of events.

Janice did not come, but a week before the wedding, a delivery truck showed up at the house. The driver announced he had a delivery from Janice Davis. It was a large crate, about waist high. I had him put it in the garage to wait for Tom to be home, so we could open it together. Inside was a lovely note saying that she didn't want anything to detract from my day, but wanted to give us a gift that would be fitting for the new house and the new life we were beginning together. As we began to take out the contents, box by box, we found that she had sent us a full 10-place setting set of Lenox China, everything from plates, bowls, serving platters, soup tureen, and gravy boat. This was a setting worthy of a table set in Downton Abby. It was gorgeous, although I didn't know when we would ever use it, but I said to Tom, "Well, I guess we're the kind of couple who hold dinner parties now, because this stuff is not going to waste. When my dad saw what Janice had sent, he went and bought us a full set of silverware to complement it.

So that was the most wonderful day of my life, of course, and Tom and I were still riding that high. For our honeymoon, we went to Australia for 5 days, and I got to see my friend Noa, then we went to Bali for a long three-day holiday before coming back to our real lives. When we returned, I was preparing my kimono to send to the dry cleaners, before putting it back in its case, and I noticed that, before she had left for home, Koharu had embroidered my name, in both kanji and English, into the hem of the kimono.

# Chapter 17

The Fall was wonderful, but stressful. Lenny was getting tired more easily. Now 95 years old, the question was ever present on my and Irma's minds: *how much longer can he continue to do this?* But I don't think the people who showed up week after week seemed to be as aware of this fact as we were. They saw him only on Saturday nights; we saw him every day. But still, his mind and voice were as strong as they ever were.

Meanwhile, the strange girls and I were really beginning to find a groove in our music. Our YouTube subscribers have reached nearly 300k. As I read through the comments on a typical video, our audience seemed to really enjoy our quirky nature, and the fact that we took our music very seriously, producing the best sound we could, but we never took ourselves seriously. At the end of each video, we would always show a few seconds of ourselves just busting out laughing at our own antics, just to show we knew we were being silly. Our viewer seemed to love that. Of course, we had the occasional negative comments, but our regular viewers would usually come to our defense without us ever needing to say anything. It was all really happening, and we almost couldn't believe how much fun we were having doing it.

Jared, from Rondo studios, worked mostly as a freelance engineer. Local music producers would bring him in to run the soundboards or help mix when recording was done, no matter what studio they were working in, and we found he was very easy for us to work with, so he became our go-to sound engineer. Eventually, he became part of our little family when he and Sany began dating and then got married. When we first began posting our videos, our site was called Kiko and the Strange Girls, but two years in, I knew we needed to just be The Strange Girls. I didn't feel right taking lead billing when the others were all playing such a big role in what we did.

Sany and Jared keep making our video capabilities better and better, adding more camera angles and really developing their editing skills. One day, they came and asked if they could rent the studio to do some video work with another artist who also wanted to make videos she could post on YouTube, so I said, "Yeah, why not?" This became an entire revenue stream for me that I had never even thought about before. As long as I had the outside entrance that could be used by visitors, I had no problem with the studio being used by others. The Strange Girls and I were using it when we needed to, and Sany and Jared had developed their own small company to produce for other artists, a win-win for all of us.

Tom and Jared figured out a way to get Ronda's upright piano down into the basement by renting a crane and lowering it straight down onto the lower landing, without needing to try and maneuver it down the stair steps, and that was just one more wonderful instrument added to our sound.

I never did very much extravagant spending with the trust money I received from Koharu every month, but I will say, my guitar collection was getting a bit out of hand. I was up to 16, but I love every one of them. I never ceased to be amazed at the variation in tone you could get just by changing the shape or the wood species used to build one. It didn't matter if it was electric or acoustic – if it was a new sound for me, I wanted it. I worked hard not to get too carried away, though.

One day, out of the blue, I got a phone call from a ghost from my past.

"Hello?" I answered.

"Kiko, hi, it's me, Derik."

"Derik… hey… what's up?"

"Umm, look, Kiko, I'm still out here in Vegas, and me and a friend of mine are trying to start our own record label. You should see it out here, the music scene is really blowing up in Vegas, Kiko. Well, I'll get right to my point. We've seen your videos with those other girls, and we want to sign you to our label, Kiko. We think we can take you guys to the next level – you know, records and touring, everything you've ever dreamed of, Kiko. What you're doing is great, and people really like it. I think you can be a huge smash."

"Oh…wow… I need to think about this, Derik. And it's not just my decision, you know, all six of us would have a say in it, so let me present it to them, and I'll let you know."

"I can fly out there, Kiko. I can talk to them, I know I can convince them."

His desperation was noticeable. I could tell that he was in serious need of signing a marketable act to his label, just by the tone in his voice, and I felt for him. The music business is hard, and labels come and go like crazy. But I know how it works as well, and when you're hot, and they think they can make money off of you, labels and agents are all over you, but if you're cool or cold, they won't give you the time of day. In any case, it wasn't my decision alone to make, so I would need to present the offer to all the girls together. We were scheduled to begin rehearsals for our next video the following Monday, so when we were all there, I presented the offer to them. The discussion was robust, but ultimately, to the person, we each decided that we were having too much fun doing what we're doing, and why mess with what's working?

Besides, we were making money now. Sponsors were contacting us – we weren't chasing them. We had developed the knack of making quick 30-second commercials before, and if we had two sponsors, another at the end of our videos, they were just as quirky as we were. Our viewers would watch to the end just to see our cute little ad spot that we had written and put together. They were paying us 30 to 40 dollars per thousand views, and our videos were breaking into the millions of views. We didn't want to mess that up.

Ronda, who is kind of the oldest and wisest of us all, pulled up a video on her phone of Paul McCartney, George Harrison, and Ringo Starr, sitting and talking, I think it was part of their Anthology documentary they did in the early 2000s, explaining why the Beatles stopped touring, and it reminded us that we could never do what we all love doing so much, in a live performance, the way we can in the studio. I'm not saying we were as good as the Beatles, god no, but the concept was the same, we just wanted to make the music that we wanted to make, and if people liked our videos, that that was good enough for us. It would very quickly become stale and boring if we had to wear the same costumes and do the same things over and over, night after night. It would lose the very thing that made us so likable in our videos. I knew, and I think we all knew, if all this went away next week, we'd be okay with that – we still had fun for as long as it lasted. So we decided that we were, will always be, just a studio band. We all had lives beyond the music, and some even had kids to raise, and we were happy doing what we loved to do. We did agree that day, however, that if any of us ever wanted to leave, to go pursue other kinds of music, then we were free to do so, with everyone else's blessing. I had to call Derik and tell him that. He sounded so dejected, but we were happy doing what we do, and that was that.

My dad was still living in the house with Tom and I, but he spent most of his time at the gardens, in the workshop with Lenny, or just talking with him, and he and Irma were no longer even trying to pretend that they were not a thing, but both refused to put a label on their relationship, preferring to just let it be whatever it was. I think Lenny was the happiest to see the two of them together, and Irma knew that she would never have to divide her loyalties between Bill and Lenny.

Suzanna was working at the hospital all day, and then had taken to sleeping in the spare room at Lenny's at night, to be sure she was close to him. I could see how much she loved him, every bit as much as I love my own Father, and watching him age before our very eyes was hard on all of us, but none more so than on Suzanna.

Zoe and Josh had moved in together, just weeks after Daddy arrived here. Josh's family-owned nursery is located in a town called Liberty Hill, just a few miles away, so it was only about a 15-minute commute for Zoe in the mornings and afternoons. We were all very skeptical of this relationship because of how young they both were, but then I reminded everyone of how young we all were in our first true love relationships. "If anyone had tried to warn us about the perils of young love, we wouldn't have listened either." They all just nodded and agreed; it had to take whatever course it was going to take on its own, and all we could do was watch and be there if things didn't go exactly as they were both sure it would.

Suzanna was the only one among us who seemed to escape the need to be in a serious relationship at a young age, but she knew what she wanted and was always content to just let things happen naturally, and never try to force a situation into a mold of her own making. I think Lenny had become so much a part of her that all that "just let life happen" stuff that Lenny talked about came very easily and naturally for her.

Lenny made it through the entire speaking season without missing a single session. But two weeks after the last session, one week after Christmas, on December 31$^{st}$, 2014, I was at home. Tom had left at 5:00 for a 24-hour shift and was dreading it, because he knew that New Year's Eve was always a bad night for the fire department. Fireworks fires, party injuries, auto accidents that resulted in injuries, fire, or both, and more than their fair share of deaths. It was never a good night to be a firefighter, but they just went in and did what they always do – protect us from our worst selves, or sometimes just be there to comfort us on the worst day of our lives. Tom asked that I stay home that night, and I was more than willing to follow his advice.

It had been a long day in the studio. I had discovered that I was actually a pretty good producer and arranger. Jared and I spent six hours mixing the sound for our latest Strange Girls video that day, and I was very tired. I wanted to just relax, and maybe I could stay awake long enough to watch the ball drop in New York before going to bed. Daddy came in at around 8:00, and he had a worried look on his face.

"What's wrong, Daddy?" I asked.

"Umm... Lenny is not doing so well today. He was breathing hard and just looked really tired. Suzanna is staying with him, and Irma is also staying in the spare room tonight, but we made an appointment to get him in to see his doctor first thing in the morning. I told Irma I'd be there to drive them. He did eat pretty well this evening, though, that was good to see."

"Oh no! I hope everything is okay."

"I'm sure he'll be fine, Sweetheart."

We both stayed up to watch the ball drop, and then I went to bed. Almost exactly 2:00 in the morning, my phone began to ring. It was Irma; she was in tears and crying uncontrollably, but managed to get out. "Kiko... Lenny's gone... Lenny Died!"

"Okay, Irma, I'm coming, I'm on my way!" I ran downstairs and found Daddy sleeping on the couch, fully dressed, maybe he had been expecting that call, I don't know. I woke him and burst into tears as I said, "Daddy, Lenny's dead!"

"Okay...Okay... Okay!" he said as he forced himself awake. "Okay... let's go, we'll take my truck."

We raced to the gardens, and the driveway was full of flashing lights and emergency vehicles. Suzanna and Irma were huddled together, holding each other. We rushed over to them, and all just hugged and cried. When the emergency crews finished with Lenny, they did not take him away right away. They said taking him to the hospital was not needed due to him being declared deceased already, so they had called the funeral home to come and take him away. We sat with him for more than an hour while we waited for the van to come and take him.

By the time the sun came up, we had all regained enough composure to know we needed to begin putting Lenny's plans in place. He had left very detailed instructions for his death and burial, and both Irma and my dad knew where those instructions were. The funeral home had his prepaid funeral instructions on file, which were just for a simple cremation, and to have his ashes spread at Liberty Gardens – no burial.

Irma called Jack Sparks, Lenny's attorney and also the attorney for the Liberty Garden Trust, and told him that Lenny had passed. He immediately put the necessary plans for executing Lenny's Will in motion and for the transfer of Trusteeship of the Liberty Garden Trust. I was in charge of writing and sending out an announcement to all the people on the Liberty Gardens email list and placing an announcement on the Liberty Gardens' social media sites. It was a simple statement. Just the date and time of his passing, and that we would be posting an announcement for his memorial service in the next few days. Almost immediately, people began calling and coming by with food and cards, and just to give condolences. Within days, cards began coming in from all over the world, people who knew Lenny, people who had seen one of his talks on social media, which I had started posting a couple of years prior. The outpouring of love and respect was amazing and went on for weeks. Some people wrote beautiful letters, telling of what they had learned from Lenny over the time they attended his talks at the Gardens. They were so wonderful to read.

Four-weeks after his death, we held a memorial service at the Gardens. The place was packed. We had nearly 200 people there. In keeping with Lenny's wishes, we fed everyone who showed up, but had it catered. Suzanna and I read a few of the letters we had received, just the most touching ones. The Strange Girls had done a version of Let's Go Down to the River a few months prior, and Lenny loved that song and told me how much he enjoyed it. So Ronda, Laura, and I, sang an A Capella version at the service. We had already spread most of his ashes at the gardens, but held back a small bit at the request of his niece in Indiana, to be buried at his family farm alongside his parents and brother.

Six weeks after Lenny had passed, Jack finally had the death certificate in his possession and could complete the final legal arrangements and formal reading of Lenny's Last Will and Testament. Irma, Suzanna, Tom and I, Daddy, and Zoe were all there, and Jack began.

"I, Leonard Edward Boyce, do hereby bequeath all my worldly possessions, with the following exceptions, to Irma Ortega Sanchez.

Exceptions,

To Suzanna Ortega Sanchez, I bequeath the house she grew up in at 718 Basswood Street, in Dripping Springs, Texas. This house is owned by the Liberty Gardens Trust, but being within my power as the trustee of the trust, and within my rights, I hereby transfer ownership to Suzanna.

I looked at Irma and asked, "Did you know the trust owned your house?"

She laughed, "Of course I knew. I finally got Lenny to admit it about 10 years ago. I mean, who else was going to let me live there and never raise my rent for all those years?"

We all had a bit of a chuckle about that.

Jack continued. "To my dear friend, Kiko Davis, I bequeath all my written discourses, and those of Sam Eustes, which have also been entrusted to me, to do with whatever you see fit. Of all my students, no one has ever expressed as intense an interest in my teachings as you, Kiko. I hope you will find a good use for them, even if only for personal study and growth. In addition, I ask one favor from you, and that is to deliver to my niece in Terra Haute, Indiana, my personal papers, such as my military documents and awards. She has requested them of me many times, to be placed in the family archives alongside my brother's, and I promised her I would make sure she received them."

"To Irma, Suzanna, and Kiko, I leave you each a personal letter, which I ask to be held in strict confidence and read only by each of you. These are my deepest expressions of hope and desire from me to each of you, but they are for each of you alone and not to be shared." Jack handed each of us an envelope with our letters from Lenny. To this day, I still have not shared mine, even with Tom, and Tom has respected that.

"With my power and authority as Trustee of the Liberty Gardens Trust, I hereby appoint Irma Ortega Sanchez as the next Trustee of the Liberty Gardens Trust, including all the properties, financial assets, and business holdings. As Trustee, you are granted the right to live on the property for as long as you serve as Trustee, disperse all funds, make all decisions and transactions regarding all legal, business, and personal matters concerning the Liberty Gardens Trust."

So that was pretty much it, just a lot of papers for Irma to sign, and everything, other than what was specified in the Will, was now Irma's to do with as she saw fit.

Irma, Suzanna, Daddy, and I took several weeks to sort through all of Lenny's papers, to determine what needed to go to his niece in Indiana, and what should remain here as archives of the trust. As I was looking through a folder, I found Lenny's birth certificate, and I almost couldn't believe what I was looking at. I asked, "Irma, do you have a copy of Lenny's death certificate?"

"Yes, it's here on the desk." She handed it to me, and I looked and asked, "Have you seen this?"

"What?" she asked.

"Lenny was born on January 1, 1919, at 1:55 AM. His birth certificate says he died on January 1, 2015, at 2:55 AM."

"Really!" Irma said.

Suzanna added, "Yeah, but he actually died about an hour before the time on the certificate; that's just the time the EMS declared him deceased."

"Yeah, that's what I'm saying, he died almost exactly 96 years, to the minute, from when he was born. How unusual is that?"

Suzanna replied, "Wow... that's rare. I'm not sure if I've ever seen that before. Kind of spooky."

Then Irma laughed and added, "No, that's just Lenny, being Lenny."

In the bottom drawer of the cabinet that contained Lenny's personal papers were small presentation boxes, containing all of the medals Lenny had been awarded during his time in WWII. I had to look them up online to even know what they were, or in some cases my dad recognized them and could tell me what they were, but among then were the Navy Cross, I discovered this was a very important one, Navy Cross, a Silver Star, a Purple heart, the Asiatic-Pacific Campaign Medal, a Presidential Unit Citation, Navy Commendation Medal, Navy Achievement Medal, and Good Conduct Medal. In a folder were all the written citations that came along with each of these medals. I almost couldn't believe what I was reading: "Extreme valor in the face of the enemy; Saved countless lives; Heroics above and beyond the call of duty." Lenny was a real, bona fide war hero. Some were from Pearl Harbor, others from the Battle of Midway Island, Gilbert and Marshal Islands, and Iwo Jima; his Purple Heart had two gold stars on it, signifying he had been wounded three times during the war. Even Irma had never seen any of these and had no idea what he had gone through during his war years. Irma just wept at finally understanding everything that Lenny had been through in those early years of his life – things he never dared to talk about.

I, of course, knew of the wound that ended the war for him, but not of any of these other battles or campaigns he had been part of. There were also some old black and white photos of Lenny in his uniform and with buddies all standing around in fatigues with cigarettes hanging off their lips, looking very seasoned and relaxed. There were even a couple of photos of Lenny and Sam when they were building this house and the pavilion. He looked so young and fit. I also found a trove of letters that Lenny had received from his brother, mother, and niece over the years. I thought Julia needed to have those as well.

After a couple of weeks, I had finally gathered everything that I thought needed to be part of his family archives and put them in a box. Irma, Suzanna, and I had agreed to take them to Indiana together.

So, at the end of February 2015, Irma, Suzanna, and I loaded the boxes up in my SUV, and we drove to Terra Haute, Indiana, and to the family farm, which was still owned by Lenny's niece, Julia, the daughter of Lenny's brother James. Julia was now nearly 70. I told her when we would be there, and she had someone come to open a spot in the family grave plot that sat under a large Elm tree, about twenty yards from the house. The once large corn farm was now reduced to only five acres of land, but the house built by Lenny's father and Grandfather, and the barn built by Lenny's father, Lenny, and brother James still stood. We had a lovely ceremony to lay his ashes in the ground, and all his extended family came to observe the occasion. It was very nice, and brought some closure to Irma and Suzanna, and even to me, I believe.

Julia said she would see that all his medals and citations were handed over to the Indiana Museum that was dedicated to preserving these records for all the sons and daughters of Indiana who ever served in the military. She had given her own father's awards as well. I learned that James, Lenny's elder brother, had served in the Army in Europe and was also quite a decorated soldier. He had died about ten years previously, but Julia always maintained contact with Lenny. This was probably one of the saddest duties I have ever had to carry out, but it was one I did with great honor and great respect.

# Chapter 18

It has been nearly 18 months since Lenny's passing. I can't possibly express how much I miss him, talking to him, laughing with him, seeking his advice. I've heard it said that at any given time in human history, there are seven living sages alive in this world. Finding one and being able to sit at their feet and study, for even a single day, is the rarest of all blessings that any human being can experience. I am honored to say that I had that privilege for six of the most wonderful years of my life.

So many changes have taken place over these months. Let me begin with Zoe and Josh. They've surprised us all. Josh is working very hard to earn his Nurseryman's certificate before taking over for his father at the family-owned nursery, one of the best and biggest in Central Texas – a very important and difficult certification to achieve, I'm told. It represents a level of expertise that people depend heavily on when seeking advice on plants and trees that are suited for certain climates and zones across the country and the world. A wonderful distinction to hold. Zoe has already earned her Texas Natural Gardeners certificate from the Texas Gardening Association, and you should see what wonderful work she and Irma are doing at Liberty Gardens.

Suzanna has decided that being a Nurse wasn't enough for her, so she took the M-CAT exam and passed with high scores, and was selected to be among the very first students in the very first class at the brand new University of Texas, Austin, Medical School that opened just last summer. We are all so proud of her.

I keep in touch with Koharu regularly. Tom and I are planning a trip to London in the Summer. Koharu tells me that she has taken up painting. She says being around all these wonderful professional artists at the Art College has encouraged her to pick up her brushes and canvas once again. "Art was my first love," she says. "I wanted to be an artist when Ao and I were planning on running away together." Now she has found that once again. I can't wait to see what will come from those incredible hands, so full of grace and elegance.

Daddy and Irma are living together in the house at Liberty Gardens. They say they were inspired by my wedding to turn the Gardens into a place where everyone from the community can come to hold weddings, or just take wedding or engagement photos, or family photos. Every event planner and photographer in central Texas is now aware that the gardens are open to the public for such purposes. Daddy is in the process of building a public restroom, converting the downstairs apartment into a bridal suite, and planting a flat half-acre lawn area where weddings can be held. Vendors can pitch large, covered, portable tents for hosting receptions, picnics, and other events. There will, of course, be a fee structure for use of those facilities. But it is such a beautiful place to hold a wedding, I can't imagine it won't be booked continually.

We still hold events at the Gardens every Saturday, from March to the end of November. I make Lenny's and Sam's discourses available for anyone to read if they want to read one at the gathering. At first, I thought, *oh, it's always just going to be me, daddy, or Irma who has to read them*, but to my surprise, people loved the idea, and they are booked weeks in advance, signed up to get the chance to read one of the discourses. People love to sit in that big Rattan chair with the fan back and read a discourse. Some even get very animated when reading, and we all enjoy the experience.

Tom's mother, Carol, works at UT and has known the Senior Librarian and Chief Archivist there for years. She mentioned to him that I had inherited Sam and Lenny's written discourses, and he almost begged me to let the library hold and preserve them as a loaned collection. He even had a student scan, digitize them, and arrange them by topic and author, into a database so I had access to print them for anyone who wants to read one at an event. He told me that they needed to be preserved so students doing dissertations and research could access them for their scholarly work. It seems he knew of Lenny and had even attended some talks when he himself was still a student, and he assured me that they would be well cared for. Officially, they are on loan from the Liberty Gardens Trust, but I was so happy to see that they would be available to so many other people. Perhaps someday, someone might even publish an entire book of them.

I still go and sing at the events, but not every week. There are others now who enjoy coming and singing as well. Irma and Daddy still serve food, but not the full hearty meal like we used to. Lenny always said, "Nothing stimulates vigorous conversation more than people sharing a hearty meal." I'm sure he was right about that, but times have changed, and people don't eat as heavily as they once did, so now it's just a light snack and some drinks, but people still come and enjoy just being together. "Robust Fellowship," Lenny called it.

The Strange Girls and I are still going strong. We have over 800k subscribers on YouTube now, and almost as many on TikTok. Our covers are being downloaded from iTunes and played on Spotify, and we still love what we are doing. Sponsors still contact us and ask to sponsor videos, and we actually hired a social media agent to help navigate all of that, and we have a website to sell Strange Girls merchandise. The extra income is nice, even though I don't really need it, but I am so happy to be able to write those checks to each of the Strange Girls every month; it makes me feel like I am really making a difference in their lives. A few of our videos have reached over 5 million views – those are nice paydays.

Jared and Sany are also growing their business. The studio is booked almost every day that the strange girls and I are not using it. If this keeps up, we may have to build a separate rehearsal space, so we only need to use the studio on recording days.

Tom and I are doing wonderful. We're trying to get pregnant, but no luck there yet – hopefully soon though. We still have a ways to go to get this house exactly like we want it, but it's coming along quite well. Thanks to Daddy, Zoe, Josh, and Irma, the landscaping outside looks incredible, and I did manage to get that ugly brown paint covered up with a nice yellow and white scheme. When artists come to the studio for the first time, they pull up into the drive and get the strangest look on their faces, like "This can't be it, this is a house." But then they see the signs pointing to the studio parking and entrance, and they relax.

Tom and I are acutely aware of how lucky we are. I have stumbled into money and success in a way most people can only dream of. Tom has a job that he absolutely loves, and I love him for doing what he does. I mean, my man saves lives for a living, who could not be in love with a man like that? We also know how hard our parents have worked to make these lives possible for us, and we feel so obligated to them and to our future children to pass that along.

Lenny used to talk about a thing he called "The ether of possibilities." He said that the universe is made up of nothing more than possibilities, and we each just carom continuously from one possibility to another our entire lives, plucking one possibility after another from that ether, each leading us to the next, until we have arrived at the very point where we stand today.

I sat with a pen and paper one day, and I tried to map out every decision point in my life, where I had plucked a new possibility that changed my trajectory, leading me to the next decision point and a new opportunity to pluck yet another possibility there before me. It was eye-opening. I made it all the way back to twelve-year-old Kiko, remembering every decision I had made, and how each of those decisions set in motion a series of events that led me to the next inflexion point in my life, step by step, leading me to where I am today. And then I started thinking of all the people in my life, and all the decisions they made that led them to be part of my life. But when I got to the point that the thought, if Lenny had chosen a different place to stand on that beach on Iwo Jima, would any of the last few years of my life have even been a possibility. And what if he didn't come here with Sam, what if he never stood up, in his drunken bravado, and said, "I can build you a house, mister."

And if I had never met Lenny, would I ever have been brave enough to go look for Koharu? If I had never found Koharu, would she still be in Tokyo, living that life of a jewelry heiress instead of living the life she wants to live in London? To be honest, all of the intertwining possibilities and decision points kind of broke my brain, just thinking about them. But that was Lenny, the great brain buster. I can't tell you how many times over the last years, Lenny, with that Urantia Book he loved so much, opened my eyes to a universe I never even imagined was a possibility before.

I have tons of unanswered questions in my life, still to this day. Will Tom and I have kids? I hope so, but I really don't know. Will the Strange Girls keep having success? I don't know, but we'll ride that wave for as long as we are having fun. So many I don't knows still linger in my thoughts, but I learned from Lenny to be okay with a life full of "I don't knows." It's okay to not have every moment of my life mapped out. "Uncertainty is the Salt of Life," Lenny would say. "It brings out all the savory flavors you never imagined were hidden inside."

But one thing I do know for sure, beyond a doubt, I Am Kiko – A Happy Child.

The End

# Other Books by K. U. Helsley

Chronicles of the Sons of Seth: Book One – Eden Lost
ISBN: 9798332608100

Chronicles of the Sons of Seth: Book Two – Nephilim Wars
ISBN: 9798332787942

Chronicles of the Sons of Seth: Book Three – Babel
ISBN: 9798333206602

Chronicles of the Sons of Seth: Book Four – Order of Melchizedek
ISBN: 9798333728715

Lucy's Joy
ISBN: 9798345895283

Made in the USA
Coppell, TX
23 January 2026

69149836R00134